Bruised Souls & Other Torments

Bruised Souls
&
Other Torments

Shannon Lawrence

Warrior Muse Press

Table of Contents

Stuck With Me

She's dead when I awaken.

At first I panic. Sobbing, I seek movement in her chest, a quiet breath. She can't be gone. I call for help, but there's no one else here. We are alone.

I am alone.

After some time has passed, I calm. I feel weak, and mourning takes too much energy.

Her mouth is open. So are her eyes, staring blindly at the ceiling, head tilted at a slight angle. I wonder what she was thinking when she died. Whether she knew this was her time. She certainly didn't when we went to bed last night. We were having an argument. Something about a guy we both like.

Liked, I mean. I guess she doesn't like him anymore.

It seems petty now, but it doesn't matter. I feel fragile, like I'm slipping away with her.

A thin line of saliva snakes its way across her cheek, puddling into the tangled black hair that nests behind her ear. I yearn to clean it off her face, but my arm doesn't want to move, resisting my attempts to lift it. With all the focus I can muster, I will my heavy hand to rise.

It does so, slow and shaky. I maneuver it to the ruffle around her neck, lifting the soft cotton. The saliva comes off with ease, and I even press it to the puddle for a moment in order to soak it up. Still wet, though it has lost its warmth. How long has she been gone?

A press of my fingertips to her throat tells me my first impression was right. No pulse. Her flesh is still warm against my fingers, though maybe cooler than my own. It hasn't been long. Perhaps I awoke at the moment of her death. It could be that her soul reached out and touched mine before drifting away.

Pain overtakes me. My chest aches. Maybe there's still room for mourning. My sister is dead. She died lying beside me. Did she whisper my name before she left me? Did she try to say something, to tell me something? Maybe some part of my brain heard it, and it will come to me in my dreams, snake in and out of my ears.

Oh god, I hope she didn't suffer. Surely I would have awakened had she whimpered or called out. If only I could lift my head enough to see the expression on her face. Whether it looks blissful, like one of our loved ones visited her and asked her to come away with them. Or frightened. The visitor might not have been a loved one. What if, instead, it was a wraith? The reaper himself. Something scaly and demonic. Skeletal. Her soul may have been ripped from her body unwillingly. Painfully. All while I slept peacefully beside her.

It's probably best that I can't see anything but her profile. From this angle, it doesn't look like she was in pain. Surely her mouth would look different. It wouldn't just be gaping open like that of a fish or an imbecile. Her lips would be pulled back, teeth clenched. A rictus of pain, they call it, right? Her eyes might be squinty if she were in pain, but I see no lines, no squints. They are wide. The lashes I was always so jealous of thrust outward, the sun lacing its way through them, casting a lacy shadow on the cheek nearest me.

Her skin is pale. The veins are visible, especially in her temple.

The blood pumps through my own veins in a sluggish manner. I can feel it pushing, shoving. The poisons are seeping through me, as jealousy once did. My own sister will be the cause of my death. Weakness already makes my limbs limp and hard to move. My breaths are slow and jagged, like knives slashing my lungs. Her last act will be my murder.

You may wonder if I killed her.

I didn't. At least I'm fairly certain it wasn't me. We fought, sure. What sisters don't? Especially sisters who are forced to be around each other all the time, her presence always by my side, body pressed to mine. We are—or were—mirror images of each other. Both with raven hair and hazel eyes. I share her pale skin. Even now, my veins may be as visible as hers, only mine still pulse with life. What life remains to them. The poison might even be visible as it moves through those pulsing veins. A different color. Does tainted blood pump as red as normal, healthy blood? Does it look bluish green through layers of flesh? If I could move better, I could check, look in a mirror.

In a test of my freedom, I attempt to lift myself up on elbows turned to taffy. The bed is soft beneath me. Too soft. But it's how she preferred it. Our life was a succession of acquiescences. A ballet of consent and resignation. "You first," "No, you first." We may have shared space, but we shared little in the way of tastes and preferences.

Mark is the exception. The guy at the supermarket. Always friendly to us. Handsome. His eyes a deep, chocolate brown. Dimpled cheeks. A smile to fight over. I wanted to be the first to kiss those lips, to feel them against my own. To taste them. But Emily said he looked at her first, smiled at her first. I was just the luggage she had to carry to grab a bag of apples. I was nothing to either of them. A skin sack of inconvenience.

She's wrong.

She *was* wrong. Death is the ultimate fight winner. There's no arguing with a corpse, even one nestled against your side. She always did have to have the last word, but this is a new low, even for her.

"I'm ugly, Melissa?" she had said. "Look in a mirror."

But she was my mirror. This argument never made any sense to me. She was ugly inside, but she missed my meaning when I said that.

"You know what I mean, Emily. You're a despicable, hateful person. How could you say these things to me?" My voice had gone higher than I wanted, slipping into a whine. It was never good to whine to Emily. It hardened her. Sometimes it made her laugh, but it wasn't a pretty, tittery laugh, like her flirt laugh. Or low and melodious, like her happy laugh. No, this was her mean laugh, accompanied by a grimace, a baring of teeth. Cruelty in her narrowed eyes.

She was like a wild animal at times, dragging me with her

on bursts of anger. I didn't want to go, but I had to. There was never a choice; I was her shadow. One time I even got punched in the face because of my proximity to one of her fist fights. Even when I wasn't the one being punched, I felt it rocketing through my body. We were one.

My backside is starting to get sore. Mostly around my tailbone, but it's begun to radiate out. I turn my head to look at her, a tear sliding out of my eye. I'll miss her. I don't know how I can go on without her. Not that this is an option. However long I have, I will be filled with this longing for her, this hollow feeling in my chest. It aches. She should be looking back at me. Her hand should be reaching over to move this stray lock from my face, to smooth it back. She'd laugh, kiss me on the forehead like she did sometimes. Be my everything, as she always has been.

The lacing on her nightgown has loosened. This time it's even harder to move my arms, but I lift them and reach over to tie the laces into a crooked, silky bow, my fingers clumsy. Her face is almost the same shade of cream as the nightgown.

Her open mouth is starting to bug me, so I press two fingers under her chin and push. Her teeth clack together, and I wince. At least she didn't bite her tongue.

When I remove my fingers, her mouth drops open again, but not as far as before. If she were alive, she'd be snoring. She always did. A snore I could feel as much as hear. Sometimes I couldn't sleep because of it. It's not like I could move to a different room.

I study her profile. The shape of her nose, her chin. Unbidden, my fingers touch on me the places my eyes touch on her. They're warm against my nose, sliding up the curve, over, down to the cleft in my upper lip. I allow my middle finger to drift over my lips, which part at the touch. Then two fingers over the line of my chin, so similar to hers. Index finger along my throat, the swell of my breast. I curl my fingers under, let the knuckles follow the curve around to the side.

Then my fingers drift farther, farther, down and over to my side, to the flesh that connects us. The bridge of skin, of muscle, that has joined us together since we developed in the womb. It's soft to the touch, yet firm underneath. We share not only flesh and muscle, but an artery that cannot be severed. An artery that pumps blood between our bodies, one heart to another. I suspect the poison I feel in my veins is her dead blood. Red and white cells with no further mission, shoved toward my heart, circulating through my veins alongside my own healthy cells.

There's no telling how long my body can perform on this mixture of cells, dead and alive. How long it will be until her body kills my cells and pushes them back through our link to overpower the living ones. How outnumbered must mine be before I die?

The rhythm of my heart has changed. The beat is inconsistent. Quick then slow, quick-quick, slow. Like a ballroom dance. Every little once in a while it even feels like a twirl or dip has occurred. My breaths are more of a struggle when this happens. I gasp for air, feel like no oxygen is coming in.

It passes.

Now that there is only one of us, could a doctor sever that artery inside of her and curl it into my body? It would be beautiful if I could live, though my body probably couldn't handle it. After twenty years of being anchored on one side, I would fall over sideways. Flounder. My heart might not know what to do without that counter pump from Emily.

My clothes would have to be remade without that hole in them. All my shirts, my dresses. There would be no one to advise me on what to wear. What colors look good with my skin tone. What patterns make me look sallow. No one to talk on the phone to a man, to flirt, to say naughty things. I've never been good at that, but it was fun to listen, to choke back giggles so I didn't give us away.

She wouldn't want me to give up. It's odd that she went first, when she was the strong one. Always so hearty and boisterous. She's nothing now. She's not funny or charming or mean or smart. She's just dead. I'm not. I'm still here. Barely.

If I can just get to the phone. Drag her dead weight far enough. It's on the table in the corner of the room. Only a few feet away. My salvation of coiled cording and telephone wires. Three numbers, and someone will come help me.

I strain to my left, away from her body. Just a little bit more and I'll be able to grasp the side of the mattress to get some leverage. Her body pulls at mine, keeps me from moving as far as I need to. My muscles feel sluggish. I'm tired. A nap would be nice, but I can't fall asleep. Not now. If I sleep, I die.

When I attempt to take a deep breath in, it ends up being a pant. My chest rises and falls so fast, yet my lungs feel as if they're stuffed with cotton, with no room for oxygen. A cough shoots out of me, and it hurts. Everything hurts, with a dull ache that seeps outward from my chest. Sand is filling me, weighing me down.

I begin to rock my upper body from side to side as much as our connection allows. More. Faster. Farther. Rock, rock, rock, rock. The bedsprings creak. I rock until the motion is enough to help me swing my arm over, and this time I do grasp the side of the mattress. It's not a great hold, but it's good enough. I heave myself over, despite the resistance. Despite the pain that makes it feel like the shared flesh between us will rend. Sharp and tearing, the sensation makes me scream. But I roll, anyway, and she comes with me.

When I peer over my shoulder, her eyes are fixed on mine. She has fallen to the side and lifted a bit off the bed. I can't look away. Her eyes are vacant; they don't really see me. But they're so familiar. These are the eyes I have looked into more than my own. These are the eyes that have cried, glared, stared, and squinched up into laughter. Eyes that have looked through mine and seen everything I bore. My deepest inner thoughts.

It would be so easy to turn toward her, embrace her, drift away with her. I could melt into the sweet oblivion that calls to me. They would find us facing each other, arms wrapped around each other. The pain would stop.

Instead, I blink and break my gaze away. I continue to pull until I'm at the edge of the bed, and all I have to do is fall. There's a brief moment to brace myself before gravity takes me, and then I'm falling.

I'm pulled up short, hovering somewhere between bed and floor. When I open my eyes and look up, I see that it's her anchoring us to the bed. The pain between us is nearly unbearable. It feels like I'm bleeding out inside, like the artery must have burst open. It pulses, throbs.

She begins to shift. The mattress is compressed at the side, and she's sliding. Now so am I.

I hit the ground, pain bursting across my shoulder and hip before my head strikes the carpeting and explodes in agony. Then Emily lands on top of me. Her head slams into mine, and I realize what I felt before wasn't agony. This is.

Her body rolls forward off of mine and hits the floor, pulling me over with a shriek. My side aches so horribly that I question whether we're still attached at all. This could have done it, severed our connection.

It only takes a second to reach for the bridge between us and confirm we are still one. The skin there is cooling, and I move my fingers to her stomach. Her skin is no longer as warm as it was upon my waking. Ice is spreading from my sister into me, frozen tendrils that tease at my insides.

I'm lying on my stomach with her on my right, between me and the phone. This is manageable. I can do this. The carpet is thick, and I stretch my fingers out, wrap them in the fibers. More pulling. One of my nails tears down into the quick with a sharp pain, followed by burning, but I ignore it and move forward. Dust fills my nose, and I resist the sneeze. A sneeze would surely finish me.

My head feels heavy. Maybe just a brief rest.

The carpeting feels cool against my cheek. Soft, yet scratchy. My hurts drift away. My brain feels squishy, malleable.

Melissa.

"Mm?"

You have to keep going.

"Tired."

Move.

"Nuh-uh."

Don't be an idiot. Go!

An idiot? Only Emily would try to wake me up that way. I force my eyes open, blink against the gumminess. All I can see is taupe carpeting and black hair. When she fell, her face landed away from me. It's for the best.

I'm cold, my whole body shaking. My breaths are now so shallow I don't know how they can possibly sustain me. But I reach forward, grab a hold of the carpeting again. Drag myself forward. Emily's head shifts sideways, not moving with the rest of her body. Each pull arches her neck more.

By the time I reach the spindly legs of the table, her entire body has folded in half, pulled by that last anchor of flesh between us. It stopped hurting a little while ago. Now it burns. I am fire and ice.

The table leg nearest me is smooth, save for one small, rough slot of missing wood. Pulling myself up it turns out to be impossible—I'm too weak, and she's too heavy—but my attempt does make the table wobble. I rest my head on the floor again and shake the table until a scrape tells me the phone has shifted. Shaking harder, I strain away from where I think the phone will fall. It scrapes again, again, again.

There's a final scritch on top of the table, then a moment of silence. The phone hits the carpeting next to me with a muffled slam. My lungs are screaming from lack of oxygen now, and I try to pull in a deep breath, which only makes me cough, a weak, yet painful, expulsion of air.

I grab the receiver and depress the button on the top. It was my idea to have an old fashioned landline instead of a battery powered cordless phone in here. I'd heard they were more dependable, especially in emergencies. Unfortunately, it came with a short cord, forcing us to keep it over here instead of next to the bed.

A dial tone greets my ear, a welcome purr. 9-1-1, and I wait as it rings.

"You've reached emergency services. How may I help you?" The man's voice is low and soothing. Calm and professional.

When I open my mouth to speak, no sound comes out. Only a rasp. My breaths puff against the mouthpiece, my own sour morning breath bouncing back into my nose.

"I can hear you're there," he says. "I'm tracing the call. You're going to be okay."

He's a reassuring presence on the other side of the phone. His fingers tap out a staccato rhythm on the keyboard. Tappita-tappita-tap.

"I show your residence as 6932 Oak Lane. An ambulance has been dispatched. Try to stay with me."

Another rasp escapes my chest. I'm suffocating. Darkness is setting in.

Emily's arms slide around me, pull me close. The scent of her lavender face lotion fills my sinuses, and I relax into her. She's warm again. How odd.

"The ambulance is five minutes out," the dispatcher says in his soothing voice.

You don't have five minutes.

I'm sure she's right.

I nuzzle my cheek into the carpeting. It no longer itches. Nothing hurts anymore, either. Or burns. No more fire and ice. No more anything. I'm floating in a liquid sea.

I'm just so tired.

I was first again. She's always so competitive. *You even lose at dying.*

What a bitch.

Miss Etta's Bed & Breakfast

Etta stood on the front porch, screen door creaking behind her as it drifted open and closed. The latch needed fixing. She made a note of it.

She gazed out over her property, checking that all was as it should be. A tidy farm was a well-run farm. The same could be said for the service she provided at Miss Etta's Bed & Breakfast. First impressions made a difference, and wealthy guests wanted to see a place that looked clean and hospitable. Otherwise, they might well turn around upon arrival, stealing meals directly from Etta's mouth.

A woman had to survive.

Chickens ran about, pecking the ground even though they'd recently fed. At least they kept the bugs under control. Their eggs came in handy and, in a pinch, their meat. Her milking cow stood in the shade of the field, jaw moving in a slow and constant motion. The garden, albeit small, grew lush and green.

Etta frowned upon noticing the still broken slat in the fence. Her handyman, Thomas, was supposed to have fixed it yesterday. This sort of slacking was unacceptable. If he couldn't do the job, she'd find someone who could.

Along the tan ribbon of dirt road came a small black vehicle. It flashed in the sunlight, glass winking at each turn in the curvy road. Her guest had arrived. A small thrill coursed through her.

Wiping her hands on her apron, she went inside, the screen door clacking behind her. A quick look in the mirror showed her hair was tidy, no flour on her face. With a fingertip, she cleaned the corners of her eyes then washed her hands. She pinched her cheeks to get a good glow going, and rubbed cherry juice into her lips. She stepped out the back door and yelled, "Thomas! Our guest." Then back to the porch she went.

The man stooped to get out of the car then stood to his full height, dragging a small, dark suitcase with him. Tall and narrow like a reed, he was neat and tidy, just how Etta liked it. His suit was mildly rumpled from the drive, but clean. He lifted his hat to her and approached the porch. "Miss Etta, is it?"

She nodded and gestured behind her. "Come on in, Mr. Lamb. Dinner will be ready soon. In the meantime, Thomas will get you settled into your room. You recall the rules?"

"Yes, ma'am. In by nine, lights out by ten. Breakfast at seven, lunch at noon, dinner at six. No smoking."

"No wandering the house at night, and no snacking. I make my meals large enough to get you through the day."

"Yes, ma'am."

"Very good."

Etta bustled inside, stopping to look pointedly down at Mr. Lamb's shoes. He paused in the doorway to wipe the soles on the mat then followed her inside. He took his hat off as he stepped inside, knocking it at his side to get the road dust off. She shot him a disapproving look, and he stopped, chin dipping.

Thomas shambled in through the back door, towering over Mr. Lamb. He wore dirty overalls, a sweat-stained blue shirt, and a pair of brown work boots. He reached one large hand toward the smaller man; they shook in greeting.

"Thomas doesn't speak," Etta said. "Thomas, please take Mr. Lamb up to his room and show him where to wash up."

Thomas nodded, picked up the man's suitcase, then lumbered up the short flight of wooden steps. Mr. Lamb followed.

Time to get to work. Etta had already set out the vegetables, so she sprinkled salt and pepper over the hunk of meat, massaging it to be sure it was thoroughly seasoned. She gently placed it in the roasting pan, giving it a quick smack.

She peeled the papery skin off a yellow onion, disposing of it in a spare bowl. Her knife bit through the crisp onion, the smell rising. Her eyes stung mildly, but not enough to make the tears flow.

Once the onion was well diced, she scraped it into the pan with her knife. Picking up three carrots, she peeled them into a bowl, the sweet scent mingling with the savory smell of the onion. She chopped the now smooth and shiny carrots into bite-sized pieces, delighting at the sound of each snap of the knife hitting the cutting board. She dropped these into the pan, as well.

The potatoes smelled of the earth, even after a good washing. These she also peeled, the brown skin pressing down on the lighter, thinner orange carrot slivers already in the bowl. She chopped the irregular white orbs into slightly larger pieces and added them to the pan.

Now she poured water in to cover the vegetables, but not quite the roast. When she shifted the pot, the vegetables moved around in the water, clunking against the sides.

With the flat of her blade, she crushed each of the garlic cloves to free them from the crinkly skin. She minced the garlic, sprinkling the sticky, white pieces over the meat. Before chopping the thyme, she held it up to her nose and took a deep breath. The simple pleasures and scents of cooking always energized her. It was also a good time to think.

The men's footsteps sounded heavy on the stairs as she slid the pan into the oven. The heat rolled out in a wave, licking in hot tracks across her face. She closed her eyes to savor the sensation, her hair tickling the back of her neck as it drifted backward.

Etta poured three glasses of iced tea. The glasses sweated, large beads of moisture rolling down the sides. Setting them on the table, she settled into a chair, hands folded in front of her. The hostess should never take the first drink.

Thomas led Mr. Lamb to the table, gesturing to a chair.

Once Mr. Lamb had taken his seat, he lifted the glass in a salute and said, "Thank you." He took a long drink before setting it on the table. "That's exactly what I needed, ma'am."

"Miss Etta is good enough for propriety's sake. After all,

you're here for some time. We should be friendly."

Thomas still stood. He stared thirstily at the iced tea she'd poured him, lips folding in.

Etta made him wait a moment before tapping a hand on the table in front of his glass, letting him know he should sit. To Mr. Lamb, she said, "Tell me, where is it you're from originally? Where are your people?"

Mr. Lamb took another drink. "I'm originally from Ohio, but I haven't had people there in quite some time. My family's all gone."

"That's right, you'd mentioned that in our correspondence. My apologies. You and I may be the last two without huge families." She laughed, and he joined her. "Seems like everyone gets on like rabbits these days. Families of four, five, and more. It's rare that I speak to anyone without siblings."

"I hadn't thought about it, but I guess you're right. Most people I talk to have at least one brother or sister. I'm not sure why my parents stopped with me. Maybe I was a bad kid."

Etta chuckled. "That doesn't seem to stop most. I figure they keep trying to get a good one."

"That may very well be true."

"Surely you have a girl, though? A handsome man like yourself." Etta reached a hand forward, setting it on his wrist.

Color rose in his cheeks. "No, ma'am...Miss Etta. My job keeps me busy. No time for courting."

"That's a shame. You don't want to waste your youth without finding a wife." She paused and removed her hand. "I'm overstepping. My apologies again, Mr. Lamb."

"No need to apologize. I don't often get to talk with someone who isn't a client or a co-worker. Talking about investments and properties gets boring."

"I'm sure. Then again, with only Thomas and I out here, I can see the benefits of having co-workers to talk to. Keeps the loneliness away, doesn't it?"

"I guess you're right. We don't see each other much. This is a pretty solitary job. And with me not from around here, I don't know anyone well enough to, say, go out for a bite after work. Which is why your establishment is such a blessing, Miss Etta."

She reached out and patted his hand, a small smile gracing her lips.

Thomas finished his iced tea, nodded to both Etta and Mr. Lamb, and stood from the table. He grabbed a straw hat from a hook by the wall before going outside.

"You're out here working on one of those investments?" she asked Mr. Lamb.

"Yes. Well, we've already signed the deal, so I collected the fee today, which I'll deposit tomorrow, and then it's a supervisor role from here on out."

"Seems dangerous to hang onto money overnight."

"The bank was closed. I'm not worried." He laughed. "What could happen way out here?"

She smiled. "True, it is quite safe out here in the country. Folks don't even lock their doors."

"Sounds like my hometown. It was small, but friendly." He took a deep breath, head tilted back, nose high. "What is that delicious meal you're cooking?"

"Why, it's a roast. They always cook up so flavorful."

"I can't tell you how long it's been since I had a decent home-cooked meal. I'm looking forward to it."

"I'm glad." The smile slid off her face, and she furrowed her brow, directing a look of concern at Mr. Lamb. "I didn't get an emergency contact from you. It's good to have one just in case. I know you don't have relatives I could contact if anything happens, but surely there's someone. A friend or co-worker maybe?"

"Just my boss, I'd say. I can give you his contact information, though I don't know what would possibly go wrong." He made as if to stand, and Etta put a hand out.

"No need to worry about that right now. Just see I get it before you leave the house next." She pointed to his now empty glass. "Can I get you another of those?"

"Oh, yes, please. The road dust settled right into my chest and throat. I can't seem to get rid of the thirst."

"Of course." She took his glass and moved to the sweating pitcher, pouring the amber liquid in a steady stream. A spoonful from the sugar bowl topped it off, and she stirred until it had dissolved. She set the glass back in front of him and settled into her seat once more. "There's nothing like iced tea on a hot day. I put a little sugar in to sweeten it."

"That's a delight. Thank you." He drank his iced tea more slowly this time, setting it down after only a sip and licking his lips.

Etta stared at his tongue, watching the pink muscle move around his lips. She remembered herself when he smiled at her, bringing her eyes up to meet his. The succulent scent of cooking meat and onions filled the kitchen now. Etta salivated. A drink of iced tea helped, so she took two more, rolling the cool, bitter liquid over her tongue. Her stomach rumbled. "Goodness. How rude of me."

"You can't help what your stomach says."

"That you can't."

There was silence for a moment, and Etta got up, bustling to the stove to check on the roast. She used a spoon to stir the vegetables around and make sure they were all absorbing some of the seasoning. By now, there was a lovely broth simmering around the roast. She spooned this over the meat, watching it sink into it and disappear. The heat and scent swirled around her, warming her cheeks.

When she sat back at the table, Mr. Lamb, whose eyes were beginning to droop, turned the conversation. "How long have you operated an inn?"

"Ever since my husband passed, God rest his soul. His heart gave out while he was working the field." She touched a hand to her chest. "I do miss him so."

"I'm s-s-sorry to hear that, Miss Etta. It's good you have help wiff da farm."

"Yes, the farm's only a portion of what it used to be. I sold off some of the land, but kept this plot for myself. Thomas, of course, is a Godsend. He helped out at harvest time when my husband was alive. He still does that now, but he also acts as a handyman and lends assistance where I need it. I'm not sure what my life would be like without him."

Thomas's boots sounded on the back stoop. His shadow filled the doorway, and he opened the screen door, coming into the kitchen. He hung his hat on the hook again and scraped his boots on the rug inside the door. He ambled over behind Mr. Lamb and stopped, looking to Etta for instruction. His mouth pulled down at the corners, eyes sad.

"Yes, Thomas, just make it quick. Mr. Lamb is such a polite gentleman. I'd hate for him to suffer."

Mr. Lamb looked up at this, eyes swimming to meet Etta's.

She smiled at him, cocking her head to the side.

At the creak of Thomas's boot on the hardwood, Mr. Lamb began to turn, his hand hitting the iced tea and knocking it over. The cool, amber liquid slid across the tablecloth several inches before soaking into the fabric and spreading. A single ice cube lay on the surface, white and cracked.

Thomas brought his belt around Mr. Lamb's throat. The smaller man fought back, but panic and the drugs Etta had slipped him kept him from doing much harm. He clawed at his own throat, gouging the skin with his nails. His eyes bulged, face turning first red then purple. He bucked against Thomas, kicking out.

Etta, accustomed to these violent acts of self-defense, had already backed toward the oven, glasses in hand. The table fell over, skidding along the floor a couple feet.

Mr. Lamb's feet hit the floor with a loud series of thunks. His movements slowed, blood seeping through the whites of his eyes in dark red splotches. His hands fell away from his throat, and he slumped, eyes still wide.

"Let him down, Thomas. He's done."

Thomas did as she asked. He took a moment to slide the belt through the loops at his waist. Then he bent over and straightened Mr. Lamb, folding the man's hands over his chest and closing his eyes. Done arranging the body, he closed his own eyes, lips moving in a silent prayer.

"Oh, enough of that." Etta strode across the room, squatting down at Mr. Lamb's side. She pinched the flesh on his upper arm, his belly, his backside, and his thighs. "He'll do nicely, Thomas. Get him down to the cellar and hang him up for draining. Can't have that blood marring the meat." She stood with a grunt. "Hurry up, now. Dinner's almost ready. We don't want to waste the last of Mr. Macy, now do we?"

Thomas shook his head, a single tear drifting down his cheek. He hefted Mr. Lamb over his shoulder and tread heavily toward the cellar, the other man's arm slapping against the back of his thigh with each step.

"We'll have his tongue tomorrow. It's been a while since I had tongue."

Thomas froze, his mouth working.

Etta grabbed pot holders, opened the oven door, and pulled the pan out, breathing deeply. She liked her meat medium rare. It was the best way to enjoy the full flavor and tenderness.

Unwelcome Guests

The raspy ding of the doorbell echoed through the room. Laura sighed at the injustice of being grounded on Halloween, and grabbed the controller to pause the movie. She eyeballed the clock. 11:30 was way too late for trick-or-treaters. And where were her parents, anyway? They should have been back from their party ages ago.

She looked at the dark front door. There were no lights on in the house except for the flash of the television set. She shrugged, turning back to the movie where a laundry list of teens was being systematically killed off in gory ways.

The doorbell rang again, followed by insistent knocking. She stood up and snuck around to the front window, peering out into the dark. At first, she couldn't see anything at all, so she pressed her face to the window and looked harder, hands cupped around her eyes.

A pale face appeared in the window in front of her. She stepped back, tripped over her shoes, and sprawled onto her butt, scurrying backward until she hit the wall.

The face remained at the window, staring back. The eyes were fully black, like pits of ink. It appeared to be a young girl, younger than Laura. Dark hair framed her face in a severe bob, and she still had the chubby face of a child. Yet there was something about her that felt wrong, sending a chill up Laura's spine. She shuddered.

The face disappeared, and Laura sat there a moment more, adrenaline coursing through her veins, heart pounding. Her hands clenched the carpet fibers, and the ache of a torn fingernail began to throb in time with her heart. It felt like she had rug burn on her palms; warmth and pain spread throughout them.

She felt like she could stay rooted to that spot forever, but then she had a thought. The front door wasn't locked.

The tile was cool on her abraded palms as she crawled along the floor. Any moment, the girl could burst in. She darted quick glances around the room for something to defend herself with as she crept toward the door, but nothing stood out.

Every particle of her being wanted to run away from the door, not step up to it, but she stood and approached it, reaching for the knob.

A voice filtered through the wood of the door. "Can we come in?"

Laura slammed one palm against the door and used the other hand to turn the deadbolt. She flipped on the outside light and stood there, unable to move, afraid to breathe, one hand still pressed to the door's smooth surface. She tasted bile in her mouth.

Her palm began to tingle. She jerked it back from the door, clenching it at her side. The tingling didn't stop, and the hairs on the back of her neck rose, goosebumps rushing up her forearms. She could feel the presence through the solid surface, malignant.

She rose up on her tiptoes, careful not to let any part of her touch the door, and looked through the peephole. Complete black met her gaze, and she stared harder, trying to figure out what was over the hole.

The darkness pulled back, light leaking in, and there was an eye, which resolved into the round face of another young girl. Laura jerked away from the door, stumbling back to stand in the middle of the tiled entryway, hands gripped in front of her chest.

If she'd needed to stand on tiptoe to look out there, how was the girl looking back in at her?

And had the girl been able to see Laura peering through the peephole?

"Hello?" The voice was young and plaintive. "Can we come

in?"

"Go away," Laura said. "I'm calling the police."

"But we're lost. Can't we just come in to call our mom?"

"No!"

It was quiet for a moment. Then came the sound of muffled sobs.

"Now you've upset my sister."

Laura gulped, the saliva sliding down her dry throat like a rock. She really could call the police, but she'd left her phone on the coffee table, and part of her feared that if she took her eyes off the door, they'd get in.

Even as she stood there thinking this, a compulsion to open the door came over her. The tingling in her palm moved to her fingers, and they began to twitch. Against her will, her arm rose, her feet moved. She forced herself to still, hand partially raised toward the door. As much as she tried, she couldn't get the hand to go down, and it was all she could do not to run to the door and unlock it, throw it open for whatever stood outside.

"Please open the door for us. We just want to call our mom."

The voice was louder than it should have been, as if the speaker, that creepy little girl, was in the room beside her. Laura's skin crawled, shoulders climbing into a hunch around her ears.

When her hand grasped the deadbolt, she realized she'd taken the three steps it required to get to the door. Once again, she stopped herself from going further, wresting her hand away from the lock.

"Let us in, Laura. We can feel you standing there."

She jumped at the sound of her name in the little girl's high pitched voice. How did she know her name?

Once again, she stood on tiptoes, putting her eye up against the peephole. She could just see the two little girls, hand in hand, the same height. Twins? They looked much the same, only one looked sad and scared, the other angry, her face pinched.

They were both staring directly up at the peephole, eyes burning into hers. The compulsion to open the door was on her once more. She felt like a puppet, unable to control her own movements. The bolt turned easily in her hand.

Light washed over the girls, making them appear briefly translucent. Laura heard the garage door opening and unconsciously pulled back to look in that direction.

When she turned back to the peephole, the girls were gone.

***

That night, standing in her darkened room, Laura was drawn to her window. Down below, in a puddle of warm light, the two girls stood, hands still clasped. They stared directly at her, unmoving for several moments. An electric shock of fear sizzled up her back, dread filling her stomach.

The girls slowly raised their unclasped hands and waved with just their fingers, perfectly synchronized, before dissolving into the night.

Laura slept with her light on that night, and for many that followed.

***

Fifteen years later...

"Mom, my dress won't stay!"

Laura looked up from the sandwiches she was hastily putting together. Her daughter, golden haired and delicate, stood before her, princess dress off-kilter, wig askew. She put down the sandwich and beckoned her daughter over to her.

"Alright, honey, let's just get that fixed." With deft fingers, she pulled the thin fabric together and pressed the Velcro closed. Once the gown was straightened, she went to work on the wig, removing the barrette from her own hair and using it to stick the wig on a mite more steadily, tucking several dark hairs back under it.

"Thanks, mommy! Is it time to trick-or-treat yet?"

"Is your dad home?"

"No."

"Well, when he gets home, it's almost time to trick-or-treat."

Lily sagged a bit, mouth drooping, and flounced out of the room in a cloud of fake blond hair and blue gauze.

Laura laughed and finished putting together the sandwiches, opening a bag of chips and dumping some on each plate before adding a handful of baby carrots. Then she pulled out a Diet Coke and sat on a stool in her kitchen, relishing the dusky light that filtered in through the small window over the sink.

She didn't get many quiet moments, and she was determined to enjoy this one.

The familiar notes of a Disney song drifted into the kitchen from the living room. Laura rolled her eyes, taking another big swallow of her soda. The front door opened, and her husband called out in his deep voice, "Where's my little princess?"

"Daddy!" The stomp of tiny feet, and her gauzy girl flew past the kitchen to the front door. Bill came in, Lily clutched in one arm, a giant bag of candy bars in the other. Laura reached out to take the candy. "Thank you. Last year we ran out, so I wanted to be sure we had enough. Don't want to get T.P.'ed like the Johnsons."

"A little toilet paper never hurt anyone," he said.

"Have you ever had to clean that mess up?" she asked.

"Nope, but I've got a blow torch."

"What's a blow torch, daddy?"

"Something you can't play with, baby girl. It's a daddy toy. Now let's have some dinner so we can go trick-or-treat." He put Lily down and she followed him up the stairs, jabbering about princesses and candy. Laura shook her head and grabbed the big plastic cauldron. She poured the candy in and set it by the front door, drifting back into the kitchen and her now room temperature soda.

It didn't take long for Bill and Lily to reappear in the kitchen and scarf down their food, him dressed in a Batman costume and almost as excited as their daughter. Laura let Lily eat only half her sandwich, but insisted she drink all of her milk. By the time her whirling dervish was out the door, Laura was exhausted from the last minute costume adjustments and constant litany of enthusiastic chatter. She settled in to read a book and await the chiming of the doorbell.

The weather was pleasant, so the doorbell dinged constantly for the rest of the evening. When Bill tromped in around eight with an exhausted Lily, Laura left the rest of the candy to him and went up to get Lily settled into bed. By the time she came back downstairs, the candy was gone. Bill had changed out of his costume into some sweats, and was lounging on the sofa.

"I figured we could watch something before I head to bed," he said, holding an arm out for her. She snuggled in against him, and they watched a horror movie before he went upstairs. She stayed behind to watch something lighter and unwind a bit more.

About an hour after Bill had gone up to bed, there was a soft knock at the door. Laura looked at the time: 11:30. She frowned and went to the door, flipping the porch light on. When she peeked through the peephole, she saw two small girls standing outside. They wore black dresses, their hair in matching dark bobs. They were holding hands and standing there quietly.

Concerned that these two were out alone at this time of night, she undid the deadbolt and opened the door.

"Girls, where are your parents?"

She immediately regretted her decision when she saw their coal black eyes staring back at her, devouring the light that poured from the decorative brass lamp on the porch. Their skin was so white she could see black veins underneath it. When she attempted to step back and close the door, her muscles strained against her.

"We're lost. Can we come in?"

Laura tried to tell them they couldn't, to push one single word out, but her throat wouldn't work. Her heart pounded, yet she couldn't close the door, couldn't do anything but grasp the edge of it, her knuckles turning white. Her throat made a clicking sound, mouth hanging open as she tried to force the words, any words, out.

One girl stepped closer, eyes boring into Laura's. She smiled and yanked her sister's arm to bring her alongside. That one stayed silent, though her eyes were wide and wet, tears threatening to spill.

Finally able to move, Laura stepped back. The dominant girl followed her, stepping up into the threshold, pulling her sister with her. The girl's gaze never strayed from Laura's, and Laura couldn't look away.

As their feet touched the hardwood of the entrance, they both threw their heads back. There was a pulse of darkness, the light in the foyer dimming.

Whatever that had been, Laura was released from her strange paralysis. She shook her head and stepped forward, reaching for the girls, unsure what to do. She screamed for Bill.

Her hands felt ice cold as they plunged through the space the girls should have inhabited. She recoiled, pulling her hands back and staring at them. They should be frost-bitten, the cold had been that intense. When she looked back up, the dominant one was smiling, the other placid.

Bill's voice sounded from the top of the stairs. "Honey? What's wrong?"

She turned to look up at him, reaching for the girls once again. She fell forward, hands not touching anything, not even the cold air. When she looked back, they were gone. Just like that.

She looked around, frantic with the fear that they were somewhere in the house, but there was no way they could have slipped around her without her or Bill seeing them.

"Did you see them, Bill?" she asked. "Did they leave?"

"'They' who?" he asked.

"The girls. Are they in here? Where did they go?"

He rubbed his face, hair standing up from having been fast asleep. "I didn't see any girls. Did you fall asleep? Maybe it was a dream." He started down the stairs, smothering a yawn and hitching up his boxers.

Laura slammed the door, locked it, and pressed her back to it, breaths puffing out like a steam engine. Her fingers throbbed with the force of the blood moving through them.

"I wasn't asleep, Bill. There were two little girls. Creepy girls. They had black eyes—"

"I'm sure they just looked that way in the dark."

"Don't talk to me like I'm crazy. There were girls out

there."

"I bet they were just playing a prank. It *is* Halloween night." He came up to her and pulled her into his arms. "You're shaking. Here, come in here and sit down, and I'll go outside and look around."

"No! They're dangerous. I can feel it. Stay in here with me." She clutched his arm, pulling him with her to the kitchen, where it was warm and bright. Her safe place. Before she could sit down, she ran in to check that the back door was locked. She pulled the shades on that and the windows so nothing could look in.

"You really need to calm down," he said. "Do you want me to call the police?"

"They wouldn't be able to do anything," she said. "I remember something like this happening when I was in high school. I swear, these girls looked just like those ones. Isn't that weird?"

Bill just looked at her, running a thumb over her forearm. "Well, they're gone now. Everything's okay. You ready to come up to bed?"

Laura nodded and followed him upstairs. She climbed into bed, refusing to look out the window. Not this time.

***

The next few days went by without incident. Laura relaxed, convincing herself it had just been a prank. Bill had been right. She caught him looking at her with concern for the first day or two, but when nothing else happened, he stopped.

On the fourth night, there was a knock at the door at 11:30 again. This time, Laura refused to go to the door, though her skin crawled, and she felt her face flush from the blood pounding behind the skin.

She turned the TV up, focusing on the screen and refusing to look anywhere else. The doors and windows were all locked. She'd checked.

After a few more knocks on the door, there was silence. She turned the TV back down, knees pulled up against her chest, chin resting on them. The sensation of being watched crept along her back and neck, and she felt a strong desire to turn around and look.

She jumped when a knock sounded on the window behind her. When she looked, all she could see were the drawn curtains.

Suddenly, there was knocking everywhere. The windows, the doors, the walls. It sounded like there was an entire army out there, pounding on her house. She jumped up from the sofa and ran to the stairs, passing the front door on the way. As she sped by it, she heard a loud whisper: "Let us in."

She yelped and ran up the stairs, slamming through the bedroom door and shaking Bill awake. "There's someone outside. They're pounding on the doors and windows."

"What? Who's pounding on the windows?" Once again pulled out of sleep, Bill struggled to sit up, rubbing a hand over his blinking eyes.

"There's someone outside hitting the house. Quick! Come downstairs."

He swung his legs out of bed and followed her, sweatpants grasped in his hand.

The only sound was the TV, which babbled on in the living room, casting flashes of light off the walls.

Bill went to the door and looked out the peephole. He pulled his head back and slipped into his sweatpants before unlocking the deadbolt. Laura grabbed his arm and pulled at him, but he opened the door and pulled his arm out of hers.

"Stay here and grab the phone in case you need to call the police," he said.

With that, he slipped outside. Laura stood in the doorway, rubbing her arms against the chill air that now crept into the house. The night wrapped around the warm glow from the lamp.

"Who's out here?" he called, moving down the sidewalk to the driveway. As he rounded the corner of the garage, disappearing from her sight, Laura's attention was drawn to the road, where she caught a glimpse of something pale against the dark backsplash of the night. There it was again. A face. No, two faces, peering at her from across the street, the figures hard to see because of the dark clothing.

"Bill! They're across the street."

When there was no response, she ran after him, no longer able to see the faces. Her stomach clenched as she moved out of the light from the front porch, and she called for him again. Looking around her with short, sharp jerks of her head, she scanned for the girls and for Bill, one hand clenching her sweater closed at her collarbone.

Something crunched off to her right. She let out a small shriek, hand fluttering to her mouth. She tried to stop, but tripped forward, slamming into a figure as it rounded the garage. Letting go of her sweater, Laura pushed against the bare arms wrapping around her.

"What are you doing out here?" Bill asked.

"I saw them, the girls. I was coming to let you know."

He frowned, puzzled. "What girls?"

"The ones from the other night. It was them." She pointed in the direction they'd been. "I saw them, there, across the street."

There was nothing there.

He sighed and cupped her elbow in his hand, gently leading her to the front door, which yawned wide open.

"I can't believe I left the door open," she said. "What if they're inside?"

No longer hiding his exasperation, he said, "They're not inside. How old are these girls you keep seeing, anyway? Teenagers?"

She thought back to their white faces, still curved with baby fat. "No, maybe more like nine or ten."

"You're telling me ten-year-old girls are tormenting you?" He removed his hand from her arm and turned to shut and lock the door. "Seriously?"

"They aren't normal kids. There's something deeply wrong with them."

"I don't know how to respond to this. I haven't seen or heard anything."

Laura placed a hand on his arm. "I know, but you've got to believe me that something's going on. I can't explain it."

"Okay. Next time something happens, we're calling the police." He shook his head and climbed back up the stairs. "I don't know what else to do."

Laura went to turn off the television, ready for bed herself, but when she got into the living room the TV was already off, the controller laid neatly on the table. Had she turned it off without realizing it? Must have.

She started up the steps, flipping the lights of the main floor off. Above her arose the sound of small feet running across the carpeted floor.

"What is that girl doing?" she asked herself. Occasionally, Lily got up in the middle of the night for a glass of water, or because of a nightmare.

Lily's door was closed, so Laura turned the knob and stepped inside. The pink flower nightlight lit the room, and her still form breathed softly from the bed. Laura moved to the side of the bed and pulled the blanket up, tucking it around her daughter. She smoothed the hair away from her forehead and rubbed a hand down her daughter's cheek. Lily didn't stir.

As Laura stood up, she noticed the closet door was ajar, inky blackness spilling from it. She moved over to close it with a gentle push. Footsteps sounded on the carpet behind her, a soft puff of sound. Without turning, Laura spoke to Bill. "I thought she was up walking around, but she's fast asleep."

When she turned to look at him, there was no one there. Obviously, her imagination was working overtime. Time for bed.

As she approached the door, she stepped into a pocket of icy air, raising goosebumps on her arm. She pulled the door shut behind her and went to her room, closing her own door and turning on the house alarm at the glowing panel. Bill breathed deeply, already fast asleep, one arm flung over his forehead.

Laura went into the master bathroom, feeling safer now that the alarm was on. She started the water in the shower and placed her clothes in the hamper. Hot water flowed over her as she stepped into the shower, pulling the curtain closed behind her. She stood there for a moment, eyes closed, letting the heat soak into her skin, the water pounding down on her head.

A cold draft drifted through the shower, moving the curtain against her leg. She tried to pull it off her skin, but touched something solid through the material.

A hot rush of panic filled her, heart pounding against her ribcage. She backed up against the cool tile wall. The curtain shifted then went back to hanging straight. A shadow moved across it. Laura reached out with a trembling hand to yank it open.

Steam curled out of the shower into the empty room. The door was still closed, the mirror fogged.

Laura turned off the water and grabbed her towel, stepping out into the bathroom. She dried her hair then reached over and wiped the condensation from the mirror. A flash of white caused her to jerk her head around to look behind her, but there was nothing there.

She hastily finished her bedtime routine before climbing in beside Bill and snuggling up against him. His warmth helped her relax, and she eventually fell asleep.

***

Laura swam up from a dream about a TV playing in a dark room. She was cold, shivering. Something brushed her face, and she swept at it with a heavy hand, still battling sleep. It touched her again, icy cold, and she opened her eyes.

Standing over her, pale faces almost glowing in the dark, were the two girls, black eyes looking even darker than before. They grinned, but it didn't change their eyes.

She shoved herself backward into Bill, who grunted and rolled over, throwing an arm over her side and pulling her in close. She struggled against him, slapped him on the arm.

"Ow, what?" he mumbled.

Her eyes not leaving their faces, Laura reached over and slapped his arm again. "They're in here," she whispered.

The quiet one opened her mouth, stretching it to the limits of her jaw, a dark maw gaping before Laura's face. The other one smiled, mouth stretching an unnatural distance, white teeth against dark lips.

Behind her, Bill rolled over, putting his back against hers. How had he not seen them?

Something wriggled in the girl's open mouth, something

pale white like her face. It pushed out, serpentine in its movement, and slid across her cheek with a dry rasp. Black tears rained down her cheeks, and Laura was afraid the tears would hurt if they touched her. She reached behind her to nudge Bill, trapped between him and the girls.

The grinning one reached a pale hand toward Laura's face, moving slowly. Her fingers were long, skeletal. Laura knew that if the girl touched her she was finished.

A scream broke through her lips and the girls disappeared. She couldn't stop herself, even when they were gone, and Bill shook her. It took a moment to calm down. Bill turned on the lamp on his side of the bed before placing a hand on her shoulder.

"What's going on?" he asked. "Are you okay?"

"They were in here. In our room. Those girls!"

He studied her for a moment, looking into her eyes without blinking. Finally, he said, "I think we need to call someone tomorrow. About these things you're seeing. Maybe there's something you can take that would help."

"You think—"

Frantic screams broke into what she was about to say. They both jumped out of bed and ran into Lily's room, Laura running straight to her bed while Bill turned on the light.

"Mommy! There were people in my room!"

Laura sat on the edge of Lily's bed and pulled her into her arms, looking over the sobbing girl's head to meet her husband's eyes. Instead of the understanding she thought she'd see, he wore a look of disappointment, lips pressed together.

"Now you've got her believing this?" he asked.

***

The next night, Laura opted to sleep in Lily's room. She and Bill hadn't spoken since their fight the night before, which had dragged on well into the early morning hours. Normally, she would have made him sleep in the guest room, but this way she could keep Lily safe.

Plus, she was too scared to sleep by herself. Not that she

figured she'd be sleeping much.

She made sure to go up to bed before 11:30 since that seemed to be the time everything began. If she wasn't downstairs, maybe they couldn't come in again.

Stretched out next to Lily, who slumbered peacefully, cheeks pink, mouth slack, Laura read a book using a small book light. She became drowsy as she read, even snorting herself awake at one point. A glance at Lily's kitty alarm clock showed 11:57.

A sense of triumph filled her. She'd made it! After 11:30 and nothing had happened. Bedtime.

Lily moved beside her with a little sound, so Laura put an arm out and pulled her in tight, chin resting on top of her head. She took a deep breath and relaxed, eyes drifting shut.

Then the cold crept in, icy fingers on the back of her neck, running down her spine.

The blankets shifted, creeping down from her neck. Over her shoulder. Down her arm.

She grasped the blanket and pulled it back up, keeping her eyes squeezed shut, body curled around Lily's.

The blanket began to slide down again, and cold fingers wrapped themselves around her foot, which stuck out from beneath Lily's small blanket. A giggle sounded behind her. Frigid fingers touched her neck again.

Unable to bear it anymore, Laura jerked her leg up and turned around, throwing an arm out. She made brief contact with something before it dissolved into cool air.

There was nothing behind her.

She lay there, heart pounding, body twisted. Then she heard it: a giggle.

At first it was quiet, and she couldn't pinpoint where it had come from. She combed the dim light with narrowed eyes, straining to see what stood in the dark corners of the room. As she scanned the shadows, the closet door popped open. Just a crack, but the darkness falling from it seemed blacker than any of the room's other shadows.

She froze, staring at the door, heart climbing into her throat.

Pale fingers slid around the door's edge, and it opened

further, gliding without sound. A thin white arm became visible, but nothing else.

The next giggle didn't come from the closet.

The hairs on the back of Laura's neck stood up. The sound had come from above her. Everything within her screamed for her not to look up, to simply grab Lily and flee, but she had to know.

Without moving any other part of her body, she brought her gaze up to the ceiling. A dark mass swirled above her, taking the shape of a girl. It elongated toward her, gathering darkness to it as it moved, sucking the scant light from the room.

When the mass was right above her, a pale face emerged from it, soulless black eyes forming voids before her. A mouth appeared and opened as another giggle sounded, blowing an arctic blast of rotten meat-scented air right into her face.

The cold air acted like a bucket of water, breaking the paralysis that held her. Laura grabbed Lily and fled the room, screaming for her husband.

Her screams awakened Lily, who began to sob.

Laura kicked her bedroom door open and found Bill scrambling out of their bed. He looked at her, standing there with their terrified daughter. Then his eyes tracked sideways and widened.

His voice was quiet when he said, "Get away from the door, Laura." His gaze stayed near the door to her right, and Laura stepped sideways, turning her head to look where she'd just left.

The girls stood there, holding each other's hands. Their eyes were massive, swallowing their corpse-white faces. Black veins throbbed in their temples, dark blood pumping into those eyes, which reflected no light, even when Bill pulled the lamp chain to illuminate the room.

"What do you want?" Laura asked, grasping Lily tightly to her.

Instead of answering, the girls both swiveled their heads to the right. The phone let out an eerie squeal, similar to an old dial-up modem. Bill covered his ears and Laura wrapped her arm around Lily's head and pressed her into her chest, trying to muffle the screeching the best she could.

Silence fell.

The phone rang.

"It's for you," both girls said at the same time, though their mouths didn't move.

Laura met Bill's eyes, and he moved over to answer the phone, stretching his arm out toward it.

"No!" The girls lifted their free hands and Bill was thrown against the wall. Plaster cracked and he slid to the floor in a limp heap.

They turned their wretched eyes back upon her, and Laura felt ice water moving through her veins. Their mouths opened simultaneously, but only one voice sounded. "Only you may answer."

Setting Lily on her feet, Laura shoved her daughter behind her. As she moved sideways toward the phone, she kept Lily safely hidden. The phone continued to ring, the girls watching her, bodies rigid, faces expressionless.

The phone was cool in her hand when she lifted it from the charger. The ring stopped abruptly, before she had a chance to push the button. She froze, phone grasped in her hand, Lily's hands clutching the back of her shirt.

"They hung up," she said, not sure what she expected from the girls in response.

Smiles stretched their mouths simultaneously, and then static burst from the phone. Laura dropped it. The battery fell off the phone when it struck the ground, but the sound didn't cease. Eyes on the girls, she bent to pick it up, but this time when her hand made contact, the phone was so cold it burned. It seared into her flesh, but when she tried to release it, the plastic had molded itself to her hand.

She brought the phone to her ear, and through the static she heard a cacophony of gravelly voices joined in a choir of hideous sound.

"Let us in."

There was a burst of sound: screams, shouts, wails. Then silence. The two girls tilted their heads, and then the windows burst inward, glass flying through the room. Laura turned and covered Lily with her body, waiting for the piercing pain of glass shards.

Nothing happened. Wind wailed through the room, but still nothing struck her.

When she dared look up, she saw the glass swirling around the girls, who were looking toward the windows with smiles on their faces. She turned and instantly wished she hadn't. Climbing in through the windows was a set of boys, as pale and empty-eyed as their female counterparts. Crashes sounded from below. Were there more?

Laura dragged Lily over to Bill, who was starting to come around, moving sluggishly. He brought a hand up to his head, winced. There was blood there, but not much.

Through the door came more children, all in pairs. Black eyes, pale skin, throbbing black veins lacing their faces. Each pair held hands and stared at the family before them. More entered through the windows. The room was filling up.

Lily stood up and pushed out of her mother's arms. Her hair rose, standing on end as if hit by a large amount of static electricity. The lightbulb exploded, plunging the room into darkness. And in front of them, Lily glowed, white light radiating out from her tiny body. Her hands flew out to her sides, fingers spread wide, and she threw her head back. Her open mouth emitted a voice that wasn't hers. Deep and sonorous, it lapped at the walls in almost visible waves, the timber so palpable that it could be felt.

"You are not welcome here."

The white light grew, filling the room, forcing Laura to cover her eyes.

The sound of something pelting the floor made her open her eyes. The pale children were gone, glass sparkling on the carpet.

Tentatively, Laura reached a hand toward her daughter. Her blond hair now lay flat, and her arms were wrapped around her stomach. "Lily?"

"Mommy?" Lily turned, her movements slow. "Mommy, I can't see."

Laura gasped as her daughter turned to face her.

Where her eyes had been, pools of darkness now resided.

Tent City Horror

"Hey, Hawk! We've got some vittles out here. Rise and shine, princess!"

Clark cleared his throat and spat into the dirt next to the overturned bucket he sat on. He stirred something unidentifiable in a pan over a small fire and surveyed his dingy surroundings. Ragged tents lined the dirt and sand banks along Fountain Creek, flanked by sleeping bags, boxes, and anything else the homeless community could possibly live in.

A graffiti-ridden portable toilet lay on its side, partially in the water. The city had provided dumpsters, portable toilets, and camping gear in the hopes that the community would keep the area clean, but many here had no interest in doing so. Some wanted to make a statement, others just plain didn't care. Those that did care were at the whims of those who didn't.

Clark scratched his chest, spat again and called more loudly, "Hawk, get your ass out here!"

When there was no answer, Clark got up and walked to the tent. Opening the broken flap, he peered inside.

The grotesque sight that met his eyes couldn't possibly be his friend and camp-mate, George "Hawk" Hawkins.

Blood and other unidentifiable substances were spattered about the inside, gore dripping from the domed roof. Hawk's threadbare blanket was shredded. One boot lay by the door, a bone sticking out of it. Other than that, no solid remains appeared obvious to Clark's eyes, just the viscous fluids and chunks of flesh that coated the nylon.

He backpedaled, a guttural groan escaping from somewhere deep inside him. He turned to the side, unable to hold back the vomit climbing his insides. The sour acidic taste of vomit flooded his mouth, and he bent over, retching into the mud.

Jorge ran over from a neighboring tent. "You okay, man? Bad can?"

"It's Hawk."

"*Qué*? What's Hawk?"

Clark couldn't answer, continued to heave into the dirt beside the creek. His head pounded, a migraine coming on.

Jorge walked up to the tent and looked inside. His startled yell brought more of Tent City's residents from their various sleeping places. As each person looked inside and absorbed the horror for themselves, heated discussions began, voices growing louder, higher from the fear that now permeated the sprawling camp.

Now that the tent flap had been opened, the scent of blood and the insides of Hawk's intestines battled the smell of decay that rose from the creek. Clark wasn't the only one to be sick. It didn't take long to empty stomachs that hadn't been full in quite some time.

Questions were fired off in rapid, panicked voices.

"What do you think did it?"

"It had to be an animal, man. He's ripped to shreds. Do mountain lions come down here?"

"How did an animal come through here without anyone hearing it?"

"I don't know, but what else could it be?"

"How could something have done this without him screaming or making some kind of sound?"

Marti, a petite blond with scars laddering up her arms and deep lines around her eyes and mouth, snuggled under Clark's arm, burying her face in his chest.

"Should we find a cop?" Clark asked the group.

"You think anyone is going to care about a dead homeless man?" asked Magnus, a sandy haired giant of a man who'd come up from farther down the creek.

Several heads shook in the negative, and they stood around

thinking, eyes downcast.

"We can't stay here," Jorge said. "How long you think it'll take 'em to blame us for this?"

"He's right," Clark said. "We have to break camp, move upstream some. Hawk would understand. Besides, we don't want to be around if this thing comes back."

Used to being rousted and having to move quickly, they broke camp, all the while watching for whatever had done this. It could come back at any moment. Most of the predators in the area were nocturnal, but there were always exceptions, and no one wanted to be part of the buffet if it returned, especially if it brought friends.

In the end, all that was left behind was that one sad tent—flaps moving in the breeze—and scattered garbage. Plus the portable toilet. If nothing else, the city would want that back.

Later that day, as the sun set behind Pikes Peak, pinks and oranges reaching up from its bald peak, fear that had hidden during the busier parts of the day seeped back through the members of the homeless community. By now, word had spread throughout the downtown area, and many had packed up and moved to find a safer place among the old stone buildings. The city was trying to clean out the homeless, though, and everyone knew they'd be back in no time if they weren't picked up and dropped off in local shelters by the police first.

Clark had no interest in being in a shelter. Unlike many of the others, he was armed. One thing that hadn't been taken from him was his gun and the box of ammo. Nothing was going to kill him in his sleep. Or out of it. This was his home. The place he'd been forced to when he'd lost his job after constant migraines took hold of him. Doctors hadn't been able to find a way to stop them, nor did they ever bother finding out why he was beset by them. Increasingly, he'd withdrawn from life, calling in to work when the pain was too much. He'd forgotten to pay bills, with more coming in every day from the medical tests, visits, and medications. Each drug they'd put him on had made him more miserable, without relieving the migraines. One had dehydrated him so badly that he could no longer go to the bathroom. Another had turned him into a mindless zombie, sleeping all day and unable to eat.

You can't sleep all day and keep a job. Or a marriage. Neither can you sleep through paying your bills and still expect to have a home, a car, or anything else.

The funny thing was, becoming homeless had eased his migraines. It was plenty miserable in other ways, but the migraines had decreased without the stress associated with bills, work, and a marriage that had already been on the rocks long before the pain had come along to steal his life. They weren't gone all the time, instead lurking in his head like sentient creatures full of spikes and claws, and an odd dampening effect on his thoughts and memory. Hunger and dehydration didn't help them, but he got much more sleep now than he had as a working man.

Hawk had been a Vietnam veteran. PTSD and bone degradation courtesy of Agent Orange exposure had landed him without a job. According to what he'd told Clark, friends and family members had allowed him to bounce around among them each time he lost a job, but they'd tired of taking care of an almost seventy-year old man, and they'd stopped opening their doors to him. He claimed to have liked the freedom living outdoors gave him, keeping mum when it got cold and miserable. While the folks who'd known him in his past life, as they referred to it, had thought him lazy and a loser, he was always quick to lend a hand or come up with a genius idea for keeping them warm, finding food, or cleaning water to make it drinkable.

He was a survivor, a fighter, yet something had torn him to shreds without anyone nearby hearing a sound. It must have been quick, because he never would have gone down without a fight. Perhaps he'd been dead before it had begun eviscerating him.

That's what Clark wanted to think, anyway. Then again, what good would his own gun do if it killed him before he awoke at all? This wasn't the best life, but he wanted to live. Some day he wouldn't be living in a second rate tent along a mosquito-infested creek, hunted by the police, spit on by residents, and generally loathed. With the migraines getting better, he might be able to find a job. Something with less stress than his previous nine-to-five. It was a matter of figuring out the logistics in between, like how to get nice clothing for an interview, and how to get cleaned up for it, so they didn't know he was homeless. Like how to stay clean long enough to get a paycheck.

"You're deep in thought." Marti walked up to the small campfire he'd built atop some dry, packed earth. She placed a hand on his shoulder. "Thinking about Hawk?"

"Some. Thinking about other things, too. Like getting out of here."

"Maybe we could figure something out together."

They'd been on again, off again, living in such close proximity. It was a way to stay warm, to have some human companionship, and to share resources. But he didn't love her, and he was pretty sure she didn't love him. Still, maybe that sharing of resources could help them each gain a foothold in the real world again. The outside world. Then what? Would they be stuck together, miserable? He didn't need another bad relationship.

His head tweaked at the thought, and he knew his blood pressure must be rising.

"Maybe," he said. "Let's worry about making it through tonight first."

"I doubt it will show up here. That had to be a fluke."

"You're probably right, but I don't want to take any chances. Why don't you sleep with me tonight?"

"I have been feeling lonely." She slid a hand down his chest and pressed her cheek to his.

Funny how things like the odors of an unwashed human body became unimportant when you were lonely and scared. And she smelled better than some. A group had come through with care packages last week. They'd included shampoo, body wash, and toothbrushes. But it was leaning toward fall right now, and the creek water was colder than a witch's tit. Still, they'd both taken advantage of the cleaning items. There'd been others who'd scoffed. The same types who didn't want the use of a portable toilet or a sturdy tent. The types who would die out here as soon as take charity.

He placed his hand over hers, stroked a thumb along her

skin. "Then it's settled."

***

Neither of them slept well that night. Every sound was the padding paws of a predator. Every shadow was the outline of a killer. Every whisper was the slash of a deadly claw.

After they'd had sex, they lay in each other's arms, ears straining. The tents were clustered closer together than usual, much like the circling of wagons. Tonight, everyone wanted to be close to others in hopes of safety. The intimacy this provided meant Marti and Clark weren't the only ones to explore their carnal desires. There was no hiding it, but they'd all long ago lost the need for privacy in the way they'd known it in civilization.

In the morning, there were no new bodies, no stories of real predators on the prowl. After several mornings with the same report, the community relaxed. Things got back to normal. Marti had been right: it was a fluke.

But on the fifth night, Clark awoke to screaming. He disentangled himself from Marti's limbs, but she grabbed him.

"What is it?" she asked.

"I don't know yet."

Clark stepped out into the cold night air, his shoes sinking into the soft earth. The screams had come from his left, though they were missing now, the night deathly silent. He grabbed the gun out of his waistband, having slept with it there every night since this began.

Others had come out into the darkness to find out who was screaming, and he followed them to a light-colored tent on the flank of the group. There was no motion, no sound from within.

No one wanted to be the first to open the flaps.

"Ah hell, I'll do it." Clark stepped forward and gripped the zipper, opening it and stepping back, just in case something waited to attack. When nothing stirred, he grabbed a flap and looked inside.

A hole in the back of the tent let in the moonlight. They must have scared the creature away; there were much bigger chunks remaining, including the rib cage, wide open and fully exposed. The head was gone, just like Hawk's. Gore dripped from the nylon surfaces.

This time, Clark held the vomit in, but just barely.

"Over here. Another one!" Magnus called. He stood in front of the next tent, about a foot away from the open flaps.

Clark made his way toward Magnus. Inside, he found a similar scene to that of Hawk's. There were no larger chunks. No head. Just viscera and torn flesh. Even the bones had been demolished somehow. The breaking of bones should have been noisy.

Something cracked behind and to the left of the tent, and several men shot away toward the sound. Others ran in the opposite direction. Clark held his ground, shouting, "Wait, come back!"

They didn't listen.

There was a high pitched shriek, followed by a garbled yell. Then scattered shouts.

Clark's shoulders slumped, but he gave chase, knowing he couldn't leave them out there, couldn't listen to the calls for help without doing anything.

The moon hung fat in the sky, and he had no trouble seeing his way. The men had crushed tall reeds and grasses under them as they ran, leaving a clear trail. He followed this, climbing a small rise that led to a field, where he paused to catch his breath.

Across the field, figures approached, heads bobbing with their rapid movement. Clark jogged to meet them. They were carrying a figure between them, of medium build. Clark squinted, trying to figure out who it was, but he didn't recognize the man. Not one of their community regulars then, but they'd joined a different group when they'd moved upstream.

"What's going on?" he asked.

"It got him!" Magnus called. He probably could have carried the injured man himself, but instead supported just the right side while others held his shoulders, legs, and other side.

When they pulled up even with him, Clark made out tears

in the man's sweatshirt. They covered his full torso, dark blood staining the shirt. He wheezed and gasped, babbling incomprehensibly.

"Here, put him down, and stand guard," Jorge said, coming up behind Clark. He'd been a nurse in his past life, before bipolar disorder had lost him a series of jobs and put him on the street.

The men settled him on the ground and stepped back. Clark watched the direction they'd come from, straining to see any movement. It was calm, wind ruffling the tall stalks along the way. Yet he felt a sensation as of being watched.

Something was out there, hiding somewhere beyond his sightline, watching them. Waiting for its chance. Gooseflesh popped out over his neck and arms.

"Shit, these are deep," Jorge said. He'd pulled the sweatshirt up, exposing five deep, jagged gouges across the man's chest and stomach. Something hung out of one of the lower ones. A loop.

"That's not what I think it is, is it?" Clark hoped the answer was no.

"If you think that's part of his intestine, then yes, it's exactly what you think it is." Jorge spoke as he worked, pulling off his top shirt, bunching it up, then pressing it to as much of the deep wound as he could cover. "I need you to put pressure on this for me."

Clark knelt beside the man and pressed hard against the shirt, eliciting a whimper. He could feel the roll of the intestine beneath his hands.

Jorge continued checking the boy over, taking his pulse and looking over the rest of him. "I can't do anything for him. We've got to get him to a hospital."

"You're right, but there's no way for us to do that. It's too far. Someone will have to run for help." Clark looked at the men milling about and raised his voice. "Who will go find help?"

No one stepped forward. A couple of the men avoided meeting his eyes.

"Someone has to go," he said. "Now. Or he's going to die."

"He's going to die anyway," a small man, also unknown to

Clark, said. He had a thick beard and brushy mustache, and wore two button-up shirts over a t-shirt and torn jeans.

"He doesn't have to," Jorge said. "This is fixable if there's no major internal damage."

"For a homeless man?" the same small man said. "They don't give a shit about us."

"You're wrong." Jorge's voice was soft, full of doubt.

"It doesn't matter," Clark said. "We need to try."

The small man stepped toward Clark. "Why don't you go then?"

Clark lowered his voice and injected it with menace. "Because I'm holding his intestines in and I'm the only one with a gun in case it comes back."

The little man stepped back.

"I'll go, but I'm slow," said Magnus. "I need someone faster to go with me."

Layla, one of their long-time camp-mates, stepped forward. "Let's go, Magnus." She nodded at Clark then at Jorge before following Magnus into the brush.

"We're sitting ducks here," said the small man.

"Then leave." Clark was done with this man's whining.

Instead of leaving, the small man pinched his lips shut, and squatted, facing away from the rest of them.

"What's your name?" Jorge asked the injured man, who drifted in and out of consciousness, but currently appeared to be awake.

"Jim." A sob followed the single, slurred word.

"How old are you, Jim?"

"Nineteen."

It felt like someone had punched Clark in the stomach. Jim wasn't the youngest kid he'd seen on the street. Not by far. But knowing it was just a kid lying before him with a portion of his intestine hanging out bothered him.

"Are you from around here originally?" Jorge continued.

"Yeah. I went to Palmer." A local high school.

Clark stayed out of the talk as he scanned the darkness surrounding them. He could still feel the malignant presence. At least that meant it hadn't followed Magnus and Layla, but he wasn't too keen on being stalked by it. The skin between his shoulders crawled.

"Palmer, huh? What are you doing out here?"

"My parents kicked me out when I was seventeen." He paused, took a pained breath. "Got in trouble for smoking pot at school."

Anger overtook some of the mental anguish at the boy's age. What a stupid reason to condemn your child to living on the streets. Pot. And now this boy was quite possibly going to die out here among a bunch of strangers. He nodded to the boy, afraid to move his hands as blood seeped through the fabric, squeezing between his fingers. "Hey, Jim, I'm Clark."

The boy smiled up at Clark. "Nice to meet you."

He was dead long before help came.

***

"Should we move tomorrow?" Marti asked.

They were sharing a tent again tonight. There'd been no sleep for Tent City residents after the events of the previous night. Clark hadn't made it back until after dawn; he and Jorge had stayed with the boy until rescuers arrived. By that time, their only job had been to remove the body.

Whatever had been watching them had disappeared right around the time the EMTs arrived.

His head throbbed, felt like it was stuffed with spiked cotton.

"I don't think we can move far enough to make a difference."

"Did they see what it was?"

Clark thought about the descriptions each of the men had given, all different. "Not really." There was no reason to scare her more than she already was, especially since there was nothing concrete to tell. They couldn't even agree on whether it was a man or an animal. Magnus insisted it was both. A couple of the others agreed, though they couldn't say what that meant.

A shudder ran up Clark's spine, and he couldn't keep it from running through the rest of his body. Marti snuggled closer, found his hand with hers and squeezed.

He kept seeing that boy's face. If Clark knew his last name, he'd be tracking his parents down to deliver the news of his death personally, to see their wretched faces when they found out they were indirectly responsible for their child's death.

Anger was a far easier emotion to wallow in than fear and grief.

***

Clark awoke to a wet gurgling. Marti twitched against him, hard abrupt movements.

"Marti?" he mumbled, figuring she must have been having one hell of a nightmare. He rolled over and placed a hand on her shoulder, intending to wake her gently.

His hand came away sticky-wet.

Her jerky movements continued.

He sat up, easing out of the sleeping bag.

There was something on top of her, molded to her body, jerking violently. Every time it moved, her body heaved.

Her eyes glistened wetly in the scant light leaking through the canvas surface from the cloud-shrouded moon. Her mouth hung open, but the gurgling didn't come from there. It came from the deeper dark of the gaping slit in her throat, a gout of blood accompanying each gurgle.

Clark pulled his gun out of his waistband and took aim at the figure atop Marti. He grasped the handle with two hands, slid the safety off, pulled the hammer back, and squeezed with his right index finger.

The blast shook his eardrums, the acrid scent of gunpowder infiltrating his nose.

The figure screeched and took several rapid steps back, slapping into the side of the tent and going down to one knee. It sprang up as soon as its knee impacted the ground, leaping toward Clark, who shot again. It jolted back, spun in the air, kept its feet.

This time it stayed put, facing him.

Clark thought about the closely circled tents, about the thin walls. He hesitated, afraid a shot would go wild, into another tent. Outside, voices called to each other, shouted.

Though he could not clearly see the thing staring at him, he could see its movements, its form. It was vaguely man-shaped, but hunched, and it moved like a bird, with short jerky motions. The head jutted forward, then twitched side to side at unnatural angles. It was dark in color, though he could not make out the exact hue.

Now it screamed again, threw out arms that ended in blades or talons—it was impossible to tell which in the dark. Either way, they looked sharp.

"Stay away from the tent!" he yelled, hoping those outside understood. "Get down."

He fired again, continued until there was nothing left.

It took every shot, juddering with the impacts, screeching at a painfully high pitch. But it never went down.

Clark threw the gun at it and dove for the tent flap. The first slash came as he gripped the zipper, jerking it upward. Pain sliced up his back, cutting diagonally across his spine. He gasped, turned to fight it off.

He held his hands up, took the brunt of the next slash through them. Two of his fingers fell to the ground with soft plops, leaving behind blazing pain.

Behind him, the zipper continued to move, the metallic teeth sounding. Someone was coming to help.

He kicked out, feet lashing at its head. He was yelling now, throat straining.

The creature became frenzied, slashing haphazardly. Each strike was a new slice of pain, sharp and horrible.

All Clark could taste or smell was copper, thick, metallic. The screeching filled his ears, made it feel like they would implode at any moment. He fought, kicked, hit. Tried to keep his hands up to shield his head.

Hands on him now, pulling him out through the tent flap.

Fire. The tent blazing.

Breaking away from the hands, the voices. Crawling.

A large stick under his shredded hands. He grabbed it, ran at the tent, yelling more, guttural, the feel of it filling him, reverberating through his insides.

The creature fought inside the tent, ripping it apart.

He had to stop it, couldn't let it get away. The stick felt

solid in his hands, splinters sliding inside open wounds. He swung, the impact solid. Swung again, again. Vaguely, he felt the others around him, helping, joining. Together, they whaled on the creature until it didn't move anymore.

Clark's stick came away in flames. He threw it down, watched the fire until it consumed every bit of the tent, until it demolished the bodies inside.

***

The hospital didn't waste time in releasing Clark. As soon as they'd wrapped his finger stumps and treated the deep cuts he'd suffered, they booted him right back onto the street. The wounds kept his movements slow, especially the ones in his back and legs, so it took him hours to get from the hospital back to the park that would allow access to the creek. He came upon the old site at dusk, finding only ashes and garbage to tell him he was on the right track.

He camped there on the bare ground, cold and uncomfortable. His sleep came light, every sound jolting him back to consciousness with a raw awareness. At dawn, he gave up on the thought of more sleep and continued south down the creek, wondering if they were even still downtown, or if they'd wandered into the industrial area on the south end.

The smell hit him first: raw meat, feces, and urine. A slight breeze blew it directly into his face as he limped along. Then there was the sharp flap of fabric sounding with the breeze. Afraid of what he was about to find, he slowed his pace, knowing that smell couldn't be anything good.

Despite his slow speed, the tent city came into his view. He approached the closest one, but didn't have to get close to see the tear in the back of it. Every tent still standing boasted large tears and holes, and the ground ran black with blood. Mercifully, he saw only a few pieces of human remains, unidentifiable. It had been a bloodbath. There had to have been more of the creatures to accomplish brutality like this.

In the center of the camp, he came across one of the creatures, dead, torn to pieces. A metallic glint caught his eye, and he bent down, gripping a section of the creature's broken skull.

Some sort of chip had been embedded in the bone. He brushed away the dirt covering it then polished the blood off on his shirt. In tiny letters, it said *Property of the City of Colorado Springs*. Beneath that, it said *Gen II*.

His head throbbed, a bright visual aura blinding him.

Let's Play a Game

gatha clapped her hands together with the rest of the crowd, only half watching the parade as it went by. Music thundered through her eardrums in an unpleasant cacophony, the band blundering past her spot only to be followed by another. It had been seventy years since the war had ended, but the crashing of the cymbals, the pounding of the drums, still brought to mind the sound of the bombs. She'd lived through many years of peace, and only a handful of war years, but she'd never forget. Times like this, the memories were brought to the forefront.

A flash of gold caught her eye. A little girl danced by her, flaxen hair catching the sunlight. She wore a simple plaid dress, square bib at her throat. Her socks were white and folded down over her ankles, touching the shiny black patent leather shoes. Her hair was cut in a short bob, a portion of it lifted in the breeze of the passing parade.

The girl looked up, eyes catching Agatha's, and all sound blended together into one background hum. The girl squinted her blue eyes, brow furrowing. She pulled her chin down and studied Agatha, lips pressed together.

And Agatha remembered.

The scent of alfalfa and cow manure.

Gray skies.

Mrs. Pettigrew's voice, full of poison and disgust.

Agatha was nine again. Before her stood the girl. The terrifying little she-beast who would haunt Agatha's nightmares for the rest of her life. Sarah. Sarah was all sugar on the outside, venom lurking just below the surface. She wore a brown and blue plaid dress with a white collar, golden hair cut into a short bob, a black silk ribbon tied into a bow on top of her head.

Her voice, sweet and clear: "Tell her what I've done, and I'll make you regret it, Aggie."

Agatha hated that nickname. But she dare not argue with Sarah. Instead, she nodded, swallowing hard.

"Good. Now give me your biscuit. Mine is simply awful." She threw the biscuit onto the grass and stomped on it, crushing the crumbs into the ground. She held out her little pink hand, fingers nearly touching Agatha's chest.

Agatha looked down at the biscuit in her hand, her mouth watering. This was the only food she'd have until supper, and the first biscuit she'd had in months. Her stomach rumbled, but she handed it over, rubbing her stomach to ease the ache that permanently dwelled there these days.

Sarah took that biscuit and dashed it on the ground. "That one's even nastier."

With a devilish giggle, she turned and ran.

Agatha let out a breath and allowed her shoulders to relax, but only for a moment. With Sarah's attention diverted from her, now was the time to find a quiet place where she might stay hidden until supper. She fled to the barn, slipping in through the opening left by two rotted planks that had been pulled loose and moved to the side. With a gentle hand, she insured neither plank had moved even a bit with her passage. It was best to leave no signs behind.

As she climbed the rickety ladder to the loft above, Agatha focused on the sounds around her. Above the gentle nickering of the horses, she heard muffled voices outside. There was no laughter. There was never laughter at Mrs. Pettigrew's, where Agatha happened to be billeted until a foster family could be found for her. There had been a mistake, and she and the other girls had been sent here instead of Cornwall. That's what the grownups had said.

At least out here there were no bombs or air raid sirens. Back in London, where her mother, father, and older brother remained, there was less food than here. There were buildings that lay in crumbles, much like those biscuits out in the grass, thanks to German bombs.

But here there was Sarah, who had arrived separately from the other girls. Agatha was convinced that she was more dangerous to her than any German bomb. There were hundreds of houses to act as targets there, but only three other girls here who could share in the negative attention Sarah cast upon them. One never knew who Sarah would choose to victimize at any given moment. Not until she was standing before you, menace in her eyes, nose smooshed up and wrinkled at the top as she studied you and schemed. Sometimes she even turned her head to the side, ever studious like a cat contemplating a furry meal.

Agatha buried herself in the mildewed hay in one corner of the hayloft and found a knothole to peer through. She could see Mary and Constance playing below, tucked into a corner near the barn. Mary was twice Constance's age, and it showed in their height difference. Both had brown hair, but Mary's was long where Constance had a bob like the rest of the girls.

She spotted Shelley over by the chickens, her back toward the barn. Sarah stood before her, face visible to Agatha, a red chicken hanging upside down from her hand. The chicken was flapping madly, cackling and calling. The other birds were pressed against the fence on the other side of the pen. Even animals feared Sarah.

Shelley's hands were clasped behind her back, and Agatha watched her dark hair swing as she shook her head at something Sarah was saying. She shook her head faster as Sarah thrust the frantic chicken in her face, but she didn't move, not even to take a step back.

Sarah shook the chicken and stomped her foot. When Shelley still shook her head, Sarah grabbed the chicken's head with her other hand and jerked, her face unchanging.

Agatha gasped, clapping her hands over her mouth as Sarah looked up. Sarah was too far away and shouldn't have been able to hear, but she was staring directly at Agatha's knothole. She even held the still twitching, limp necked chicken up in a triumphant salute before turning her attention back to Shelley.

Whatever Shelley had refused to do would get her in trouble later. Sarah never punished you right away. She made sure you had time to worry.

***

At supper that night, Shelley stared at the carrots on her plate, pushing her fork through them.

Across from her sat Sarah, who had a healthy appetite. She ate her food, smiling around at everyone at the table. The tension was palpable, and no one but her seemed able to eat much. Agatha shuffled her own carrots around before taking a bite. Though she usually enjoyed the flavor of the fresh vegetables—so much better than the tinned carrots she got at home—tonight they tasted bland, developing into mush as she chewed, and choking her on the way down.

When Sarah had cleared her plate, she turned to Mrs. Pettigrew and said, "Thank you for the yummy food, Missus. It tastes ever so much better than the city food."

Sarah was the only one who seemed capable of eliciting a smile from their sour, shriveled benefactor, and tonight was no different. Mrs. Pettigrew pushed her gray hair back and smiled at Sarah, saying, "Thank you, my dear. My little Annie loved her carrots. You remind me so of her." Her eyes lingered on the beaming Sarah for a moment before shifting away. The smile disappeared as she looked pointedly at each of the others, eyes flicking down to their plates then back up to their faces. "What's wrong with your food, girls? Not good enough for you?"

Shelley's head jerked up for the first time since the meal had commenced. "No, ma'am. I mean, no, Mrs. Pettigrew. My stomach is feeling off today is all." The others concurred in mumbled voices.

"Maybe you need some extra chores tomorrow to increase those appetites."

"Yes, Mrs. Pettigrew," they said together.

Mrs. Pettigrew nodded, sent a fond look Sarah's way, her eyes big and dewy, and returned to her food, ignoring the girls again.

Agatha looked at Constance and Mary, both of whom were staring at their own plates. Now that the dark cast of Mrs. Pettigrew's eyes had passed over them, they were shoveling in their food as if they were starving, though she imagined their appetites to be much the same as her own. Mary briefly looked up, nodding toward her plate in silent encouragement before returning to her own food.

When they were all finished, Mrs. Pettigrew excused them to take their plates to the sink for scrubbing. "Wash those nasty little hands and faces while you're at it," she called as they gathered around the sink. They stood back to allow Sarah to wash her hands and face first. Once done, she pushed her plate into Mary's hand, and Mary washed it without question.

As they shuffled from the room, Sarah traipsed over to Mrs. Pettigrew and placed one hand on her arm. "Goodnight, Missus."

Mrs. Pettigrew leaned her cheek down for Sarah to kiss and gave her yet another smile as she raced off to join the others. Her gaze hardened when she saw Agatha looking. "Off to bed with you lot. I'll have a list of chores for you tomorrow to be sure you've earned your supper."

Shoulders sagging, they climbed the narrow stairs to the attic, where each had a bedroll to sleep on. Sarah led the way, as always, selecting the space she wanted to sleep and the bedroll she preferred for the night. Once she had chosen, the rest could each find their own.

They all got their nightgowns on and had begun to settle in when Sarah's high, clear voice sang out. "Oh no, Shelley, I want you to sleep here by me."

Shelley's shoulders tensed, but she picked up her bedroll and carried it over next to Sarah. Spreading it out, she knelt to say her prayers, grasping the bracelet her mom had given her as she did so. Sarah, who never said prayers, sat upright in her bedroll, hands folded in her lap, watching until Shelley had finished.

Agatha said her prayers with the other girls then climbed into bed, trying hard not to look in Sarah's or Shelley's direction, but failing miserably. Shelley was lying on her back, staring up at the ceiling. Sarah, who had the sole candle, was on her side, staring at Shelley. She scooted the candle closer to the other girl before snuffing it out. The scent of the candle's last smoke curled around the room, tickling Agatha's nose.

The darkness was deep and complete. There were no windows here in the attic, and no light breached the room from the downstairs. Agatha listened for sounds of movement, but heard nothing, so she shut her eyes, forcing her breathing into a relaxed pattern.

Only a moment had passed when there was a scrape, followed by high pitched screams. A muffled giggle sounded between screams, followed by the slap of running feet, bare on the floorboards. A cool breeze blew past Agatha before one final scream preceded a series of thumps and bangs.

There were no further sounds.

Unable to see in the dark, Agatha lay motionless, waiting, afraid to breathe. A snick was followed by a bright flare and the fizz of a match, and the candle lit the room. There sat Sarah, a grin splitting her face, and in her hand was Shelley's bracelet. Agatha watched as she fastened it around her wrist and examined it before looking at her. Sarah held a single finger up to her lips, exacting a promise of silence.

"Oh, lord, what has happened, you little wretches?" Mrs. Pettigrew's voice sounded from the bottom of the staircase. There was a shriek, then: "This girl is dead. How am I supposed to explain this to the authorities? They'll have my head! Get over here and explain what you've done."

The girls stood and quickly made their way to the top of the stairs. Shelley lay at the bottom, body twisted. Across her eyes was a bumpy mess. It took Agatha a moment to realize what it was: candle wax. There were bloody scratches on her cheeks and forehead.

"I think she knocked over the candle, Missus. We couldn't stop her from running." Sarah said this in a little girl voice. Tears poured down her cheeks, and her body spasmed with her fake sobs.

Mary pulled Agatha and Constance into her arms. Together, they cried silently.

"Is that what happened, girls?"

"I don't know, Mrs. Pettigrew. It was terrible dark," Mary

answered.

"You girls should have been more careful. I'll have to ring the doctor. Back to bed." She shook her head and wandered away from them, leaving the girls to gaze down at their friend's lifeless body.

Why hadn't Shelley given Sarah what she'd wanted?

***

The next few days went without incident. Sarah was on her best behavior. Agatha, Mary, and Constance kept away from her as much as they could. And she let them.

Shelley's body had been removed the next morning, the girls clustered in the attic to avoid seeing what they did with her. All, that is, except for Sarah, who sat at the top of the stairs, legs crossed, watching with interest. She even called down questions a few times. "Why is her neck bent like that, good sirs?" "What will you do with her now?" "Did she scratch her eyes out?" Agatha never heard any answers.

Other than a lecture on proper candle usage, Mrs. Pettigrew said nothing about the incident. Figuring it best to do the same, Agatha stayed mum during the day and cried quietly in the attic at night.

After five days of tense peace, Sarah grew bored. A bored Sarah was a restless and irritable Sarah. And dangerous.

At first, it was small things. A tack in Constance's bedroll. Pepper in Mary's porridge. Dirt in Agatha's brush. Still, all told, the little pranks that occurred weren't terribly harmful or dangerous, and the girls took them with grace, afraid to show a bad reaction.

Agatha was the first to realize the mistake they'd all made. Sarah needed to be entertained, and by not reacting, they had unwittingly made the situation worse. The next time Sarah played a prank on her, she made sure to play up her reaction.

It was the morning of the eighth day after Shelley's death. Agatha went to take a drink of her milk, usually fresh, warm, and frothy. What she found, instead, was soured milk, thick and awful in her mouth. Instead of swallowing it down and pretending all was well, she choked and sprayed the milk across the table, gasping and coughing.

Mrs. Pettigrew, of course, was livid. "What in heaven's name are you doing, Agatha Miller?"

"My milk is sour!"

"It's no such thing. How dare you waste good milk."

"Taste it yourself," said Agatha, thrusting her partially emptied glass toward Mrs. Pettigrew, who jumped back just as the soured milk splashed onto her dress.

"How dare you!"

Her punishment was to clean the table, chairs, and flooring in the kitchen. As she scrubbed on hands and knees, Sarah skipped merrily about her, singing a song.

"Agatha got in trouble,
Agatha got in trouble.
She spilled her milk,
She spit it out,
Who gave her spoilt nasty?"

While Sarah wanted a reaction, Agatha still feared being impertinent to her. Being punished by Mrs. Pettigrew was one thing. Being punished by Sarah was a terrifying prospect she hoped to avoid, so she kept her eyes downcast and hoped taking the punishment was enough to entertain Sarah, at least for a little while.

Once her punishment was completed, Mrs. Pettigrew sent Agatha outside with the others, Sarah trailing behind her.

"What shall we do now, Aggie?"

The pet name rankled even more than usual.

"I'm rather tired, Sarah. I was just going to sit under the apple tree and rest a bit."

"Well, I don't want to rest. I want to play. With you."

Agatha sighed. What was she to do? She couldn't turn her down, but nothing Sarah wanted to play could end well.

"What do you want to play then?" She stopped and turned to face the other girl.

Sarah looked at her, a thoughtful expression on her face. Her eyes seemed to go far away for a moment, and then a smile spread slowly over her face.

"Want to go pinch the cows?"

"Why would I want to do that?" Agatha asked, without

thinking. She realized her error when Sarah's face scrunched, brows knitted.

"Because I said so."

With a resigned huff, Agatha turned toward the field, figuring Sarah would follow. When she reached the side of the barn and found herself alone, she turned to look back at Sarah, who stood in the same place she'd left her. Her fists were curled at her sides, her shoulders raised and tense, and her face was dark like a thunder cloud, features tiny and scrunched.

"Aren't you going to come play, Sarah?"

"I don't want to."

"Oh, please, won't you come play? I'm sorry I angered you."

"You will be."

They stared at each other a moment longer before Sarah turned with a swish of that golden hair and stalked off in the direction of Mary and Constance. Agatha felt a tweak of remorse, like whatever happened to them now would be her fault for setting Sarah off, but she brushed it off. They wouldn't get anything she wouldn't suffer twice as much of later.

She went into the barn and climbed back up into the hayloft, her favorite place on the farm. The sweet scent of the hay surrounded her. Oh, when would they find her somewhere else to billet? How much longer would she have to deal with Sarah's cruelty and Mrs. Pettigrew's indifference?

***

Agatha awoke to a darkening sky and the sound of footfalls in the hay below. Shush-shush.

"Who's down there? Is it time to go inside for supper?"

No one answered her call. The only sound was the shush of shifting hay.

"Mary? Constance? Is that you?"

Still no answer.

"Sarah?" This time her voice came out in a low trembling whisper. "Is it supper time?"

Shush, shush.

And then the ladder creaked, moving slightly as some weight rested upon it.

"Please, who's there?"

The ladder continued to creak and shift, just a little, as someone moved slowly up its length.

Agatha scrunched back into the darkness.

"Sarah, if that's you, I'm sorry. We can play whatever you like tomorrow."

This time, a voice did answer from just below the loft. "Anything?"

"Yes, anything you like." Hope flared in her breast.

"Okay. Meet me under the apple tree after breakfast then."

Sarah's movement down the ladder was much quicker than her climb had been. Agatha heard her jump off into the hay with a hushed thump, her feet clapping all the way out of the barn. Her voice drifted in through the door. "You'd better come in for supper, or you'll be in trouble."

Agatha hopped up and ran to the ladder, turning to climb down. As she put her foot on the second to last rung, it hit something slick and she slipped. She lost her grip, sliding down the rest of the ladder onto the ground. She landed on her feet, but scraped her palm. Examining it, she found a thick splinter embedded under the skin.

Sarah had made her point. She wasn't happy.

***

The next day, Agatha made her way to the apple tree directly after breakfast. Sarah was already waiting there for her. She was hopping from one foot to the other, staring intently at the ground.

She didn't look up as Agatha approached. Agatha drew up next to her and looked down, searching for what so interested Sarah. There, between the other girl's feet, was a toad. Sarah was hopping over it, back and forth, back and forth.

"Hi, Sarah."

Sarah continued hopping for a moment, still not looking up at Agatha. Hop. Hop. Hop. Hop. Then she let out a drawn out sigh and landed on the toad, which exploded out from under Sarah's tiny shoe. Something pink dripped down the patent leather, and the grass was a deep red. She looked up at Agatha with a giggle and wiped her shoe in the grass next to the murdered creature. Agatha did her best to hide the dismay and disgust she felt at this, and stared back at Sarah. Inside her was a roiling sea of fear, her stomach sick.

Sarah didn't speak to her, instead picking up the tattered remnants of the little creature she had killed. She cradled it in her hand and lifted it to her face. Her lips were moving, and Agatha realized she was singing to it, very quietly, just under her breath. A whisper of sound. As she sang, she walked over to the well, the metal lid having been removed, and dropped the frog inside. She stood there for a moment, looking down, and Agatha studied her back, waiting.

Finally, she took a breath, shoulders rising then falling again as she exhaled. Agatha felt a jolt when the other girl turned toward her with an abruptness that seemed impossible, her movements fluid.

"I want to play a game, Aggie."

"What game?"

"Let's call it 'Fool's Errand.' How does that sound?"

"How do you play it?" Agatha chewed on her lip and waited.

Sarah clapped her hands and did a little hop. "You'll be 'it' first. Ready for your fool's errand?"

"I think so."

"Your errand is to go into Old Pettigrew's room and get a trinket from there. Then I want you to bring it to me."

"She'll never let me go in there!" Agatha cried.

"She certainly won't. That's why it's a fool's errand."

"Can't we play another game? How about hopscotch?" Agatha's stomach turned as she said this, envisioning the poor toad exploding once more.

The smile on Sarah's face fell. "I said I want to play Fool's Errand. Do it or you'll pay."

Agatha closed her eyes and took a deep breath, then another. She didn't have much choice in the matter. Denying Sarah would only cause her behavior to escalate, and who knew what she would come up with next.

"Fine. Do you have a preference for what I get?"

"No, but make sure it's shiny. And pretty!" Again, she clapped and hopped. "Oh, this will be so much fun!"

Fun, sure.

Agatha turned away from Sarah, and headed back toward the house. Mrs. Pettigrew would be going to tend the horses soon, which might be her only chance to get into her room. She'd just have to be ready.

She sat on the bottom step of the porch, dragging her toe in the dirt to form shapes. First, a large circle, two smaller ones inside, followed by a half moon shape. Studying it, she realized she was drawing a face and finished it out with a nose and straight hair. Then wrote "Sarah" in the dirt beneath the face and stomped on it. Dirt puffed out from the drawing, some settling on her shoe in a light dusting.

A rustle nearby made her jerk her head up. She looked around, but didn't see anyone. Had Sarah seen? Quickly, she wiped out everything she'd drawn in the dirt and pulled her knees close to her chest, arms wrapped around her legs.

The door behind her opened, and she scooted to the side to allow the Missus to pass by her. Mrs. Pettigrew let out an irritated noise, almost a growl, but didn't so much as look at Agatha or speak to her. When she disappeared into the shadows of the barn, Agatha jumped up and ran inside.

It took her eyes a moment to adjust to the dimness of the house, but she knew her way through it well enough by now. She continued walking forward until the grays separated into the shapes of furniture. The bedroom was through the kitchen and down a hallway to the back of the house.

As she approached the doorway, she realized there was a chance it could be locked. The knob stood, stark against the whiteness of the door, and she reached out with a trembling hand to grasp it.

A creak sounded behind her, and she jerked her hand away as if it had been burned, turning to look down the hallway.

Nothing there.

She wiped her hand on her dress then reached out again, this time grasping the doorknob with purpose. She turned, and found that it moved easily beneath her palm. The door swung open with a creak, and she shot a look behind her again before slipping into the cool darkness beyond.

The room was simple, made up of a bed, a bureau, and a vanity table. Clothes lay strewn about on the floor and the bed was unmade. It smelled musty and unpleasant. She glanced around, looking for anything that might claim Sarah's fancy.

There, on a cabinet. A locket. Agatha ran over to the cabinet and snatched up the locket, stuffing it into the pocket of her dress without studying it.

Footsteps sounded in the hallway. Agatha looked around for a hiding place, her gaze sweeping the room. A pile of clothes lay by the closet, and she dove beneath them, rolling onto her back and covering herself the best she could. The smells of cow manure and hay filled her nostrils, warm and dank beneath the pile of clothing.

The footsteps stopped at the doorway, and Agatha heard Mrs. Pettigrew say, "Hm? I thought I closed this." There was a second of silence, and then a bit of a snort, followed by the footsteps coming into the room. "Now, where was that silly thing?"

Agatha kept very still, afraid to breathe. If Mrs. Pettigrew caught her in here, what would she do? She'd only used the strap once, on Constance, but the look on her face had said she'd enjoyed it. At the very least, Agatha would receive a beating for being in here.

There was shuffling and the sound of things being moved about. The steps drew nearer, and Agatha was certain she'd be revealed at any moment. Her whole body tensed as she waited for something to happen, her pulse throbbing in her throat and temple. Her skin crawled as she imagined Mrs. Pettigrew standing over her.

Any moment.

Instead, she heard, "Ah ha!" Then Mrs. Pettigrew left the room, a solid click telling Agatha she'd shut the door.

With a loud exhalation, Agatha crawled from beneath the stinking pile of clothes and brushed herself off. She felt in her pocket and found the locket still there. Carefully, she opened the door a crack and peered out. No sounds, no one there. She forced herself through the doorway and into the hall. Any moment, Mrs. Pettigrew's form would steal the meager light coming from the front of the house, and she'd be discovered.

It took forever to move down the hallway, her feet filled with lead. Her ears picked up at the tiniest sounds and amplified them into footsteps. The shadows danced, changed shape. But Mrs. Pettigrew never appeared, and she made it to the door without incident.

Outside again, she made her way back to the apple tree, hand on the outside of her pocket to keep the feel of the locket. She didn't want to lose it.

When she arrived at the tree, Sarah was up in its branches, dangling like a cat, arms and legs on either side of a thick branch. Her cheek was pressed to the wood and she was facing the house.

"What did you bring me, Fool?"

Agatha's shoulders bunched up, but she reached into her pocket and held the locket up as high as she could. It glinted in the pale sunlight, and fell open. A child's face looked back at Agatha, and she realized that this must be the daughter Mrs. Pettigrew had spoken of in the past, Annie, who had died in the well as a toddler. She really did look like a younger version of Sarah.

A warm sensation flushed through her system, and she knew she had to put the locket back. She pulled it toward her as Sarah reached for it, and Sarah overreached, slipping on the branch. She fell on the ground with a horrible thump, breath escaping her with an "Oof!"

And then she was still.

Agatha went down on her knees beside her, checking to see if she was okay. Sarah didn't move for a moment, eyes staring up at the branches of the tree, mouth opening and closing like a drowning fish's.

Sarah took a deep breath. As Agatha knelt there, Sarah's eyes darted to her face. The pupils enlarged, filling her eyes, making them black as night. Agatha gasped and pulled back, away from what she saw there. She fell on her bum and back pedaled.

"I'm sorry, Sarah! Are you okay?"

"You. Will. Pay. For that." Her words were gasps, strained and wheezing.

Without looking back, Agatha got to her feet and ran. She kept on running until she was as far from the apple tree as she could get, and then she hid. If only she never had to go back.

Sarah would be waiting for her.

***

Supper was quiet. The other girls kept sneaking looks at both Sarah and Agatha, but they kept their mouths shut.

Mrs. Pettigrew was tense, fidgeting with her dress, her utensils, her hair. She barely ate, pushing the food around on her plate. Had she discovered the locket was missing, or was there something else wrong?

Agatha's stomach and chest burned as she looked between Sarah and Mrs. Pettigrew. Every time she looked at Sarah, she was staring at her, eyes dark, just as they'd been under the apple tree. She had no expression on her face, and as Agatha watched, she continued to eat, calmly forking food into her mouth and chewing, swallowing, and sticking the next bite in, all without looking down at her plate or away from Agatha.

As the fear grew inside Agatha, something happened. The fear began to change, to morph within her.

She became angry.

Sarah couldn't keep doing this. She wasn't even the oldest girl here. In fact, Constance was the only one younger than her. Why should they all be afraid?

The acidic burn within her ceased hurting, instead becoming a burn of passion, of righteous anger. The warmth that filled her now was pleasant, a throbbing that made her want to act.

And as this feeling grew, Agatha tilted her head to study Sarah right back. She ate, eyes never leaving Sarah's.

Two could play at this game.

***

Mrs. Pettigrew went to bed immediately after supper,

mumbling something about cleaning up. There was a wrinkled sheet of paper clutched in her hand.

Agatha and Sarah continued eyeing each other, a wicked smile playing across Sarah's face every time Agatha lifted her chin and stared back. It faltered when Agatha smiled back.

Once they were upstairs, Sarah patted the spot next to her. "I want Agatha to sleep next to me tonight."

"I don't think I will." It had been months since she'd felt this good about anything, and the look on Sarah's face was even better. Her mouth gaped for a moment before clamping shut. Then her eyes narrowed to slits.

"We'll see about that later, dear Aggie."

Constance stared at Agatha, for once not intent on their nemesis. Mary's gaze slid sideways between the two of them, brow furrowed. Her quizzical expression was the last thing Agatha saw before the light was blown out and darkness fell.

And then she listened.

It was quiet for a few minutes, long enough for one of the girls to fall asleep, her deep measured breaths filling the room.

There it was. Something stirring. The sound of wool sliding over cotton. Shuffling.

Agatha reached under her pillow for the fork she had hidden there. Sarah had washed the knives, but left the other utensils to the rest of them. The fork felt cool in Agatha's hand, smooth to the touch. She rubbed her thumb over the handle, her grip tightening when a scuff sounded near her. Cool air washed over her from a nearby disturbance.

Something swiped by her face, so close she felt a tingle across her cheek. She jabbed out with the fork, sinking it into something soft. A gasp sounded above her, and she rolled away, toward the door, fork still in hand.

"Agatha?" A whisper. Mary.

Agatha crouched against the wall, shushed Mary.

Bare feet slapping the floor. Away from her.

A sharp smack. A scream. A scuffle. Mary?

She needed to get Agatha away from here, lead her out. The soothing sound of Constance's breathing had ceased. Whimpers had taken its place.

"You want to play, Sarah? Meet me under the tree!" And

Agatha ran. Through the door, down the steps, feet light on the rough wooden stairs. One step creaked as she neared the bottom. She froze, waiting for Mrs. Pettigrew's voice or the sound of her footsteps.

Nothing.

Off again, like a shot. Feet patting the ground behind her. As she reached the back door, she heard a creak, knew Sarah had reached the bottom of the stairs.

She threw the latch, opened the door. Cool air embraced her, mist dotting her face as she stepped out into a thick fog. She could barely see in front of her, everything gray and featureless. So she ran down the stairs and aimed to her right, stumbling blindly across the damp grass, the cold infiltrating her skin. Her night dress clung to the skin of her legs.

The fog dampened sound, and Agatha couldn't tell where Sarah was. Sounds and shapes moved around her, echoed off the droplets of water in the air. She refused to look behind her, afraid she'd trip over something hidden in the fog. It wasn't until the apple tree loomed ahead of her that she stopped, throwing herself against its rough bark, pieces breaking off under the clutch of her hands.

"What game are we going to play, Aggie?"

Agatha turned around, now pressing her back to the tree. "Hopscotch, Sarah. Why don't we play hopscotch?"

Sarah giggled, a sound that carried no joy. It made Agatha's skin crawl, her neck tightening. Her breaths were coming in pants as she tried to catch her breath despite the pounding of her heart. But Sarah didn't seem winded at all.

"Okay! You first."

"I don't know how to play. Can you show me first?"

Sarah turned away from Agatha and began to hop. Agatha walked behind her, bare feet soft and silent on the wet grass. When Sarah reached the well, she stopped and hopped into a turn, once again facing Agatha. But she hadn't expected Agatha to be standing right behind her. She jerked her head up and looked into the other girl's eyes. They studied each other for a moment, then Agatha reached forward with both arms and shoved as hard as she could.

As Sarah fell into the well, Agatha glimpsed a flash of gold.

The locket? She heard her say, "Aggie?" And then there was a splash. No screams. No further sounds. Agatha picked up the cover and slid it over the mouth of the well, goosebumps rising when metal grated over stone. She padded back toward the house, following the bent grasses to find her way back.

Shivering, she made her way back inside, closing the door behind her, and up to her pallet. Mrs. Pettigrew hadn't woken, but Mary had lit the candle and was waiting, back against the corner. Constance was snuggled into her lap, fast asleep again. Relief shown on Mary's face when Agatha was the one to enter, and they bedded down for the night, no questions asked.

***

They never found Sarah. Not even when they checked the well.

Agatha overheard the constable speaking with Mrs. Pettigrew the next day, voice gruff. "One girl dead was bad enough, but now another girl missing? Worse, we can't seem to find where this child was sent here from. How will we reach her parents? The warning we sent you wasn't enough?"

"Please, Mr. Owens, how could I have stopped either one? She ran out in the middle of the night. Was I to get no sleep? To guard them every moment?" She dabbed at her soggy, red eyes.

"I'm taking these children with me when I leave. Fetch them, and have them pack their things."

Agatha jerked back behind the side of the building as he turned, jowls wiggling with the movement. She watched his ample back as he moved down the steps and into the yard, turning his head to study the other two girls, who stood next to the chicken coop. He didn't turn when Mrs. Pettigrew called out to them. "Girls, come pack your things." Her voice was choked, shaking, but it firmed when she said, "At once!"

Mary and Constance ran inside. Agatha made her way around the porch and up the stairs, a few steps behind them. As she packed her meager belongings into a sack, the other girls did the same, no one speaking. Agatha slid into her thick brown coat, making sure the large cream tag with her name on it was pinned to the front lapel.

There was a weight in her pocket, and she stuffed her hand inside to investigate. Something smooth and cool met her fingers. When she pulled it out, she discovered the locket. It dangled there, swaying below her palm, until she threw it across the room to where Sarah had slept each night. The other two looked at her, eyes wide. She shook her head, signaling them not to say a word.

***

Agatha was pulled from her reverie by the feel of a cold hand on hers. The band had moved away, the sound dampened, blunted. She looked up to see the young girl there in front of her, a smirk on her face. Her eyes were dark. Hadn't they been blue?

The girl leaned forward, giggled, and said, "Let's play a game."

Dearest

My Love,

    The need for your touch is a craving I cannot withstand. I hunger for you each moment we're apart, imagining your tender hand upon my cheek, your soft, hungry lips upon mine. I want nothing more than to feel the hard lines of your body pressed against me. It won't be long now until we're together forever.

I remember the first time I saw you, sitting at that bistro on the corner of Baptist and Red Oak, your chestnut hair haloed red and golden by the sunlight. You sat deep in conversation, eyes intent, leaning forward. No one could ever say you're not a good listener.

Then you smiled.

The first time that smile graced your lips it caressed my insides, stroked every single inch of me. I froze where I stood, letting the heat of you fill me, build to an eruption. You stole my heart in that moment, imprisoned it. We're soulmates, the passage of time having only made this all the clearer to me.

Nobody can ever keep us apart. We are one.

My memories have all been tied to you. There is no moment I remember without you in it somehow. You are the sun of my emotional solar system, the bright shining beacon that gets me through each day. My every need is fulfilled by you. I can't imagine life being just me ever again.

It is you and me forever.

There have been dark times through these many months. I'm the first to admit that things have not been perfect. Hard times have come and gone. Times I thought we'd be kept apart, that our bodies and minds would be forever estranged. We've made it through the bad, survived it and come out the other side. True love brought us through.

You are my destiny. And I yours.

Soulmates.

Flowery words don't forge relationships. You already know we're meant to be together, though sometimes your behavior makes me wonder. At times you can be so aloof, so self-involved. I don't understand why you do this to me, why this selfish beast tears forward from inside you. What have I done other than adore you?

When you ignore me, fail to acknowledge my feelings for you, fail even to acknowledge *me*, my presence, it hurts more deeply than you could ever imagine. It shreds my soul, rips my heart out. I have ruined more pillows with the stains of my grief than you could possibly grasp. Love should not be buoyed by a sea of tears. It should be made of laughter, smiles, and kisses. I should be able to come to you when I hurt, not flee, hide, because it is you who hurts me.

Through much soul searching, I know there's only one way to fix this, to strip away the distractions and make us one soul as we should be.

I need to take care of Her.

I know all about you two. She may temporarily possess your heart, but it's on loan from me. Always from me. You have allowed her to steal from me for the last time. I have given you time to work through this on your own, but it seems I allowed you too much rope. It has reached the point that I either let you hang yourself with it or save you from yourself.

And, my love, I cannot let you destroy yourself or us. I must do whatever it takes.

I look at Her and see what it was that attracted you. Believe me, I do. She's the type of woman they cast in movies, with a face meant to be on screens and billboards, and curves that would stop traffic. It's true She bears more physical beauty than I do, but I can give you so much more than She can in the way of love, of consistency, of dedication. I am smarter than She will ever be, and you and I have more in common.

From that moment on the street corner you were mine.

Even as you sat across from Her, we became one.

When you married Her, I thought I'd never breathe again. I watched, you know. The audience at these weddings is so big that anyone can lose themselves in the crowd. I sat in the back next to your great-aunt Sandy and her breathing apparatus, her wheezing a steady background to despicable vows being exchanged at the front of the church. It took everything within me not to kink that tube as I rolled it between my fingers, to let her suffocate, much as my heart was doing right then. But sense prevailed, and I held myself back. You should be thanking me. That old wretch begged for it, sobbing away, the scent of mothballs a suffocating cloud of putrescence around us.

You put on a good show with those empty vows you spoke at the altar. That woman you call your wife ate it up, lapping at your voice like a dog at the water bowl. The dress was perfect, and She was flawless in it. I bet Her brain weighs half what a normal person's does, and it showed in the vapid expression She fixed on you as you spoke those falsities, poisonous vows pouring from your tongue. I nearly threw up on your Uncle Gene, there in the pew ahead of me, his bald dome reflecting the church lighting like a beacon. How I wanted to eradicate that light, to crack his skull, to flail at anyone near me and kill the smiles they wore in their ignorance.

You looked so handsome in your tuxedo. I want you to wear it when our time comes to wed. We'll need to exorcise Her stink from it first. Then again, there's probably no way to clean that off. We'll find you an identical tuxedo instead. I don't want a church wedding. Rather, a small wedding on a vineyard is my preference. Rolling hills of green, luscious grapes, the blue sky above us.

Yes, we'll make this right. She can take the baby with Her when She leaves, that devilish spawn. No child should be born of false love, but that will be Her problem, not ours. You and I will have our own children, products of real love. Forget that ugly, squalling little wretch. Who knew babies could be so hideous? Ours won't be. They'll have your hair and lips, and my nose and eyes. They'll be healthy and quiet, not like that thing currently sleeping in its crib, snot-stained and foul. I hear it breathing, smell the spoiled milk odor it constantly exudes.

It's time for me to clean up this final mess, as I am always forced to do when it comes to you. I'm not sure you understand how much I do for you. How much time I've put into this relationship, what an investment I've made. It all seems so one sided when I think of everything I've done and how little you've given. A true relationship takes two, not one slaving away and the other taking advantage.

That all changes soon.

Tomorrow, we meet in person. I will finally get to touch your skin, feel that smile directed at me. It will be me you embrace, me you caress, me your voice strokes. I've waited all this time for you to look at me the way you look at Her, but without the deception. All this time I have been right here, sometimes inches from you, and you have looked right past me, ignored my presence. Surely you've seen me in all those public spaces. I can't have been invisible to you, not really. You just had to act like I was so She wouldn't know what existed between us.

I'm sure it will be a relief for you to be able to stop play acting this way. You want me as much as I want you. I know this. Every touch from Her must feel like sandpaper across your skin. Every laugh must grate on your nerves the way it does on mine. The time for pretending is done. Your freedom awaits, along with our future together. The gods smile down upon us, urging us toward our destiny.

You'll know when the time is right, when the clock chimes the time of our first meeting on our anniversary tomorrow. I'm ready for you, for us. As I lie here in the spawn's closet, listening to the sound of your voices downstairs, I steel myself against the false sounds of happiness, knowing that at every moment you await our meeting, that every touch and laugh is one you intend to share with me.

While neither of us wants it to come to this, I am prepared in case She fights to stay. How deliciously ironic that it may be Her own gardening tools that end Her life. And the baby, if it comes to that. If She dies, so must the baby. After all, we can't move forward saddled with baggage from the heresy of your flawed relationship. It would be a curse upon us.

Wait for me tomorrow, dearest. For I will come for you once I have finished here, so that we may forge ahead with this love that was meant to be, released from the shackles that have held us for the past two years. Our destiny will be realized.

All my love,
The Woman of your Dreams.

A Cold and Carnal Hunger

One
Water rushed by at knee level, spurring Gray to work faster to board up the windows of the old stone church. He'd already sealed the large double doors at the front. Around him, fellow residents threw their belongings into vehicles, set livestock free to take their chances, and packed their families out of the drowning town of Sweetwater. But for Gray, nothing mattered more than putting protections in place.

It was essential the *being* trapped inside this church not get out. Wooden boards wouldn't last forever, but it was the most he could do in the time he had. Later, he'd find a way to block it up more thoroughly, to ensure the evil within couldn't harm anyone else. He had one more window to cover, then he could recite the blessing and flee with his neighbours.

The water had risen to his waist by the time he'd nailed the final board into the crumbling mortar. The cold ate through his flesh to infiltrate his bones. October was no time to go wading. A child's doll, its haloed hair full of leaves, bumped his leg before drifting away. Branches, golden leaves, and other detritus moved with the current. The dark gray water reflected the ashen sky above. He couldn't see his own feet, nor could he tell what touched him at times.

From inside the building came a cacophony of sound. Pounding, crashing, screeching. She – *it* – had awakened, and now fought her bonds. He couldn't be sure they'd hold.

The wood directly in front of him splintered outward, a

sharp, dark piece of metal jutting through, stopping mere inches from his head. He stumbled in the water before righting himself, then felt around with his feet until he found another board trapped beneath some rocks. He shoved the rocks off, lifted the board with his foot, and leaned down to grasp it, soaking himself to the shoulder. It took a moment to hammer the metal spike back through the wood, a clang sounding from the other side. Slapping the board across the damaged wood, he nailed it into place.

The job done, he stepped back and pulled the vial of holy water out of his pocket. He struggled to uncap it with his cold, wet hands, but managed. Drops of holy water pelted the stone, but just as he opened his mouth to speak the words that would shore up the protections he'd put in place, something large and heavy rolled into his legs beneath the water, bowling him over. He slipped beneath the surface.

The jolt of cold water closing over his head shocked a gasp out of him. Icy fingers of water filled his lungs, and they began to burn. He struggled to plant his feet to stand, but the current pulled him backward. A force pushed at his head, keeping him submerged. No matter how he tried to get his footing, the water stymied him. One small inch reclaimed would allow him to breathe.

The last thing Gray saw before the darkness overtook him was a green glow shining through the cracks between the boards and emitting from the small steeple, visible through the thin shimmer of water above him.

***

Two

The sun shone off the surface of the lake, creating an emerald sparkle, but not penetrating the thick, algae-filled depths. Small waves lapped at the dark soil lining the edge. Lauren dipped a toe into the tepid water, her other foot sinking into the moist mud which seeped between her toes. The rich, loamy scent tickled her nose.

"I can't see the bottom," Lauren said. "And it looks filthy. You sure you want to swim here?"

"Everyone swims here," May said.

"But it smells."

"You get used to it."

Footsteps sounded behind the two girls. "What's the problem?" Chris asked as he approached.

"Lauren doesn't want to go in." May pulled her tank top off, beneath which she wore a purple bikini top.

Chris laughed, his gaze lingering on May's slim figure. "Because of the ghost town?"

"Ghost town?" Lauren asked.

May rolled her eyes. "Oh great, now she'll never go in."

"Seriously, what ghost town?" Lauren looked around, trying to see what they were talking about. Low, tree-covered hills surrounded the lake. There were no buildings visible.

"It's under the water, silly," May said. "And it's really not a ghost town. I don't know why they call it that. I'm sure there's nothing left."

Lauren stared at the murky water, squinting as if that would show her the hidden town.

"You might as well tell her since you brought it up, Chris."

"Okay." Chris sat down in the grass and patted a spot in front of him. Lauren sat down across from him, followed by May. "There used to be a town where the lake is now. An old mining settlement. When they built the Roughton Dam they screwed up. The river diverted the wrong way and started flooding the populated town in the middle of the day."

"There were other towns," May broke in. "Officials emptied them first, moved the bodies from the graveyards, tore down and burned the remnants of the buildings, and cleared them out. They were supposed to be covered by the water."

"Right," Chris said. "But not Sweetwater. So, unlike other reservoirs, this one has a full town still standing beneath it. There's supposed to be a stone church, and that, at least, has to be there, even if the wooden buildings have fallen apart. Even better, they never moved the bodies from the graveyard like in the other towns."

"Tell her about the priest."

"Oh, yeah. There was a priest who stayed behind. He said he had to secure the church, wouldn't let anyone help him, wouldn't tell them what the big deal was. No one ever saw him again. They say he drowned."

Lauren had been watching the lake throughout the story. The usually soothing shush of water lapping the shore sent a shudder up her spine. "So you have no problem swimming in water that could be full of dead bodies?"

"It's been a long time since a body washed up." A huge grin split May's face.

Lauren frowned at her. They picked at Lauren sometimes, treated her like she was naïve, like they knew so much more than she did. It bothered her, but she tried to shake it off. After all, she was the new girl in town. At least they'd brought her into the fold, even if not yet entirely. "But... I mean, there are buildings under there. That doesn't freak you out? People used to live in those houses, shop in the stores. There's an entire history under there. There's—"

"Ghosts?" May interrupted.

"That's not what I'm saying." Lauren sighed. "Have you ever had a relative die, and you go to their house afterward, and the emptiness feels unnatural? Like you can feel their presence and the absence of their presence at the same time?"

May frowned. "I've never been to a dead person's house."

"Never mind," Lauren said. "You guys go in. I'll explore out here for a bit. Maybe I'll come in later."

Chris stood up, removed his shirt and tossed it to the side. He was slim with lean muscle. He offered May a hand up. She wiggled out of her jean shorts and chased him into the water.

Lauren ignored their yells and splashes. She walked along the edge of the lake, avoiding the water. It looked deceptive to her now, as if it were hiding something. The waves reached for her, crawling up the muddy banks. She found it disturbing that the energy of so many lives swirled about beneath the placid water. It was like feeling a presence on the other side of a door, a thin plank of wood the only thing between you and it.

Try as she might, she couldn't make out anything beneath the surface. And where were the turtles, the frogs, the birds, the fish? It was only now she noticed the complete lack of animal life around the lake, and she shuddered.

The sound of her friends' voices had become distant, a

whisper behind her. Waves lapped at the shore, leaves rustling in the occasional breeze. Her footfalls sounded muffled.

Ahead of her, a log lay close to the water. She walked over to it and took a seat, her body pressing into the damp, softened surface. A strong scent of decay hovered in the air. Looking out at the water, her mind strained for some confirmation of a presence below the surface. There was nothing, just as her conscious mind told her there couldn't be, and she relaxed, allowing the timid rhythms of the water to lull her to a more peaceful state. She closed her eyes and revelled in the warm wind on her arms. Stretching one leg out, she slid her foot into the water.

A cool sensation crept up her foot. She pulled it back, but the coolness didn't leave her. It moved higher, covering her heel, then her ankle. Now it was on her other foot as well.

She tried to open her eyes, but couldn't. Nor could she move her feet again. When she whimpered, she felt the vibration move up her throat and into her mouth, but her lips wouldn't part.

The cold continued upward. Her calves, her knees. Her thighs. Here it caressed her, slowing its progress. Her breath caught in her throat because now it felt like cool hands. They moved up her outer thighs, lapped at the edges of her shorts. The cool on her inner thighs was shocking, gliding along her sensitive, goose-bumped skin.

She fought to move, to call out, but each time she tried to move she felt a firm pressure, as if she were not so much paralysed as being held back. Even her eyelids felt pressed down. The moment she stopped trying to move, the pressure eased.

The chill spread, its icy touch swirling around her breasts until her nipples stood painfully erect. When it reached her throat, it became hard to breathe. She realized with a panic it could get inside her if it reached her mouth. She fought harder, tried to move, to scream, but once again the pressure increased, and this time it compressed her throat, cutting off her breath.

She had no choice but to keep still and let it move upward.

The cool reached her chin, creeping to her bottom lip.

She willed her mouth to stay tightly shut.

Now it was over her lip, poking at the corners of her mouth. Exploring, pressing.

She tried to squeeze her mouth tighter but felt her lips parting.

The cold flowed over her tongue, down her throat.

Even worse, it simultaneously moved between her thighs and plunged inside her, filling her with ice. She felt the urge to gag, but was unable to even do that. It thrust down her throat, filled her lungs, then her stomach. Infiltrated every inch of her body, pulsing through her bloodstream.

Green light burst behind her eyes.

Then nothing.

***

"Lauren, are you okay?"

A hand grasped her shoulder, shook her.

She opened her eyes. Everything was tinted light green. May's green eyes looked more vivid than before, her tan skin the colour of olives, making her appear ill. Behind her, Chris hovered. He too looked green, as if Lauren was looking through a piece of coloured plastic. May squinted in concern, but Chris looked to be holding back a laugh.

"I must have fallen asleep." Lauren sat up. She'd slid to the ground, her back against the soggy log. Mushy bark coated her back in lumps, and mud pressed coolly into the skin of her legs. Water lapped gently at her feet. "I'm okay, really."

Chris and May helped her stand. Lauren brushed at the mud on her shorts, only smearing it further.

"Are you guys already done swimming?" she asked.

The other two exchanged looks, then Chris said, "It's been a couple hours. How long did you sleep?"

Lauren shook her head, unsure. It hadn't felt that long before she'd heard them calling for her. Then again, she'd been having a crazy dream. Didn't it take a while before dreams kicked in during sleep?

"Let me just rinse off." To Chris and May's surprise, she stepped into the water. It no longer felt weird to her. Instead, it embraced her, welcomed her in. Moving deeper, she washed the mud off, let the water lap at her waist, sucking at her shorts, now sodden and heavy. "Sure you guys don't want to come back in?"

"I've got to get to work at the theatre," May said. "But we can come again tomorrow, if you want."

A wave of contentment lapped through Lauren at the thought of returning.

***

Away from the lake, Lauren felt empty. All she could think of was getting back into its waters. The green tinge had faded, and she suspected it was a kind of migraine aura. She took ibuprofen and downed some Coke, but it didn't help. There was also the issue of the marshy taste in her mouth. No matter how many times she brushed her teeth and gargled mouthwash, the taste remained. It tainted everything she ate, as if algae coated her tongue.

Then there were the urges. Her eyes lingered on every young man. She yearned for them, the feel of them, the press of their bodies. Instead of warmth, cold filled her, yet her body responded to it as pleasure. Need filled her, deep and unsated. She knew how it felt to be attracted to a man, though she was a virgin. This was different; desperate.

Unfamiliar.

May had to cancel the trip back to the lake the next day. She'd been called into work to cover for a sick co-worker. It wasn't until a week later they made plans to return. The interim had been torture for Lauren. She didn't have a vehicle of her own, and her bike needed a new chain, so even riding there was out of the question. Her mom hadn't had a day off yet—the joys of being a single mom—so Lauren was stuck at home, the lake too far away for her to get there without transport. She'd asked if she could drop her mom off at work for her 6:30 AM shift, but her mom had turned her down, citing *wonky hours* and the fact that she might get off work early. Her mom, always the optimist.

The day of the return trip, Lauren sat at a café table under an oversized umbrella. Beads of moisture rolled down the outside of her glass. She traced a path with her finger, the glass pleasurably smooth and damp against her skin. May would be getting off work soon.

Lauren felt someone watching her. Slowly, she raised her eyes. A man with dark hair and a neatly trimmed beard sat at the next table. His eyes were a startling blue, and one of his ears stuck out slightly more than the other. He wore a white t-shirt and sipped from a steaming cup of coffee. He continued to look at her when she met his eyes, and a thrill coursed through her, chased by an icy chill.

Dizziness overtook her, and she gripped the icy glass, trying to will away the nausea and ground herself. Green tinted everything in her sight, and the world shifted before dissolving.

***

Lauren's phone rang. She stirred, moving her right hand, which slid through something cool and tickly that rustled at her touch. She opened her eyes and stared up at the sky, blue and cloudless. Water lapped nearby. The rich, unpleasant scent of pond scum surrounded her.

She shifted her legs to sit up. Her thighs felt tacky. Grass tickled along her bare skin. She still wore her bikini top, t-shirt, and skirt, but they were damp and dishevelled, and her swim bottoms were missing. Confusion flooded her at her lack of swim bottoms, and the first tentative fingers of panic feathered out from her chest.

Her phone stopped ringing.

Lauren scrambled to her feet, looking around for some indication of what had happened. The lake stood before her, sunlight glinting off the peaks of a few ripples. The last thing she remembered was waiting for May at the café and a bearded man staring at her over the rim of a coffee cup.

Something felt very wrong. She panted, struggling to catch her breath.

She walked to the lake's edge, pulling the hem of her skirt down, all too aware of her nudity beneath it. She added the mystery of where her bikini bottoms had gone to the list of questions running frantically through her head.

She slid her sandals off and stepped into the lake, moving waist deep. Scrubbing at her thighs until they stung, she made sure every trace was gone. As much as she willed it not to be so, the dull ache told her she'd had sex. But with whom? The man from the café? A stranger! All without any memory of it. Yet here she was, alone. She could see for some distance on every side, and no one else was visible.

"Hello?" she called out. She tried again, louder. "Hello?"

No one answered.

Had she been drugged? Raped? Dread filled her, clawed its way up her throat.

Her phone rang again. It took her a moment to find it, but there it was, hidden in the grass near where she'd woken up. Lauren hesitated, took a couple deep breaths, then answered it, her voice coming out in a choked whisper. "Hello?"

May's voice on the other end sounded frantic. "Lauren, where are you? I got off work over an hour ago, and you weren't here."

"I'm at the lake." She needed to ask for help, but fear held her back.

May's voice hardened. "Well, thanks for letting me know you didn't need a ride. Real nice. I thought something happened to you." She hung up.

How could Lauren explain this? She didn't even know what had happened. She ran her hands along the back of her wet skirt to pull it down then sat in the grass. Staring at the phone, she considered calling back, but she couldn't come up with anything to say that would make sense. She needed time to think, to figure this out. Her cheeks warmed at the thought of telling May she'd woken up several miles outside town with missing bikini bottoms and semen on her legs, unable to remember what she'd done, with whom, or even if it had been willingly.

No, May could wait. Lauren needed desperately to get home. She had a long hike ahead of her with no one to call for a ride and a lot to mull over.

It struck her that she might not want to be around when

the person who'd brought her here returned, having no way to know who it was or whether he'd be violent. She took the path to the parking lot, glancing over her shoulder to be sure no one followed her. One car sat empty, haphazardly parked across the line on the driver's side. She took a moment to peer inside and try the handle. Locked, and the fast-food wrappers inside didn't tell her anything except that her missing bottoms weren't in the car.

The car might belong to whoever had brought her here, but it also might belong to someone who could tell her what had happened, maybe even a witness if her fears were founded on truth. Had they seen what happened? Her cheeks warmed, heart pounding. Horror and humiliation replaced the initial embarrassment she'd felt, and she fled.

***

Lauren clawed her way out of sleep. She couldn't breathe. Her lungs burned.

She sat up, leaned forward, and vomited onto her bedspread. Gasping and choking, she reached for the lamp on her bedside table and turned it on. Dark chunks of what looked like algae rested atop the liquid soaking her white bedspread. It smelled like the lake.

She'd been dreaming of the lake.

After she'd cleaned everything up, including herself, she slid between the fresh sheets and rolled into the foetal position. Focusing on the dream, she tried to bring the tattered edges of it back together.

She'd been drowning. That much came back to her. Trapped beneath the surface, bubbles roiling up from her mouth as she struggled. Light sifting through the green water. A neon glow below her, moving toward her. Someone or something had been wrapped around her ankle, pulling her down.

And then she'd awakened, spewing what looked and smelled like lake water. Her lungs burned, as did her throat and nose. Despite the horror of this, she had to go back to sleep. She turned to her side. Sleep lapped at her mind like water on the lakeshore, and she drifted, the soft sound of waves lulling her.

***

She knew May would be pissed, but Lauren wasn't willing to tell her the truth yet, even to save their burgeoning friendship. Chris had taken on the role of go-between, trying to make everything right, but Lauren could tell he resented being put in this position.

As much as she hated being in a fight, Lauren had bigger problems. It had been three days since she'd woken up at the lake, and now flyers adorned every pole and storefront downtown, all featuring a photo of the man from the café.

He'd been reported missing.

Not only that, but according to the news, his car had been found in the parking lot at the lake. The same car she'd peered into... Had he been injured? Maybe an accident had occurred, and they'd both been knocked out. Was he lying out there, hurt? Dead? She'd seen no sign of him.

She sat on her bed, staring at the flyer she'd stolen from a light pole. He had kind eyes. It said he was an artist and an accountant. That he had a twin sister who missed him. No mention of a wife, a girlfriend, kids. He was last seen that same morning three days ago.

Was she the last to have seen him alive?

Of course, that assumed he was the one she'd been with at the lake. He might have nothing to do with her or that day, other than a passing glance. It could have been someone else. It could be nothing had happened at all, that she'd misconstrued the signs. She might have walked to the lake, passed out from the heat, fallen in a damp, awkward heap on the grass. Someone could have dropped her off there.

Sure... without her swimsuit. With semen on her legs.

Lauren knew she should go to the police, but what could she tell them? She had nothing helpful to say. They wouldn't find him based on one glimpse at a café and a bizarre story about waking up at the lake. She examined the photo again. It looked like him, but there, was that a mole? Her memory didn't include a mole. Lots of people looked similar, and nothing about him stood out apart from the neatly-trimmed beard, and no feature screamed, "This is the guy!"

She folded the flyer into quarters then tucked it under her mattress.

***

Blinding white, then blue.

Sound muffled, pressure against her ear drums.

Cool embrace.

Lauren gasped, flailed. Her face went beneath the surface, water filling her mouth.

Pressure from below lifted her, fresh air hitting her face as she expelled the water. Something wrapped around her ankles, sinuous in its feel and movements. It stroked along her skin, seeking.

She looked down, tried to see what was touching her. The water was too dark; she couldn't see past her own torso, pale against the green murk. When she attempted to swim away it held her fast, the tip feathering along her flesh. Desperately, she plunged her hands downward, barely registering the fact that she stayed upright despite no attempt to tread water.

The object moved ever upward, but she couldn't reach it. It now tickled along her inner thigh on one side, her knee on the other. She felt helpless against it, yet still she fought, finally shoving her face into the cool liquid surrounding her. A gentle force pressed against her face, then increased the push, trying to get her back up to where she could breathe. She refused, seeking the thing that held her.

A green glow rose from somewhere below.

A pale blob emerged, surrounded by darkness. It came closer. Closer still.

Features filled out. A face, mouth wide, eyes dark, empty, like the fathoms below. A figure, shrunken, diminished. A skeletal arm reached back toward Lauren and she screamed, bubbles fleeing her mouth, bursting with air from her own lungs.

Back up she went, fighting harder now. The things around her legs loosened, releasing her with a final caress. She pinwheeled her arms in a frantic stroke to the shore. Her muscles burned with the effort, but she got there, flinging her body onto the damp earth, digging her fingers into the muck to pull herself free of the water's suction. She felt a tickle on the bottom of her foot as she drew it out. A quick goodbye.

This was the third time in six days she'd awakened here. Dread filled her. There would be another flyer soon.

***

"May said she's willing to meet you at the lake to talk," Chris said, his voice faint.

Lauren sighed, adjusting the phone so she could hear him better. "That's not a good idea, Chris."

"This is your final chance, Lauren. Either you want to make up with her or you don't, but I'm done." A sharp edge of frustration underlined his words. "It's not my job to babysit the two of you."

"Babysit us? I didn't ask you to do any of this. You're the one who keeps calling me."

Silence greeted her words. For a moment, she thought he'd hung up, but then he spoke. "Tomorrow at five. Your choice whether you show or not. You won't hear from me again."

"I can't—"

A dial tone told her he'd hung up.

The thought of purposely going to the lake with anyone was too much. What if she blacked out? What if she saw green? But May and Chris were the only friends she'd made around here. Maybe if she told them what was happening they could help her.

If only she knew what was happening herself.

***

Lauren arrived to find May's car already in the parking lot. Lauren locked her repaired bicycle up on the rack and walked toward the lake. Sweat trickled along the small of her back, glided down her neck and between her breasts. Her hair was matted to her forehead, and she swept the damp bangs away from her face.

May and Chris sat on the ground in the spot they'd all first gathered. They talked and laughed, voices dancing through the air. Chris reached out and touched May's arm, and she smiled up at him.

May stiffened as Lauren approached, causing Chris to look up. He smiled, but it was a forced stretching of the lips that didn't reach his eyes. He looked from Lauren to May, and back again.

This'll be fun, Lauren thought. She had to force her feet to keep moving across the dirt path, pebbles crunching beneath her sandals. *Why did they even come?* She wrapped her arms around her middle for comfort and stopped in front of the others. "Hi."

Chris stood. "Hey."

"Hello." May also stood, but slower, her eyes not meeting Lauren's.

"I'm sorry. Can I explain?" Lauren asked.

They all sat down together. Lauren told them about her blackouts, but nothing more. She'd decided this was the best thing to do. They wouldn't believe the rest, but she couldn't help a medical condition, could she?

"I hate to ask, but have you been using drugs or something?" May asked.

The accusation hurt, but Lauren swallowed her pride. "No. Nothing. Not even alcohol."

"What does your mom think is happening?" May leaned toward her, seemingly forgetting her anger in the face of curiosity.

"I... I haven't told her yet."

"Why not? You should go to a doctor."

"What if a doctor tells me I'm crazy? That I'm imaging all this?"

"And what if it's serious?" Chris ran a hand along the side of his face.

Lauren followed the hand with her eyes. She was suddenly all too aware of the blunt thickness of his fingers, the stubble on his cheek. Chris, who she had no sexual interest in. Chris, who had a thing for May. The more she tried not to look at him, the harder it became to stop. Cold swirled around her insides. Was that a touch of green over everything?

She jerked her eyes away and looked at May. Focused on her friend's face. "There's more."

Oh no. Why did I say that?

Lauren swallowed and took a deep breath. "I think I'm doing things during the blackouts."

"Well, obviously, if you're waking up somewhere different than where you started," said May.

"No. I mean, I think I'm doing something bad. Maybe hurting people. Have you seen those flyers for the missing men?"

Chris laughed.

May tilted her head and raised one eyebrow. "You think you're kidnaping adult men and overpowering them?"

"For nefarious purposes?" Chris added. "You think you're some kind of siren or succubus or something?"

A succubus? Lauren wondered. That might be it. Why else would she be luring men to a lake, having sex while blacked out? But she didn't feel energized afterward. If anything, she felt tired and confused. Sore. From the little she knew of succubi, they fed off the sexual energy.

The cold spread, pulsed. Lauren tried to push the green away. She didn't talk, instead looking at the water. But that made it worse. It was hypnotic, lapping at the shore, swaying this way and that. She fought to focus, to bring herself back. If she went under now, something terrible would happen to her friends. She was sure of it. The taste of lake water pushed its way up from the back of her throat, clawed its way across her tongue and through her sinuses. Something bad was coming. She'd never felt it like this, creeping up on her rather than knocking her straight out.

"Ah, you know him."

It took her a moment to realize these words hadn't come from May or Chris. This was a new voice. Feminine, but crusty, like a long-time smoker's. It rasped across her nerves, made the hairs on her neck rise.

"I want him."

She couldn't hear anyone else now. Distantly, it sounded

like they were talking to her still, but it was a rumble, muted thunder over the sound of a radio. The woman's voice came from inside her own head. No, not a woman— a succubus. Lauren wasn't feeding off the men; this *thing* was. Certainty filled her. It had used her.

Lauren dug her fingers into the grass. It felt cool, even on this hot day. The thick, sharp blades cut her finger, drawing blood. The pain kept her grounded.

"I'll let you stay awake with me while I play with him."

No, she thought back. *Leave him alone.*

"You have no say, girl. I'll take what I want."

He's my friend. I'll find someone else.

The succubus didn't answer back. Instead, the green increased until there was no question it was coming again, the cold filling her. The wave of absence. Soon, she'd be gone. Wherever it was she went when this happened. That couldn't happen. She fought back.

"You guys need to leave." Her mouth barely moved when she spoke, teeth pressed together, gritting. "Now."

She managed to look away from the water, to their concerned faces. Chris helped May up, but then he reached for Lauren to do the same.

"No. I said go!"

"We're not going to leave you." May sounded fuzzy, far off. "I can get you to a doctor. There's an urgent care right up the road."

Chris's hand wrapped around Lauren's upper arm. He pulled at her, trying to get her to stand. "Come on, Lauren. Let's go together."

His hand felt so warm. His touch sent a frisson of electricity through her. Unbidden, her arm moved, hand wrapping around the taut muscle of his forearm, thumb stroking the firm skin. She stood, and the voice inside her laughed.

"Good, now bring him to the water, and I'll do the rest."

No.

She may have said no, but her feet moved toward the water. Her friends followed, Chris's arm locked in her grip, his own hand still strong on her arm.

"Where are you going?" asked May. Her smaller hand took Lauren's other arm.

"Please leave me here." Lauren could only whisper. "I can't control it."

"Control what?" asked Chris.

Her eyes filled. Everything around her formed green puddles in her vision, distorting as a tear fell. Mud squelched over the sides of her sandals. It felt warm compared to the ice inside her. They were close to the water.

May pulled at her. "Let's go to my car. Come on."

Directed at May, rage swept over Lauren. May needed to go away, to leave them. Her presence was an irritant, a deterrent. Get rid of May, and Chris would be all hers.

Even Chris's tug didn't alter Lauren's path. They were at the water now. Just a couple more steps and they'd be in it. Lauren knew he'd be done for as soon as he touched the water. A thrill went through her, but it didn't feel like her own emotion. It felt somehow removed from her. She was painfully aware of his body heat near hers, the feel of his skin. Even his scent. She could smell his natural musk beneath the sunblock he wore. Lauren wanted to touch him, to feel more of him. Needed it. Needed him.

Lauren wrenched herself free of both of them at once, her own hand the hardest to disengage. He yelped, and she was certain she'd taken a piece of him with it.

She leapt forward into the water, splashing through it until she got deep enough to dive.

"Get back there, you little bitch."

I won't.

She opened her eyes under the water. The green glow came from below, pulsating. It pulled at her, drew her.

Particles floated about, creating clouds against the glow. Lauren swam through them, lungs burning as she went farther into the lake. A structure became visible, vague in the murk. She kicked her feet faster, pulled as hard as she could against the water with her arms. Every part of her body strained. For distance, for oxygen, for the structure.

The water grew colder the further she went, but she swam anyway. Water seeped into her nose, and she forced air through her nostrils, sending bubbles past her eyes. The urge to inhale strengthened.

Panic overtook her. She froze for a moment then tried to change direction. The compulsion was still there, but her need to breathe, to survive, was stronger. Now she just flailed, fighting the urge to inhale, seeing the lake's surface above her.

When she could take it no longer, she sucked water into her mouth. Ice filled her throat, her lungs, and it burned like cold fire. She struggled against it, tried to expel the water, but more flowed in until she couldn't fight anymore.

Lauren stilled.

She floated, an ice-cold calm overcoming her. A figure emerged from the glow below, floating steadily closer. Lauren's body jerked, fighting the lack of oxygen in her bloodstream, but she couldn't move.

Fear faded as death crept upon her. All she could do was watch, numbed, and wonder in a vague way what it could be.

An appendage extended from the form. Shaggy, flimsy material drifted around it, tendrils writhing with the motion of the water. Everything existed in shades of black and green. The appendage took the shape of an arm, skeletal fingers outstretched from a wizened hand. It reached for her, getting closer.

It covered the space quickly, hand touching first her toe, then stroking up along her foot, her ankle, even colder than the water.

Then she was being pulled out, the air smacking her like a warm wall. She felt heavy, weighted down, and she couldn't move her limbs. Her rescuer dragged her out of the water until her entire body lay on dry ground. Dank lake-water burbled up her throat into her mouth. She rolled onto her side. Coughing and heaving, she forced the water out, gasping in her first rush of oxygen.

Chris and May hovered over her. Chris was soaked, water dripping off his face. His cheeks were flushed, chest heaving.

The green tint over Lauren's vision had disappeared. She sat up, wrapping her arms around her torso.

"Are you okay?" May asked. She reached a hand out and pushed the hair back from Lauren's forehead.

Lauren took a deep breath, which hurt her throat and lungs. "Yes." She choked, spitting out more water. "I think so." Her voice rasped, abrading her throat with its passage.

"We need to get you—" May jerked backward mid-sentence, out of Lauren's sight. A splash and a hollow crack followed.

Chris turned toward the water, his back to Lauren. "What the hell?"

A desiccated hand wrapped around the back of his head and pulled him away from Lauren. The thing from the water held him despite his attempts to get free. He pounded on it, shoved against it, kicked it. The sodden, blackened fabric of an old, tattered dress hung from the scrawny form, a flash of bone visible through a tear over the chest.

The creature pulled him to its mouth where a smattering of teeth remained under paper-thin flesh. One empty eye socket showed beneath the tangled hair, a leech squirming within, black and shiny.

Lauren screamed and ran to Chris. She grabbed his upper arm and jerked backward. He barely budged. The creature was strong, and Chris had stilled, no longer struggling. Under Lauren's fingers, his arm slackened. She threw her weight backward, hoping it would be enough to break its hold on him.

It wasn't.

Instead, a high-pitched moan sounded. The succubus backed toward the water, pulling both Chris and Lauren with it. His skin felt hot to the touch, beads of sweat rolling off him. It was increasingly harder for her to hold on.

Beyond them, at the edge of the lake, May lay half-in, half-out of the water. Blood shone at her temple where her head rested on a rock. Lauren looked between the two of them, but Chris needed her help more.

Lauren dug her fingers into his skin, trying to keep her hold on him. No matter how hard she pulled, the thing dragged them inexorably toward the lake. Lauren's feet slid down the muddy embankment before plopping into the water. She lost her grip and fell backward onto her butt.

Chris and the succubus were now up to their waists in water. It wrapped its arms around his torso then lifted its legs, enclosing his body within the musty folds of its tattered dress before drawing him down below the surface.

Lauren splashed into the lake and dove, certain she wouldn't be coming back. Chris and the succubus were visible against the green glow that still pulsated in the distance, and Lauren swam for all she was worth to catch them. Through the tatters of the dress, something beat in its chest, pulsing with the same rhythm as the glow at the bottom of the lake.

This time, instead of trying to pull Chris back, she circled around the succubus and felt along its head until her fingers slipped into the eye sockets. The slimy hair tickled along her arm, wrapping around her wrist. Disgust filled her, but she didn't pull away, instead bringing the head back as far as she could. With her other hand, she felt for the mouth, shoving her fingers through the papery skin of its cheek with a pop. She gripped the lower jaw and wrenched it down.

The succubus bucked against her, but she kept pulling in opposite directions. The jaw gave with a crunch that unsettled the water around them. Lauren let go, bits of skin floating past her.

Chris, released from the succubus's grip, floated up and away, bubbles rising from his mouth.

Lauren couldn't hold her breath much longer. She wrapped her body around the succubus, who struggled, lashing out with fingers so sharp they felt like talons. Cuts opened along Lauren's arms and cheeks, blood rising in the water, dark clouds against the glow.

Steeling herself, Lauren pushed her hand against the succubus's back, just below its rib cage. She pushed as hard as she could, weakened as she was from lack of oxygen. The skin here was thicker than that on the cheek, but a final press punctured it, and her hand slipped inside. Angling up, she reached into the chest cavity, nudging aside withered tissue that must have been the organs, long gone to rot.

One organ still worked, though. Plump and pumping, the heart beat against Lauren's palm, emitting a pale, green glow. She squeezed it as hard as she could until it split, the tissue sliding through her fingers, its glow fading. The succubus stopped fighting.

Lauren's body defied her, drawing water into her lungs again. She let the corpse drift away from her and swam upward in a frenzy, fighting to expel the water from her chest, which felt ready to burst. Below, the green glow died out, leaving only shades of gray, tinted by the faint sun above.

It was too far. Her movements slowed, weakened, but she couldn't stop. Not now.

She bobbed to the surface, coughing water out. Taking a deep breath, she flipped onto her back and floated, unable to do anything more. She heard Chris coughing, the sound of May's voice, but was too tired to call out to them. It didn't matter. She could float here forever if she had to.

Something caressed her leg. Something cold. It wrapped around her ankle.

Screaming, Lauren kicked, thrashing. Water filled her mouth, and she spluttered. Whatever held her, it was still there.

She reached for it, scratching at the slimy substance encircling her ankle. It came away easily in her hand, and she held it up before her.

Nothing but algae.

It was then that the water bubbled around her. A large object surfaced a few feet away, and she stared at it, petrified. Covered in algae, it looked like a lump of red fabric.

May shrieked, "Get out of the water!"

Another object popped up next to the first one. This one had a distinct pattern of yellow stripes across a blue surface.

Lauren swam for shore as fast as she could, unsure what was rising, but certain she didn't want to be in the water anymore. Her entire body tingled with the knowledge that one of these things might come up beneath her, touch her. She kicked harder.

Directly in front of her, a massive bubble rose then popped. She froze before pushing backward, trying to get away from the bubble. Something grazed her leg as a pale oval loomed out of the murky water. It broke the surface. A man's face, white and swollen, dark beard full of algae, skin torn in gashes. A mole upon his cheek.

It was the man from the café. These were her victims, then,

emerging from the lake in accusation. Men she had lured to their deaths to feed a hungering creature inside her. A creature who had used her unwilling body as a means to draw them in, who had masked itself beneath the surface, hidden under her skin to entrap them, robbed her of her virginity and innocence.

Staring into his milky eyes, bubbles tickling her legs, a part of Lauren broke.

There were bodies in this lake, after all, bodies she'd put there.

Night Shift

By day, the psych ward was bright, almost cheery. The walls were cornflower blue, the trim and floor tiles white. Windows lined the exterior walls, letting the sunshine enter in a merry dance. Residents could be found gazing out the windows. Catatonics were placed in front of them to stare blindly at the green foliage and distant purple mountain range. Whether they actually saw anything was another question, but they were made as comfortable as possible, and were well cared for. The patients enjoyed many activities, from bingo to light yoga. There was both a fully stocked movie room and a fully stocked library. There were even board games and video games, though Rose had yet to see anyone playing these. The smell was clean and sharp, lemon and cleaning products mixed with the scent of fresh laundry.

Her bright-eyed optimism initially had her in awe of the pleasant ward, the effective way it seemed to run during her interview and day-time trial period as a new CNA. The staff were friendly, the patients quiet and malleable, willing to let her take their blood pressure, test their pulses and O2, and overall check them for wellness. The life of a CNA wasn't glorious, but Rose had been awakened to this truth during her training and clinicals at a local nursing home. It wasn't pretty being the one to bathe residents, change their padding and sheets, feed them, and empty the urine from the bags that hung from their hospital beds and wheelchairs, a constant reminder of what age wrought, no matter the type of life lived up to that point. Age held no bias.

Once she was hired on full-time, having passed her trial period with flying colors, they moved her to nights. It seemed to her as if the day folks suddenly looked at her in a different way upon hearing her new assignment. They gave her one more week on days so she could prepare for the schedule change, but the warm glowy feeling she'd gotten steadily diminished each day leading up to the new assignment. The other CNAs, and even the RNs, gave her more distance. The playful chitchat she'd partaken in with them came to an end. Their glances became wary, pitying. She couldn't imagine why they would behave this way, and it hurt, as she'd thought she was making friends at this new job.

She had the thought that, perhaps, she had done something wrong and they weren't telling her. Had she unknowingly crossed someone, some line, and now they were banding together against her? This had happened to her in a waitressing job she'd held back home, but this was supposed to be a fresh start in a new place. No more bullying and cliques. No more melting into tears each morning before work. She'd fit in right from the beginning here, only to now feel entirely isolated once more.

The doctors showed her the same level of professional indifference they had the entire time. They weren't much for socializing with the lower echelons, despite the fact it was the grunts that kept their jobs running smoothly. They weren't unkind or even rude, save one man who occasionally came in as an expert, and who treated everyone abusively, no matter their status. He even spoke to other doctors as if they were filth beneath his feet, and a hardship to deal with. As for the others, their continued apathy reassured her.

Rose continued with her work, though everything seemed a bit dimmer, the patients more restless. What had initially been excitement evolved into a type of dread, though she had no concrete reason for it.

She told herself she was seeing something that did not exist, imagining ills that were not real, all because she was sad to be leaving her friends. She would, of course, make new friends on the night shift. Sure, there would be fewer staff around at night, but one only had so much room for friendships. Plus, this was a job, not a friendship factory. It was okay to hope for more from the job, but not to expect it. She figured there was also the natural hesitance about change. Even the pressure of proving she was up for the job wasn't as heavy as the pressure of now having to prove they were right to have chosen her.

On her last day, Beth, a slight, mousy CNA Rose had previously become close to, edged up to her during end-of-shift paperwork. Beth's large eyes appeared even bigger than usual, damp and shining. She placed a hand on Rose's upper arm and gave a gentle squeeze. "Be safe."

Rose couldn't take the weird behavior anymore. She'd suffered for an entire week. "What's wrong with the night shift?"

Beth didn't answer right away. Instead, she glanced along the hallway to each side of them, hunching her shoulders and dipping her chin.

"Well?" Rose asked. "Why is everyone acting so strangely? I thought we all got along."

"It's not that. It's just...nights are different."

"How so?"

"I've never worked them. But, it's just, night CNAs don't last long. Something changes them." She looked around one more time before continuing. "You know the lady we always sit in the best place in the sunroom? The spot where that one peak is at its most glorious, and the trees frame it perfectly?"

"Yes."

"She was on night shift. A CNA like you and me."

Rose's stomach dropped, plumbing the depths of her insides. The woman in question didn't even blink. Staff had to regularly put drops in to keep her eyes moist. They had to wipe her mouth and chin of drool. Her hands had clenched and tightened into twisted claws.

"That can't have been the job. It's the same facility, same patients. You're all being ridiculous."

There was nothing more to say. After a quick hug, Beth walked away from her, steps still uneasy. She looked back once, called up a strained smile, and waved.

"Ridiculous," Rose whispered. There was no way one shift could differ so fiercely from another.

***

What Rose discovered upon entering the psych ward her first night on the new job was that it was a wholly different place once the sun dipped behind those same mountains, now black, threatening masses. The windows gleefully let the darkness of the night leak inside, overtaking the bright white flooring, and they stared at those trapped inside with the same soulless gaze as the catatonics. The walls became drab, stained and marred, as did the floors. Everything looked gray and filthy, and even the smells had changed, attacking her senses with body odor, excrement, and something dank and dusty beneath it all.

You're being silly, she told herself. *It's the same damn place.*

A grim-faced RN named Autumn greeted her at the nurse's station. "Put your things away. You'll be doing rounds with Karl to check that everyone's ready for dinner, and then you'll bring them to the dining room except those who eat in their rooms."

No hello. No welcome. Business up front. Well, Rose could deal with a grouchy nurse. It certainly wouldn't be enough to turn her catatonic, but it was a stark change from the day nurses, who had been friendly, albeit efficient. Apparently, Nurse Ratched here had never gotten the memo that you could be both friendly and efficient.

"Yes, ma'am."

Rose ran into the small staff room to put her things into a locker. She washed her hands, as they were always supposed to do when coming onto shift, scratched an itch on her nose with the back of her wrist (they weren't allowed to touch their hair or faces once they'd washed their hands, yet something always managed to itch as soon as the faucet shut off), and tucked her pen and stethoscope into her scrub pockets. All set, she went back to the nurse's station to await Karl.

He arrived only about one minute after her, saving her

from Autumn's icy, awkward silence. He had light brown skin, dark eyes and nicely trimmed hair that lay close to his head. A blue, long-sleeved shirt ran out of from under the short sleeves of his regulation black scrubs. His shirt, unlike hers, had a pocket on the breast, and out of it poked a pen with feather hair and googly eyes. He nodded in lieu of a handshake that would force them both to re-wash their hands, and said, "Hey, name's Karl. I see you're Rose, my trainee for the night. You ready?"

"Sure am." Relief flooded Rose at the discovery that not everyone was as unfriendly as Autumn. "I worked day shift the last month, so I'm familiar with the facility, at least."

"Good. Let's do our rounds and get everyone ready for dinner."

Rose followed him to the rooms, where they checked each person's vitals, helped some on with sweaters, got some into wheelchairs, emptied catheter bags, etc. Most could take care of themselves, but their vitals still had to be checked and logged.

"We'll plug their vitals into the computer then get everyone to dinner. There are some part-time CNAs who help with dinner and bed before taking off. Then it will be just the two of us."

"How long have you been on nights?" Rose asked.

"Six months."

Instantly, Rose felt better. He seemed nice and normal, not like he was cracking at the edges or preparing for catatonia. "Do you like it?"

"It's quiet. Anything I can say that about is going to rank high. Less staff, most of the patients sleeping. Gives me time to think. Having said that, we still have to be on our toes, maybe even more so than day shift, because we're listening for anything out of the ordinary. You learn to depend on all your senses to tell you if something's wrong, so listen to your intuition. If anything feels wrong, check it. Better safe than sorry."

"There's nothing...weird, is there? Nothing I should be afraid of?"

"Like what?"

"I don't know. It's just that the day staff were odd when they found out I'd be working nights. One of them made it sound like I was walking into Purgatory."

Karl laughed. "No, nothing like that. This is a psych ward, so of course there are weird things, and often unpleasant things, but it's all part of the job, and you experience that during the day, too."

"That I'm prepared for."

"Great."

They completed dinner with no incident, though she couldn't say it was as smooth a process as lunch and breakfast had been. Some of the patients were more restless than they'd been earlier in the day, some less willing to cooperate. Still, it was all in the job, and she knew from her class that this could happen. Now they had to get everyone ready for bed. For those who took care of themselves, she gave them ample time to get ready before checking in on them. For those who needed full care, the catatonics mostly, she provided ADLs (activities of daily living, like tooth brushing, hair brushing, cleaning, peri-care, etc.). It took about two hours, but once everyone had been safely tucked into bed, lights out, vitals taken once again, she and Karl got to take a lunch break. The three other CNAs said their goodbyes, retrieved their items from the break room, and took off.

While things felt less oppressive than when she had first arrived, Rose couldn't help but feel on edge now that they'd completed the busy work. She and Karl took turns doing rounds and responding to call buttons. It was a lot like her time in the nursing home had been, only she was keenly aware that these folks were mentally ill, some possibly dangerous, though she hadn't seen any hint of that during the day. For those who were prone to violence or escape attempts, there were notations in their files. However, the full files, the ones showing what they had done to land here, were not available to CNAs.

Karl ran over what she could expect. "Mr. Petersen has a tendency to take off all his clothes and streak down the hall. You'll also want to watch for his busy fingers. He's a bit of a perv, but maybe you've experienced that during the day. Ms.

Lansley sporadically cries and sometimes has issues with night terrors, so if there's screaming, always check her room first. Mr. Danzig is another insomniac. We give him a sleeping pill, but there are nights it doesn't work. The ones you need to watch for violence are Mr. Samson, Mr. Bevans, and Ms. Yakimodo. She'll claw you, but it's what's under her nails you should worry about, more than the scratches themselves. Mr. Bevans used to be a pugilist, and probably quite the scrapper outside of the ring, based on the delusions he has about who he's fighting. Mr. Samson is the one to really watch. He can be incredibly violent, and it comes out of nowhere. He will kick, hit, tackle, pinch, scratch, and bite." At this point, Karl pulled up his sleeve. He had a series of scars in the shape of a bite mark. "Got me my second night."

There were a few more patients with issues, but overall it wasn't so bad. Some of these behaviors were found in the nursing home, as well. Not a big deal. In fact, it would break up the monotony if someone started screaming.

The rest of the night went well, with Autumn checking on them from time to time. No screaming, no attacks. Rose resisted the temptation to pop in on the day folks and say, "I told you so," since it was only her first day.

***

On Sunday, her fifth day, Rose showed up to work feeling cheerful and ready for the night. She'd adjusted to nights for the most part, and she enjoyed Karl's company. Autumn hadn't gotten any friendlier, but Rose didn't care. She figured she'd get under the ice queen's exterior eventually.

As usual, dinner service went well, bed time went well, and Rose settled in for the rest of the night. She and Karl had taken to sneaking travel games of Scrabble and chess during the early morning hours to keep themselves occupied. Tonight, they were playing a game of Uno at the main desk, each keeping an ear open for the squeaky approach of Autumn's shoes, so they could swipe the cards into the drawer and look busy with charts. There'd been quite a few minor interruptions—the patients were more unsettled than usual—

but they had all been sorted easily enough, sending Rose and Karl back to their game.

Karl won the hand and gathered the cards, handing them to Rose. "Midnight. My turn to do rounds."

He disappeared down the hallway, shoes silent on the tiles. Rose pulled out a chart to make a note from earlier. Whenever Karl left Rose alone, the darkness of the ward crept up on her. Shadows slithered closer. The silence grew deeper. Tonight was no different. A single desk lamp lit the nurse's station. Beyond that, all was dark to encourage the patients to sleep. Rose had a hard time seeing anything outside the small, warm cocoon of light, and it felt like she was perched inside a precarious bubble of safety. Outside that bubble, something could be staring in at her, invisible against the light shining into her eyes. Anything, or anyone, could sneak up on her. That didn't seem terribly safe when dealing with dangerous people.

Rose closed the folder and re-filed it. She tapped the pencil on the counter, waiting.

A creeping sensation of dread came over her. It had no source, save the darkness surrounding her. She felt like she was being watched, like something stalked her.

Displaced air drifted across her face, stroking along her cheek. She jerked backward.

She stood up, covering the top of the lamp with her hand to deflect the light and help her eyes adjust to the dark. Her chair bumped into the wall behind her, startling her.

There was no one in the hall or the area around the nurse's station. She stood there for another minute, straining her senses. Nothing. She settled back into her chair to wait.

Fifteen minutes later, long after Karl should have returned, a call light popped on. The small, smooth red bulbs were aligned in two rows down a switchboard on the backsplash of the desk, which rose up to a secondary desk just below chest height. The red was a bright beacon against the faint amber glow of the lamp. Rose took note of the room, 12A, stood up, and made sure her pen and stethoscope were in place. It felt colder outside the lamp's light, and she shivered.

The soft fall of her footsteps bounced off the walls. Snores and peaceful breaths alternated from the rooms she passed.

12A belonged to Ms. Lansley, who preferred to be called Rhonda. Rose used the wall dispenser to get hand sanitizer, rubbing her hands together as she peered into the room. A gentle green glow came from an electronic clock that shined the time on the ceiling over the hospital bed. The sheets were in disarray, the bed empty. The call light glowed red on this end, and Rose pressed it to turn it off.

"Rhonda? Where are you?"

There was no answer, save a creeping sensation up Rose's back, so she walked over to the door, shut it, and turned the room's overhead light on. The fluorescents flickered, as they were wont to do, and Rose stood still to adjust her eyes before stepping farther into the room.

Aside from the bed, the room held a nightstand, a desk, an easy chair, and a single desk chair. An e-book reader rested on the nightstand next to a plastic cup of water. No picture frames were allowed, as they could be broken and made into weapons, but Rhonda had taped up a couple photos of her late husband. To Rose, he looked aggressive and angry, dangerous, but she couldn't say that aloud to anyone. Still, sometimes she wondered if Rhonda's night terrors stemmed from life with a man like him.

A quick sweep showed an empty room, so Rose checked the small bathroom. There was no one there, but the toilet ran as if it had been flushed within the last few minutes. She jiggled the handle, just in case, more out of habit than anything, and returned to the hallway door. She sanitized her hands once more, as required, shut off the light, and opened the door into the hallway. All was quiet out there, and the room's emptiness at her back pushed her out, eager to escape the hollow feel of it.

She went back to the nurse's station to find Karl, but he still wasn't there. Nor was Autumn. Not that Rose had expected to find her there, other than the fact that it was past time for her usual walkthrough.

Something was wrong. Karl had been gone far longer than usual, Autumn hadn't checked in for a couple hours, and now a patient had gone missing. Rose pulled out the binder that held information on their codes and protocols. She hastily flipped through the pages, trying to find anything that might tell her what to do. Should she turn on the main hallway lights? Call for backup?

No, too early. Probably Karl had just found a restless patient who wanted some company. She needed to find him so he could help her search for Rhonda. This was a locked ward, so she couldn't have gotten far.

Rose couldn't turn the main lights on. If there was one thing she'd found in the notebook, it was that turning on the lights, which could wake all the patients, should be kept as a last resort. They would be anything but orderly if awakened in the middle of the night. If she couldn't find Karl, she would shut the doors and turn the light on. And she would page Autumn. She hoped it wouldn't come to that, as she didn't want to get Karl into trouble for disappearing. Her absolute discomfort with the darkness and the odd consequences was not allowed to overrule her common sense.

Back down the hallway she went, this time with the intention of checking each room for any sign of Karl or the missing patient. She'd check A—the left side—first, since that's where Karl had gone, and where Rhonda was missing from. In fact, it might be that the two had found each other and were having a late night chat. Rhonda wasn't typically talkative, but sometimes she liked a chat, especially when she couldn't sleep. Management usually frowned on this, but Karl had taught Rhonda that some rules were meant to be bent.

The first room she came to was pitch black. Most patients had an electronic device or night light that shed a little light on the room, but not all of them. Mr. Danzig liked his room as dark as possible, often complaining about the small amount of light coming from the nurse's station. Rose didn't understand why they couldn't just move him down to the end of one of the hallways so he had nothing to complain about, but apparently once you were in a room, you were there to stay.

She stepped inside to listen for the sounds of breathing. It took a moment, her ears straining, eyes widening to compensate for the darkness, but there came a deep, slow breath, let out in a faint snore. If Karl or Rhonda were in the room, surely they would be able to see her, even if she couldn't see them, so she decided the room was empty save for Mr. Danzig.

Her room by room search continued until she reached about three-quarters of the way down the A hall, a few doors past Rhonda's room. First, she heard heavy breathing, panting. She froze where she stood, trying to pinpoint the source of the sound.

A pulse of adrenaline shot through her body, and she realized how vulnerable she was, standing in the dark. She backed against the wall, looking straight ahead so she could hear on both sides. No one could sneak up on her this way.

The breathing continued, and now a faint voice joined it. No words, only sounds. Moans.

Shit.

In the nursing home, it wasn't unusual for patients to have an active sex life. Though the nurses were not to encourage it, they also were not allowed to break it up if they discovered someone having sex. After all, they were consenting adults. Here, in the psych ward, they were most definitely not consenting adults, being mentally ill, most of them forced to stay here against their will. Problem being, that most of the folks here in the psych ward were younger than those in the nursing home, and several had no self-control due to their particular flavor of mental illness.

And what if it wasn't sex? What if something else was going on, and she stood out here and ignored it? She had to at least be sure.

Convinced that it was, in fact, what she had initially thought, Rose left the wall to follow the sounds to their origin. She still felt exposed and vulnerable, but just knowing someone else was awake and not far from her helped. She crept along, her shoes as quiet as Karl's, until she got to a doorway, as pitch black as Mr. Danzig's, where the sounds came from. She stood outside for a moment, trying to get a better feel for what she was hearing. A mewling had been added to the mix of panting and vocalizing. There were several voices involved, and a slapping, as of flesh on flesh.

Once again, she hesitated. Surely, no one was being

murdered in a pitch dark room. Still, there were dangerous offenders here, people who had committed violent crimes, though they were here in this particular psych ward because they were not thought to be repeat offenders, or to need actual prison time, and it wasn't expected that they'd commit those same crimes here. Once again, she knew she had to be sure. Steeling herself, she moved into the doorway, where heat pulsated, surprising her. If anything, the ward usually ran cold. They weren't allowed personal heaters, so there was no reason it should be so damned hot. Now she knew something weird was going on. Reaching over, she flipped on the light, only to stand transfixed in the dim glow from one flickering fluorescent; the others refused to light, though a low hum told her they were trying.

Before her, on the hospital bed, knelt Rhonda, on her hands and knees facing the door. She made the noises Rose had heard in the hallway, her skin glistening with a sheen of sweat, breasts swaying in rhythm with her movements. Her eyes were closed, a big grin stretching her face.

Behind her was Mr. Petersen, sweat running down his face, dripping from his chin. He had a hand wrapped in Rhonda's hair and pounded away behind her, his eyes also closed. His other arm stretched above his head, stroking the throat of a being that made no sense. It was large, covered in wiry muscle, its skin gray. Wings spread out behind it, one folded against the wall the bed leaned against, the other high and outstretched, the tip grazing the ceiling with its own thrusts. The creature stared directly at her, smile stretching abnormally across its face, revealing pointed teeth and a black tongue, which protruded and swept across its lips.

Rose choked. She couldn't make any other sound, couldn't move. She stared, transfixed, at the copulating threesome, one otherworldly. If she tried to stop them, she risked angering that thing.

She backed out of the room, eyes never leaving the being's, until she hit something solid. A hand clamped down on her shoulder.

"What are you doing down here?"

Rose whipped around, darting away from the person

behind her to once again put her back against the wall. "Get away from me."

Karl stood before her. His face had changed, mouth elongated, eyes deep set. He rubbed a hand over his head, smiling at her in a drowsy, contented manner. "What's wrong?"

"Where have you been? What were you doing?"

"I don't think you're ready to know that."

"Do you know what's happening in there?"

"Yep. We all pay a price in this place."

"I don't belong here." She was certain of that.

"You don't end up here unless you belong. You're not as pure as you pretend to be."

"Where's Autumn? Does she know about this?"

"Know about it? She's the head nurse. It's her job to ensure everything goes as planned. The price must be extracted, and she's the bookkeeper."

None of this made sense. There was only one reason she might be here, and no one knew about it. She'd kept it a secret from everyone, and she'd covered it up thoroughly. Even the police and fire marshals hadn't caught on that a crime had been committed. It had been declared an unfortunate mistake, a fluke.

"I see the wheels turning in your head. Thinking about your sins?"

"I don't know what you're talking about."

"Funny, that's what everyone says. But you know exactly what I'm talking about. Each person here has committed at least one of the cardinal sins. I bet you can guess the prime sin of the two in that room. But what's yours?"

Behind her, the noises in the room grew more frantic, escalating.

She didn't want to think about what she'd done. It had been wrong, she knew that, but it had felt right to be vindicated in the end. Those women had deserved what she'd done. After the way they'd treated her, not even giving her a chance.

The sounds and smells came back to her. Screams. The pop and hiss of flames. The smell of burning human bodies, of smoke. The rush of heat and the flutter of ash, fine and gray. The almost blinding glow of the flames as the restaurant burned down, the waitresses inside. The waitresses who had made her feel like trash, like she wasn't good enough to be in their presence. The rage rushed through her body, full of heat and spikes, and she remembered how she'd felt each day on the way into work. When she woke up knowing she had to go in and deal with those bitches again.

"That's it. Now you've got it." He closed his eyes and took a deep breath, like he was enjoying the smell of a rich stew. "Keep focusing on that."

All along the hallway, there were more sounds. Screams, groans, impacts. There were cries for help and cries of ecstasy. The entire ward came to life in horrible ways, and behind her, in that room, they were still going at it, the sounds now all pain, no pleasure, no sign of waning soon.

Now there were grunts, the impacts harder and harder. Whimpers.

She broke and ran back toward the nurse's station and the stairs that would lead her to the main floor and an exit. She tried to ignore the sounds coming from each room, refusing to look over lest she see something she didn't want to see. Still, her senses were assaulted. In one room, wet sounds followed impacts, as of someone being stabbed or bludgeoned repeatedly. In another, someone prayed in a high pitched shriek.

The walls closed in on her, rends and tears appearing in their surfaces. The floor tiles shifted, breaking and sliding, and she leapt forward, trying to get away. She hit a crooked tile hard enough to cause her to fall. She sprawled, cutting her hands and knees on shards of ceramic.

It grew hotter and hotter. Sweat slid down her back, her forehead, between her breasts. It dripped off of her, and still it grew hotter. Her skin blistered, pain so intense she couldn't think past it, couldn't try to get away.

She crawled forward, frantic to escape the searing heat. The ground burned every inch of her it touched, turning her scrubs into ash.

Before her, a figure appeared, similar to the one who had

been with Rhonda and Mr. Petersen. Its large feet had talons on the tips of all six toes. Hairy legs gave way to scales at the groin. It squatted before her, put a claw under her chin, and forced her to look up at it. "Do you admit your sins?"

They had deserved what they had gotten. Surely it was no sin to take retribution on women who were victimizing others, victimizing her. They'd stolen her tips, put all their dishes on her table, messed with her orders, stolen her tables, harassed her, mocked her. They had been the sinners, not her.

"No," she choked out.

"Then you shall burn."

The screams tore from her throat as the heat increased. Her very blood boiled. Her eyes blurred more and more, until full blindness hit, and she could feel her eyes, boiling, running down her face. And then it was her skin. All of her flesh, running like lava along her nerves. Either she no longer produced a sound, or her eardrums no longer existed to convey the screams to her brain. She tasted char until she could taste no more.

The agony didn't stop, but it rewound, over and over. The heat didn't go away, but it faded then resurged. Her vision came back, only to disappear again.

Her pain was everlasting.

Finally, she realized what she had done, but it was too late to end this.

***

By day, the psych ward was bright, almost cheery. The walls were cornflower blue, the trim and floor tiles white. Windows lined the exterior walls, letting the sunshine enter in a merry dance. Beth rolled Rose up to the window with the best view, tucking her blankets around her thin body, nice and snug. She wiped Rose's mouth, ran a hand through her silky hair, and walked away to get the next catatonic. Outside, the trees wavered in a slight breeze, fanning the highest peak.

Where I Woke Up

D^{ay 3} I don't know where I am or how I got here. What I know is that I'm in a comfortable, well decorated, one bedroom ranch-style house with a bare basement. Outside I hear children playing, cars driving by. Sun filters through opaque windows, letting in light, but not allowing me to see outside. Or anyone to see inside, I suppose.

The doors and windows are all sealed tight. There are no other exits.

There's lots of food in the fridge and pantry. I don't think I hate anything in there. Clothing hangs in the closet, is folded up in the bureau. The shoes vary from flip flops to sneakers to high heels. Various bits and baubles rest in a jewelry box. I even have an orange tabby kitten. The collar says her name is Carrots. Not terribly creative. She's fully stocked with food, treats, and a cat box.

I assume these things are mine, because I'm the only one here.

Muted blues and purples decorate the house. The sofas are oversized and soft. Everything is pristine. The artwork appeals to me, draws my gaze. Does that mean I decorated it or simply that whoever did knew my taste? Or neither?

See, I don't know, because I can't remember who I am.

I'm trapped in this house, and I don't even know my name, let alone why I'm here. I found this journal today in a drawer in the bedside table, so I'm going to try to keep track of my days from now on.

***

Day 4

It's been four days since I woke up in an unfamiliar bed. That first morning, the sun was streaming in through the window, and the room was suffused with a warm brightness. Despite the comfort of the bed and the sunny greeting, it felt wrong immediately, though I couldn't figure out why. I had no idea where I'd gone to bed the night before, no memory of where I was from, but I knew this was not it. This was not home.

It actually took me longer than I care to admit to notice that I didn't know who I was. It's not something a person thinks of regularly—who they are. I was too busy trying to figure out where I was, and why my bedroom and clothing were unfamiliar. Of course, perhaps it all truly is mine, and whatever has robbed me of my memory makes it feel wrong. I doubt that.

I don't know what day it was when I woke up here, but I've decided to call it Sunday. So it's Wednesday now. What would I be doing on a Wednesday if I weren't here? Would I be on a date? Working late? Watching TV? There's no television set. No radio or telephone. I haven't spoken to another human since I've been here. No one has even knocked on the door.

There's a CD player in the living room, along with a shelf of CDs. I haven't found one I don't like yet. It helps to keep music playing. Otherwise, it's too quiet, and unwelcome thoughts drift into my mind. Not that I'm able to keep them away, but the music still helps soothe me when I need it. Plus, I can sing along. The louder the thoughts get, the louder I sing.

Every single day I walk a circuit of the house and try each window and door to see if there's a weakness. There never is.

The milk in the fridge is getting low, as is the lunch meat and bread, the salad mix. What will I do when my food runs out? There's no guarantee I'll get more food, so I've been rationing. I have to eat the fresh stuff before it goes bad, so that's harder to ration. I figure apples and carrots will last, so I'm saving those. The freezer's packed with meat and frozen vegetables, and I haven't touched much from the pantry yet.

I'm afraid of what starving to death would be like.

I'm so scared. Who did this to me, and why? Sometimes I feel like I'm being watched, but there are no cameras I can see. I've checked.

***

Day 7

Last night I woke up because I heard a sound. A creak. The kitten even woke up, ears perked, body tense. I thought I saw a shadow in the closet, but when I got up and turned the light on, there was nothing there. The clothes were still. I felt so panicked that I moved them around and checked the walls, floor, and ceiling. Nothing. No door, no seams, no body. I tried knocking on the wall to figure out if it was hollow, but honestly, I don't know what it would sound like if there was something behind it.

Carrots fell asleep within a few minutes, rib cage drifting up and down. I kept my hand in her warm fur, let the softness and the rhythm lull me toward sleep. But I kept jerking awake, because I'd feel something or think I heard a sound. The house creaks sometimes, which is what must have woken me up. It wasn't until dawn's soft light pushed through those damn opaque windows that I fell asleep.

It feels like I slept late this morning. The light seemed different when I finally got up. I think I forgot to mention that there are no clocks in here, either. It feels like I'm in a cocoon or a womb. With no outside influences, including my own memories and routines, I've found a natural rhythm to my days. Get up, shower and get dressed, check the doors and windows, feed Carrots, eat breakfast, do some yoga, read for a bit, eat lunch, clean the cat box, read some more, write crappy poetry, write in this journal, play with Carrots (there are cat toys), wander around the house, eat dinner, read, go to bed. There's a deck of cards, so sometimes I play Solitaire, but I only know the one kind. There's also a puzzle. I'm going to start that tomorrow.

I've tried free writing on a separate pad of paper from the

living room. I start every sentence with "I." Occasionally, it produces something that surprises me, but feels right, like "I like buffalo wings" or "I used to play lacrosse." Yesterday I looked into the mirror for a long time, willing my face to become familiar. Sometimes my "I" statements are things about my appearance. Like this:

I have green eyes.

I have dark brown hair.

I have a narrow chin.

I have deep set eyes.

I have a mole on my right ear.

It hasn't led to anything interesting yet, but I'm determined that it will. When I look in the mirror, I get a jolt, a sense of something more. It feels like my brain is nudging me, a section of it rolling, especially when I look into my eyes. I see something familiar there, but only there. It's like I'm looking through a window into a house that's similar to mine, but has different furniture. The familiar and unfamiliar mix together to form something almost right, but completely wrong.

The salad is long gone, as is the meat. There was a frozen loaf of bread, which I've thawed. There's plenty of peanut butter and a few slices of cheese. The milk and bananas are gone. Luckily, the cat has plenty of food. She won't be running out any time soon. I ate a few pieces of it as an experiment last night. It wasn't great, but it's better than starving. She looked at me like I was on crack, head tilted.

Sometimes I look at her and I wonder which one of us will be eating the other. I've heard it said that cats will eat their human owners if they're trapped inside after they die. She seems so sweet, I can't imagine her taking that first bite, tiny needle teeth digging into my cheek or somewhere fattier. I also can't imagine ending her life so I can have one more meal. Would I strangle her? Hit her over the head with something?

It makes me sick to think these things, but they come unbidden to me. For now, petting her is a way to soothe myself when the fear sets in and my stomach twists up into knots. Her soft, rumbling purrs bring a smile to my face. I think they even lower my blood pressure. It feels like it.

The garbage can smells really bad. It's full of cat shit. I

pulled the garbage out and washed anything I could, so that way it stops smelling of rot. Any food stuff goes down the garbage disposal. As long as that doesn't back up, I'll be okay. I think I'm going to have to try to put the cat crap into the toilet, but I'm afraid to clog it up. There's only one toilet.

My second day in this house I tried using a knife to wedge open a window. I've since tried it on several others and around the doors. I couldn't break any windows with furniture when I tried. There are no tools in here for me to use. There are no screws for me to remove, no hinges inside the house. Even the front door has no hinges I can get to. In fact, I think the door is on backwards, which means it would be easier for someone to break in than for me to break out. The back door is sliding glass, but it's the weird, thick, ripply glass that's in all the windows, and it's stuck. I can't get it to budge.

The front door is super thick. I suspect it's got a metal core. I've hit it with everything I've got. Now there are two broken chairs, the pieces stacked in a corner of the basement. They were the only ones in the kitchen, so now I just eat on the sofa.

It seems to me that someone with a memory who was in my position might evaluate their life while stuck with all this unused time. But I can't, because I can't remember anything about my life. If there were things I needed to resolve before my death, I'll never know, never be able to make it right or come to peace with it. I should probably feel good then, but I feel the opposite. There's dread and panic in my stomach, and my chest burns all the time with heartburn. Some days it seems like my heart is beating too fast all the time, and on the worst days my brain is fogged up, thick, and I have to work to make up my mind on simple things, like what to make for dinner or whether tonight is a good night for a bath.

My body feels restless, like I'm not accustomed to all this sitting. In fact, my tailbone hurts from all the sitting, so now I try to recline sometimes instead, and to frequently change position. I get dizzy from walking in circles through the house. At times, Carrots follows me around, trilling at me in an interrogatory tone. "What are we doing?" I imagine she's asking. "Are we going to go outside today?"

I suspect neither of us will ever see the outside again.

***

Day 9

The basement is dank, all gray concrete and sweating metal support poles. There are no windows or doors down here, no furniture. There's nothing except the broken items and now the garbage. Let it smell down here instead of upstairs. A single bare lightbulb in the center of the room sheds light that stops short of the corners and under the uncarpeted stairs. Every time I come down here, I'm afraid something will grab my ankles through the gaps between steps. It gets harder each time to force myself to start moving down the stairs. I'm as terrified of the basement as a toddler would be.

Happily, the single bulb is controlled by a light switch at the top of the stairs. If I had to walk down into a completely dark basement, it wouldn't happen. I'd just throw everything down the stairs and hope it went as far as possible. I don't know why I don't do that anyway, considering I'll run out of food long before the basement fills up. I guess it's because I need to know there's somewhere I can go in the house other than the rooms I spend all day in. If I were to lose this space, my world would get exponentially smaller, closing in on me.

I can't breathe when I think about that. My throat closes.

Carrots likes the basement. She runs around, investigates under the stairs, meows at me from the shadows. I bet she enjoys the additional freedom, too. We don't come down here every day, because then it would be just one more room we're stuck in. For now, this awful place is my only refuge against this cage dressed as a home.

A cage is made to trap and observe. Am I being observed? Is there something I've missed? There must be. Tomorrow I'll find out.

***

Day 10

It's strange to feel so empty about myself. It's almost as if I don't feel as strongly about my plight because I don't know who I am. Who I was, I guess. Like not knowing what kind of person I was makes it harder to care for myself. Did I like who I was? Was I a good person? Or did I do something to deserve this?

I searched myself for scars, hoping they'll tell me a story. They aren't speaking, so far. There's a long white one on my knee, but I can think of about a billion ways I could have gotten it. I have two small round ones on my right arm, one on my bicep, one on my elbow. Other than that, I don't see anything. Maybe I wasn't much of a risk taker.

I've gone through the house again in hopes of finding something I've missed. I still can't find a way to force a window or door, nor have I found evidence of a camera. I checked all the furniture and the paintings. Of course, I don't exactly know what I'm looking for. It could be right in front of me and I'd never know, but everything seems as normal as it's supposed to be. There are no holes in the walls or ceiling that don't belong.

I had an idea today. There's makeup and nice clothing among my things. Up to now, I've been wearing the clothing that looked most comfortable. Sweat pants, cotton shirts. But today I put on lacy red underwear and a slinky black dress. I put my hair up to expose my neck, allowing a few tendrils to drift freely. I put on smoky eye makeup and blood red lipstick then slid my feet into a pair of shiny, black heels. A spritz of perfume finished it all up, a musky citrus cloud drifting around me.

Sitting on the sofa, my legs crossed, I spoke aloud. It wasn't the first time—I talk to Carrots all the time—but it still felt weird, like my voice box was rusty. I guess I talk to the cat differently.

I said, "If you can hear me, I'd love to meet you. I've waited ten days now. Please come talk to me."

There was nothing to do after that except run through my usual daily routine. I made double of everything for every meal and spoke aloud to tell my captor what I was doing. "If you like steak, I've got more than enough. Steak, mashed potatoes, corn. Please share dinner with me."

No one came. No one except Carrots. I gave her a small

piece of the steak, which she worried at for a time before she was able to finish it. She ate in jerky motions, working to chew it up. The rest I put into the fridge for tomorrow. At least I'd have a day off from cooking.

I stayed up late to wait and see if anything would happen, but I gave up long past dark, when Carrots had stretched herself out against my thigh and gone to sleep, her orange fur clinging to the black of my dress. Finally, I slipped the heels off and carried them to my bedroom, where I put them away in the closet. Carrots ran in there and started sniffing around the back wall. There's something in there she likes; she goes in there regularly. It's probably a good thing I can't smell whatever it is.

The tears came when I was looking at myself in the mirror to wash my face. I put down the cloth I was using and watched as the mascara streaked down my face like black fringe. My eyes became an almost translucent green, and my cheeks and the whites of my eyes reddened. Even my nose was red. This face was even less familiar than my normal one, and I turned away.

I couldn't stop the tears, and they triggered sobbing. My body heaving, I started the bath, a hand trailing in the water, waiting for it to warm. The enamel of the clawfoot tub was cool against my skin, and I stripped, pressing my body more fully against the side. The temperature in this house stays at a steady, comfortable level; it felt good to have a drastic change in sensation. Steam rose from the water, and I climbed in, hissing as it scalded my skin. It took me a moment to fully immerse myself, and I shut off the flow with my foot.

Carrots stood up, paws on the lip of the tub. She mewed, as she always does when I'm in the bath. I scratched her head with the tip of my index finger so she wouldn't get too wet. She still backed away, dropping back to all fours on the tile floor and shaking to dry off. The look she gave me as she curled up on the black dress made me feel mildly chagrined, but it wasn't long before she closed her eyes and went to sleep as only kittens can do.

Once my sobs stilled to occasional shudders, it also wasn't long before I fell asleep in the bath.

I awoke to something crashing in another room. A startled yelp shot from my throat, and I sat up, water shooting over the side. Carrots arched her back at the door and backed away, the fur along her spine standing on end, tail fluffed out. Hastily, I grabbed a towel, wrapped it around me, and stepped out of the water, careful not to slip on the slick tiles.

I didn't hear anything else. It felt like my heart would rip its way out of my chest, like my breaths would flay my throat. I had nowhere to run, and there were no locks on the inside doors for me to lock anyone out.

I couldn't just stand here.

I ran back to the bedroom and grabbed one of the high heels I'd worn all day, gripping the toe end in my right hand. With the left I held my towel in place. Carrots followed me out the door and down the hallway. I turned on every light I passed, brightening the house bit by bit. Each new room triggered another shot of adrenaline, but I checked them as I went. Nothing in the laundry room. Nothing in the kitchen. At one point I heard what sounded like a metal door closing, a sound of finality.

I jerked the basement door open, leaping backward, away from it. Nothing jumped out at me, so I approached again, shot a hand out to turn the light on. The little of the basement I could see was empty. After some debate, I shut the door again, but left the light on. Grabbing the broom, I leaned it against the door so that if it opened, I would hear it.

The only thing left was the living room. I stopped in the kitchen long enough to grab a knife from the drawer. I switched the heel into my left hand and clutched the knife in my right, raising it just above my head.

I paused in the entryway, eyes scanning the dark. Nothing moved or stood out. My breaths puffed out in quick succession, and I tried to still them so I could hear better. I felt exposed here, like something could attack me from any direction at any moment.

A flick of the switch, and light flooded the room.

The CD player lay in pieces on the floor.

The closest thing to human company I'd had, and it was gone. How? Carrots had been with me the entire time, so it hadn't been her. I searched the room, but found nothing else. The CD player was still plugged in, so I unplugged it. I searched the house again, leaving the basement to last. It was hard to decide what to do. Should I go down there? What if I got trapped down there? What if someone was down there? What would I do if I found someone?

Who was I kidding? No one could get in any more than I could get out.

I sat in the doorway at the top of the stairs for far too long, trying to decide what to do. Ultimately, I decided there was no good reason to go down into the basement. Instead, I shut the door, leaving the light on, and shoved the dining room table against the door, stuck between the end of the counter and the door so it couldn't be opened from the other side.

Carrots was totally relaxed now, and I took my cue from her, but only after I'd checked every room yet again, searching every crevice. Not that there were very many in this tiny bungalow.

We are alone. Well and truly alone. I don't know how I feel about that. I know I need to try to sleep, but I can't bring myself to turn off the light, close my eyes. I feel so vulnerable.

***

Day 11

Today is a new day. I've decided that I must have just left the CD player askew last time I used it, and a minute shift in the house knocked it down. It happens. I cleaned it up after breakfast, threw away the pieces, then put the table back in place.

I've been singing all day, because the quiet is oppressive, a physical presence. My voice has become hoarse, and I don't think I can keep this up every day. So now I whisper the words to myself, singing my favorite songs from the CDs in a softened voice. Carrots purrs and rubs against my legs, following me throughout the house.

I've got nothing else to report. I don't know what to write anymore. What does it matter?

***

Day 15
The lack of sound has really started to bother me. My voice is raspy from days of trying to defeat the quiet. I tried running the blender for noise, but it made me jumpy, so I shut it off. I spent way too long laying against the front door to listen to the kids outside. Something hit the side of the house, and it gave me an idea.

The walls. Maybe I can get through the walls.

So far, the knife has failed, but the meat tenderizer has chipped away at the plaster, even though it didn't work on the windows or doors. There's a hole in the wall in the middle of the living room. I've been making it bigger since dinner time. The walls are the old kind—lathe, I think? Thin pieces of wood are covered over with plaster. There's no sheet rock, which makes it easier to get through, but the tenderizer can't seem to breach the exterior wall. My hands ache and bleed in a dozen places.

Tomorrow I'll start on a different wall. I will get out. Freedom is so close I can taste it. It tastes like dust.

***

Day ?
Carrots is missing and the water has been shut off. All I have is what was in the toilet, plus a pitcher in the fridge since I like cold water. Oh, and the ice cubes in the freezer tray.

Her collar was lying on the closet floor when I woke up. Along with one of her mouse toys. I figured she'd just slipped out of it in there, but I've checked everywhere, and she's not there. Someone has been in this house. My captor. If they can get in and out, so can I. I haven't found where they got in yet, but I will.

***

Day ??
The electricity was off when I woke up today. Who would

have thought it could get even more silent? Everything in the freezer is going to go bad. I have no way to cook it anyway. I guess I should have expected to be punished for trying to escape. My captor must have seen right through my attempts. But what did they expect? Anyone would try to get out. I don't know what to do anymore except try to find a way out. How many times can I check the same things over and over to try and find an exit? How many times can I pace this house? How much longer can I pound away at the walls before the bones in my hands and arms shatter?

I don't remember what day it is. When I'm not searching or working at the walls, I'm sleeping or eating. If I open and close the fridge fast, I can keep it cold longer.

***

When I got up this morning, the fridge and freezer doors had been left wide open and someone had urinated in the toilet. (I'd been using the tub). My captor wants me to die. Joke's on them. I'll drink the water anyway when I get desperate enough. One more day, and I'll find a way out of this place. I know I will. I have to.

***

I found a passageway in the walls. It was full of spider webs, dust, and mouse droppings. I followed it until I came across a door that led into my closet. When I closed the door, I couldn't see it anymore. All it took was a hard push in the right place, though, and it opened right up. My captor was coming in through my bedroom closet all this time. It makes me sick to think about whoever it is looking at me while I was sleeping. Would I have woken up if they'd (he?) touched me? How often did they come in, moving around in this house while I was completely vulnerable. Every time I think about it, a massive shudder works its way up my spine until my whole body shakes with it.

I followed the passage the other way. It leads to a thick metal door. I pounded on it as long as I could. Pounded until my hands bled and throbbed. I think I may have broken something in the right one. It hurts so badly, and my pinkie won't move like normal.

In the face of the door, someone has carved one word: Why?

I miss Carrots. Without her warmth, her breathing, living soul, I'm entirely alone. If she were here, I could snuggle with her. She'd know I was in pain and scared; she always did.

I picked up her collar and realized it was heavy. There was some sort of wiring in the tag. I guess this is how my captor listened to me. It might not be the only bug here.

I hope Carrots is okay. It's not her fault I tried to get out. She was perfectly happy existing in this house. The thought of what this sick bastard might have done to her makes me ill. It also makes me wonder what this monster will do to me.

***

The water's gone, and I'm so thirsty. The exterior walls are too thick for me to get through. There is plaster and wood everywhere from all the walls I've torn through. There must be a weak place somewhere. I tried kicking through the walls, but I'm too weak now. I've been eating the previously frozen vegetables to draw the moisture from them. I even sucked on some of the meat. It tasted like rancid blood and made my stomach turn over, but if it will keep me alive, it's worth it.

***

How long has it been? I don't know. I don't think I wrote anything yesterday. Or the day before. How many days?

There are no more vegetables. I've eaten the canned goods. There's a lot of dry pasta, so I'm working my way through that now, but it won't matter if I can't find something to drink. It's hard to swallow.

I found a weak spot in an exterior wall. It was in the laundry room. When I ripped out the vent I could see outside, see the light, a tree. It rained last night. Just for a minute or two, but it was enough for me to lick water off my hand with my dry, swollen tongue. I haven't peed in two days. Everything burns. My skin is weird. I feel dizzy, and my heart is beating so fast.

I'm pretty sure I can get more of this wall out, but I keep falling asleep, and I'm so incredibly weak. I don't have the strength to wield something well enough to rip out wall.

Tomorrow. I can do this tomorrow. First I have to sleep. It's dark.

I can feel the air from outside. It caresses my skin, and I curl up against the wall, inhale the smells of grass and dirt and wood smoke.

It's hard to write now. My hand.

Sleep. And then I'll be free.

I know how to get out now.

Tomorrow.

A Doomed Affair

Darla shut down her computer, grabbed her things, and leaned over the top of her cubicle wall. "Off to my appointment. See you Monday!"

The petite blond in the next cubicle nodded, placing a hand to her headset to make sure it stayed in place. She sent a quick wave Darla's way then returned to her call. "Yes, sir, I can see how that would be a problem."

Darla wound through the warren of fabric cubicle walls, the sound of fingers tapping keys and murmuring voices following her out. Someone must have made a fresh pot of coffee, as the rich scent filled the space by the break room, a relief against the wretched backdrop of bodies forced to share space for hours each day.

Leaving the office behind, Darla had a bolt of exhilaration, chased by guilt. She felt compelled to check her texts in case her husband had tried to reach her, but she left the phone securely nestled in her purse and climbed into her car. She had an hour long drive ahead of her. Far too much time to think, to doubt, to obsess.

She wasn't taking this decision lightly. Lord knew she'd been considering it for some time now. A marriage on the rocks. A man who thought everything she did was priceless, that she was the most beautiful woman he'd seen. She'd fought it, told him she wouldn't be untrue to her husband, Stan, no matter how much they fought or how indifferent he might be to her at any time. She and Stan had discussed separation, even divorce, but he refused, saying he didn't believe in divorce. What was she supposed to do with that? His insistence against divorce didn't make his behavior any better. Or hers, for that matter. She hadn't deluded herself enough to think she wasn't equally at fault for the state of their marriage, but at least she was willing to end it, to free them both. Stan's determination to remain married had them both trapped like flightless birds in an open pen.

On the other side of it all stood Rigoberto. They'd met through mutual friends. In fact, Stan had been present for their first meeting. The two of them next to each other—Stan with his stooped posture, consummate frown, and damp, pasty skin versus Rigoberto, the bronze god of a man, quick with a smile and a compliment—were a study in contrast, a film and its negative. Where Stan never heard a word she said unless it was negative, Rigoberto really listened to her. He wanted to hear her thoughts. He told her she was intelligent, asked her questions that prompted long, deep conversations. She had yearned for treatment like that from Stan for years, her whole marriage of fifteen years, really.

Scenery flew by the windows in a blur of green and brown. Castle Rock was approaching, which meant she didn't have long before reaching Denver. It was easy to drive mindlessly along this stretch of I-25, where large plots of land went unbroken save the random cow or rocky hill.

Despite the rationalizations and desire for something positive in her life, Darla knew the affair she was about to embark on wasn't truly justified. It was just that she'd reached the point where she didn't care anymore. She was one step away from gnawing off a limb to escape her marriage, but maybe taking the time to glory in the respect of a man like Rigoberto would carry her through, buy her time to find a way out.

Every woman had the need to be worshipped in some small way by someone who didn't notice her flaws, who only focused on her positive attributes. Someone who looked at her the way Rigoberto looked at Darla, with hungry eyes that looked right into a woman's soul. His look could warm her from head to toe, cause her to flush like a school girl, while simultaneously responding in ways only a fully grown woman could. A heat burned inside her every moment she spent around him. She could feel his eyes on her the moment they touched her skin, like a physical caress, even when her head was turned.

She wanted Rigoberto, plain and simple. After nearly a year of resisting him, it was time to let him in, to feel that body pressed against hers. To finally touch those full, firm lips with her own, to feel them on her flesh.

Darla shifted in her seat, wiping sweating palms on her skirt one at a time, the other hand firmly on the wheel. She'd dressed up a bit for Rigoberto, but not so much as to stand out at work. Her fitted pencil skirt, kitten heels, and tucked blouse weren't out of the ordinary for work dress, though she usually wore flats and pants. Underneath told a different story: office babe on the outside, woman of passion on the inside. Red lace and silk slid over her skin, a caress that promised of things to come.

The speed limit decreased as she hit Castle Rock. Wary of the heightened police force the smaller town allowed for, she slowed from eighty-five to sixty-five miles-per-hour, staying firmly in the middle lane. Traffic picked up now that she drove through a medium-sized city, and she had to pay a bit more attention than she had before. It would only take a few minutes to get through the city, and then she'd have twenty minutes to the hotel.

Twenty minutes in which to consider turning back.

She'd laid the groundwork. Work thought she was at an appointment; Stan thought she was at work. If he happened to call her office—something he hadn't done in years—it would be easy enough to say she'd forgotten to tell him about the appointment. Rigoberto might already be at the hotel. She couldn't abandon someone who had been there for her all these months, humiliate him by leaving him to wait for her.

No, she'd made this decision, had in fact invited him to meet her. There would be no reconsidering now.

The road opened back up, the speed limit increasing, and Darla sped up, moving into the passing lane to climb the steep hill leading from the city. Not much longer now.

The hotel was one she was familiar with. She stayed there each year for a work convention. Though there were several restaurants nearby, it had its own restaurant inside. Even so, she was looking forward to ordering room service. Maybe a bottle of wine, or even champagne. There hadn't been anything to celebrate in so long. Did hotels really serve strawberries and champagne upon request? If so, she'd never experienced it, even when her marriage had been good.

She didn't have to deal with Denver traffic for long before reaching the hotel, which was on the south side. It being the middle of a Friday, the parking garage wasn't empty, but she easily found a spot near the elevator so she wouldn't have to trek far. She was accustomed to coming for a weekend for the convention and struggling up the far side of the lot, pulling a suitcase behind her and dodging cars in the narrow concrete tomb of the garage. It felt freeing to not have a suitcase. Her purse held everything she'd need.

A wide, carpeted hallway led to a spacious lobby with a double staircase going to the second floor. Three check-in desks stood off to the right, one of them manned by a woman with shoulder-length blond hair and a quick smile. Darla hesitated, unsure what to do next. Should she check in or wait for Rigoberto here? They probably should have discussed that in advance.

A warm hand on her shoulder saved her from making the decision. She turned into Rigoberto's comforting embrace, allowing herself to be entirely wrapped in his strong arms. He smelled faintly of cologne, and beneath that, sawdust. His beard itched against the top of her head until she tilted her chin up, stretching onto her tiptoes to touch her mouth to his. His lips were warm and soft.

He pulled back and smiled down at her. "We're on the eighth floor. Want to get a drink in the bar first?"

She smiled back, feeling safe. "I'd rather go to the room."

He kissed her again, this time a quick, but solid meeting of lips. "Let's go then. Do you have a bag?"

"Nope. Just this." She held up her purse.

A bank of elevators stood against the back wall. They rode up in the middle one, bodies pressed together along their sides, her arm wrapped through his.

"Were you working on one of your sculptures today?" she

asked.

"Yes, I had a commission for one of the bears. You know how people like those."

She did know. He made wooden sculptures for a roadside stand along Highway 24. He'd told her in the past how he yearned to make real art, but the pay was in generic commissions, like bear and deer. "Are you working on any personal projects right now?"

"Actually, I've been thinking. How would you feel about posing for me?" He looked the shyest he had since she'd known him, gazing up through his long, dark lashes, head tilted down. If his skin had been lighter, she might have seen a blush. "I've never sculpted a bust before. You'd be perfect, beautiful and symmetric."

She'd never had a compliment quite like that before. Symmetric? Artists.

The elevator opened on their floor with a ding. He led her to the room, strong, scarred fingers wrapped around her slim, smooth ones. She waited while he unlocked their door, focusing on the scent of grease and meat from the room service tray sitting outside their neighbor's room. The nerves were flooding through her now, filling her mouth with acid. This was a mistake. She shouldn't be here.

Then he was pulling her into the room, into his arms, his lips on hers again, hands questing over her body. Her nerves disappeared, the fluttering in her stomach full of heat instead of trepidation, and she returned his kiss, ran her hands over his chest, his stomach, the solid bulge of his jeans. Everything but the urgency of her need for him fled her mind, all fear, all thoughts of her husband, her job. Passion consumed her, and she shoved him onto the bed, climbed atop him, hands working to undo his pants, pull his sweater up, free him.

He grabbed her hips then slid one hand up her back, bracing her as he flipped her over. Stepping back, he undid his belt then his jeans, sliding them off. He pulled his sweater over his head, threw it to the floor.

Darla reached to remove her heels, but he moved forward, touched her hand. "Keep them on." With gentle fingers, he undid her blouse, sliding it down her arms. He pushed her skirt up around her hips and lowered his weight onto her.

She ran her hands up his back, closed her eyes, enjoying the sensation of his hands and skin on her body, reveling in the sensations she hadn't felt in so long. Every inch of him was exquisite, soft yet hard in all the right places.

When she opened her eyes, a second face hovered over Rigoberto's shoulder, black holes where the eyes should be. She screamed, shoving him off her and scooting backwards along the covers to the head of the bed, her back slamming into the wooden surface.

Rigoberto looked back at her, an expression of stunned hurt on his face. The second face was no longer there. No one else was visible.

She scrambled off the bed to look at the floor and check the room. No one hid under the bed (they couldn't, it went to the ground), in the closet, or in the bathroom. She even checked the tiny mini fridge, just in case. The door remained securely locked.

When she finally calmed down and exited the bathroom, Rigoberto sat on the bed, his jeans back on, but chest still bare. "What happened?" he asked.

"I thought I saw something. A man behind you."

He stared at her, then toward the window, open to another tall building across the way. The sky was iron gray, a storm moving in over the mountains.

"I'm not kidding. There was a face behind you."

He looked back at her, lips turned down. "Listen, I know this is a hard situation. I understand if you don't want to do this."

"It's not that. I want this more than you can know. I just..."

Of course it looked bad. They were in a hotel room, alone, and she had screamed and basically fled as soon as they started to have sex. She must have imagined the face. Obviously she had. There was no one else in the room.

She sighed. "Why don't we order some room service and try again?"

"Okay." He patted the bed beside him. When she sat next to him, he took her hand in his. "I mean what I said. I will understand if you change your mind."

"I haven't." She shivered. The temperature in the room had plummeted. She hadn't noticed before, her blood pulsing warm through her body, heating her skin, but now that she was sitting here without her blouse on the cold had caught up.

"I'll turn up the heat. Why don't you find the menu." He stood from the bed and went around the corner into the short hallway leading to the door, closet, and bathroom.

"Rigo?"

"Yep?"

"I don't think I want to go home tonight."

He came back around the corner, eyes intent on hers. "Are you sure?"

"I don't know."

He nodded, sat beside her again. "Okay."

They called their order in, turning on the TV to wait for the delivery. Static bounced across the screen, voices fading in and out. Every channel turned out to be the same, so he turned it off again, silence filling the room.

Darla put a hand on his thigh, thumb rubbing at the fabric. She rested her head on his shoulder and sighed with contentment. "I need this, you know. It's past time for me to move on."

"I know." His arm came up behind her, and he slid it over her shoulders, pulling her closer to him. "We'll move at your pace."

Tears stung her eyes. She didn't deserve this man. It had been so long since she'd had the type of kindnesses he showed her, she hadn't even remembered what she was missing.

The TV turned on, flipping through the channels rapidly, the volume shooting up. They both scrambled to find the remote in the blankets, underneath themselves, but it wasn't there. Finally, Rigoberto found it on the nightstand and pushed the power button. Nothing happened. He jumped up and ran to the TV, but pushing the buttons didn't stop it.

"Unplug it!" she yelled, trying to be heard over the noise of the TV.

He leaned over the TV, reaching behind it, but when he pulled the plug, the screen stayed on, the volume now all the way up.

Darla put her hands over her ears, the sound a cacophonous roar that hurt her eardrums. She watched as Rigoberto scrambled at the TV's buttons again and pulled every plug he could find. Nothing turned the TV off. She got up to join him, searching the wall for a switch that might turn it off.

The TV abruptly shut off, the silence a roar of its own. A moment later, someone knocked on the door. "Room service."

Heart pounding, Darla hurried behind Rigoberto and waited as he peered through the peephole. He opened the door to a young man in black slacks, a white button-up shirt, and a black vest. His nametag said "Devon." A smattering of acne covered his cheeks and chin, but he had a friendly smile. "You guys ordered room service?"

"Yep, we did," Rigoberto said.

"Great." Devon lifted a large, rectangular cover. Underneath it were two plates, one with a big, juicy burger, leaf lettuce hanging out, the other with a club sandwich. Both were adorned with golden fries, the scent of grease and salt heady. There was also a silver bucket full of ice, a bottle of white wine rising from it. Two wine glasses were stem up on the rolling tray between the food and the bucket.

Darla's stomach rumbled. "I didn't realize just how hungry I was."

Devon chuckled, then handed a plastic rectangle with a receipt tucked into it to Rigoberto. "If everything's correct, please sign here. It'll be charged to your room."

The food signed for and carried into their room, they sat down on the bed to eat, glasses of wine sitting on the nightstands. Darla ate fast, hardly tasting the sandwich, though the first bite, with its salty bacon and savory deli meat, made her moan. The wine was heavenly, the fruity tang instantly relaxing her, the alcohol working its way through her tense muscles to loosen them up.

Soon they were laughing together and necking, plates discarded in the hallway, wine bottle empty. When they kissed, Rigoberto tasted like wine with a salty undercurrent. Darla felt tipsy, lightheaded. Every touch on her skin sent a thrill though her nerves.

At first, she didn't notice the motion of the bed for what it was. Part of her subconscious registered it, but it didn't seep through to her conscious until the jittering increased. Their lips separated, then they bumped noses, sending a shock of pain and a sensation of water up her nose. Blood gushed from her nose onto his chest and her blouse, a Rorschach splotch, vivid against the brilliant white.

Rigoberto scrambled off the bed, disappearing into the hallway to the bathroom. The bed continued to shake, intensifying. Darla, hand clutched to her nose, scooted to the side, but the bed rose into the air, the shaking becoming more like a bucking bronco. Her legs were thrown into the air, sending her tumbling backward onto the bed, where she came down with a hard enough impact to make her back pop painfully. Her hand slipped off her nose, blood still leaking down her lip with a tickle.

Rigoberto ran back into the room, a handful of tissues clenched in his hand. He froze, staring at Darla, mouth agape. He was only visible from the chest up, the bed had risen so high.

"Help me!" she screamed.

It broke his paralysis, and he dropped the tissues, moving to the foot of the bed. He put his hands on the mattress and leveraged his weight, but the bed bucked, knocking him backward. He disappeared from view, a loud crunch ringing out.

At that moment, the TV turned back on, still unplugged. The telephone rang, shrill and continuous. The radio turned on to static, flipping through stations as if the dial turned back and forth nonstop, random chitters of voices or music breaking through. Blood rained around Darla, speckling the taupe comforter as the bed continued to throw her around and the nosebleed picked up again.

Her head snapped back, sending a pulse of dense pain down her spine.

She had to get off the bed. Gathering herself, she waited until the motion took her near the edge then threw herself forward. She hit the ground with a deep thud, pain exploding everywhere, air forced from her lungs. The bed landed loudly on the floor, sending vibrations through the ground that rippled across Darla's already punished nerves. In that same instant, all sound from the phone and electronics stopped, causing her ears to ring.

Darla rolled over onto her side then pushed up, climbing slowly to her feet. She could just see Rigoberto lying on the floor at the base of the bed, his head blocked by the bureau upon which the TV sat. His chest moved with slow breaths, but he was otherwise still.

It wasn't until she had limped over and knelt beside him that she saw the wound on his head. His dark hair was flattened on one side, blood pooled under his head. The bright white of bone showed through the hair in places. And something else. A light pink.

"Oh God," she said, clapping a hand to her mouth. She limped to the door, unlocked it, and attempted to open it, but it wouldn't budge. She pulled, twisting the doorknob. When that didn't work, she pounded on the door, screaming for help. How had no one heard the cacophony from the bed? Her screams?

There was no dial tone when she tried the phone. She checked that it was plugged into the wall and tried again. She pressed "0" with no effect. Frantic, she pushed every button on the phone and tried "911." The plastic sat dead in her hand, not even static coming through the earpiece. She slammed the receiver down on the base.

Then she remembered their cell phones. Both were dead. She pushed the power buttons, but got nothing. Her charger was in her purse, so she grabbed it and plugged her phone in before running back to the door to try the knob again. Even though the knob turned, the door wouldn't move in the frame. She flipped the lock the other way, but nothing changed.

The phone still wouldn't turn on. Maybe it just needed more time. Or the outlet was dead. She switched it to a different outlet and went back to Rigoberto with a towel from the bathroom. The prospect of pressing anything to his head was terrifying. What if she did more damage? But head wounds were bleeders, and it seemed important to staunch the flow of blood. Usually, it was best to put pressure on a wound, but she feared it would cause brain damage to do so in this case, so she only pressed lightly.

The towel flopped over his face, so she moved it, startled when she found his eyes wide open and staring. They didn't fix on her at all, the pupils dilated.

"Rigo? Rigo, can you hear me?"

No response.

A gurgle sounded from his throat, incessant and consistent. His eyes didn't move.

Darla began to cry, not sure what to do. She pressed a finger into the pulse at his throat. It seemed weak to her, but she was no doctor. Pounding on the wall behind him, she screamed for help. Then she stomped her foot on the ground, still screaming. Someone had to hear her. The hotel had been filling up when she'd arrived, people in line to check in. How could there be no one in adjoining rooms, above or below her who could hear everything going on?

She made sure the towel was secure on his head and moved to stand up, using a hand on the ground as leverage. Rigoberto's hand shot out and gripped her forearm, fingers like metal bands. She tried to pull away, but his fingers tightened painfully. His eyes still didn't focus on her, but he sat up, face close to hers.

"Rigo, are you okay? I think you should lie down. Rigoberto?"

The gurgling continued, now joined by the hiss of escaping air. The towel fell off, and she picked it up with her free hand and attempted to put it back on his head. His other hand came up and wrapped around her throat, fingers digging into the soft flesh at the back of her neck. He squeezed harder, blocking the air and suffocating her.

Her mouth gaped and she drew desperately at the air, trying to pull some into her lungs. A trickle made it in. Not enough. He still held her arm, so she struck at him with the other one, struggling against him with her entire body. His grip held steady. Blood ran down his face from his wound now that he sat upright. It flooded over one of his eyes, dark against his tan skin, drops clinging to his beard like red pearls. He didn't close his eye against the flow of blood, and his other eye remained unfocused.

Rigoberto stood, lifting her with him. He finally let go of her arm, but his grip on her throat remained strong. He walked to the window, ignoring her struggles, and slammed her against it.

She froze, aware that they were eight stories up. Darla wrapped her hands around his arm and pushed. Then she hit him in the face, over and over. His nose broke with a sound like peanuts being crunched, and he didn't even blink. She kicked him in the balls, but that didn't garner a reaction either. Continuing to rain blows on him, she felt herself growing weak, tunnel vision closing in on her. Her lungs burned.

This wasn't Rigoberto. She had no idea if he was in there somewhere, if some part of him knew what he was doing.

He pulled her back from the window then slammed her into it again. After three more hits, her head swam, vision diminished to a pinhole. Her struggles weakened, stopped. She willed her arms and legs to move, but couldn't make them. Her mind grew sluggish.

She gathered her strength for one last action. Concentrating as much as she was able, she lifted one arm, reaching blindly. Her fingers ran over his face, his beard tacky with blood, through his hair, and into the dent on his head. She fisted her hand and shoved it into his head as hard as she could, feeling the spongy firmness give under her knuckles. Bone scraped her skin, but she ignored it and persisted.

All at once, the pressure released. She dropped to the ground, crumpling in a pained heap. She couldn't move, despite her fear at where Rigoberto might be, nor could she see yet, though it was impossible for her to tell whether her eyes were even open.

Her throat felt raw, scratchy. Everything hurt. She was too exhausted to feel any real panic, though part of her knew she should. She floated in her own mind, no idea how much time had passed. When she finally opened her eyes, the room had darkened. Rigoberto lay beside her. She jerked back, but when he didn't move, she reached a tentative hand out and touched his chest. It was still. He felt unnaturally cool.

A sob wrenched from her damaged throat. He'd had a pulse before. She'd killed him to save herself, but there might have been a different way.

It took great effort to move, but she crawled over him, disturbed at the limp flattening of his body under her weight. She made her way toward the door, the rug burning her knees and elbows when they dragged across it.

As she got to the place Rigoberto had hit his head, his blood soaking the carpet, something grabbed her ankle. Expecting Rigoberto, she pulled her leg toward her while kicking out with the other. It didn't hit anything, and she kicked again, multiple times, never making contact. A small amount of light shone through the window, but she couldn't see him. Still, her foot was held in an iron grip.

She was pulled back toward the window, scraping over the carpeting. Bending her fingers, she tried to get a grip in the carpeting, but it was too short. One of her nails tore into the quick, followed by another, and she cried out.

Something grabbed her other ankle and flipped her over onto her back. A dark figure loomed over her, yet she could see the window through it. There were no discernible features, no true shape to it. It appeared humanoid, but the form flickered and changed.

"What do you want?" she asked, her voice coming out as more of a croak.

It lifted her up by the ankles, seemingly growing taller until she dangled, head just above the carpet. She swung her arms and body, trying to hit the form, but just as with her feet, her hands didn't come into contact with anything.

How could it be firmly holding her ankles, but her hands went right through it when she attempted to hit it?

Blood filled her head with intense pressure, and she feared her nosebleed would restart. She wasn't even sure when it had stopped, but the dried blood encrusted on her face itched. At this point, she was so exhausted she couldn't figure out how to fight this thing. Part of her wanted to give up, let it kill her. Surely, that's what it wanted. Darla didn't want to die. She was determined to find a way to live. If she could get to where it held her, perhaps it would be solid there. She tried bending upward, but didn't have the core strength to get far enough. With no other options, and unsure what this form wanted to do to her, she tried again. This time she got farther, fingers reaching, straining, but she couldn't quite reach her ankles.

As she straightened out again, it swung her up and around. She was able to get her hands up just before making contact with the window, but it was still a hard hit. Her face slammed into the backs of her hands before she fell to the ground, her legs landing on Rigoberto's body. Once again, the air was knocked out of her, but she fought it, scrambling back the way she had come, despite her inability to breathe. The form had disappeared, or it was somewhere she couldn't see it.

She got to the door, and this time it opened, surprising her. She limped out into the hallway, the bright light stark against her eyes after the dark room. "Help me!" she called. "Someone help."

No one came. The hallway remained empty. She stumbled forward, trying to get to the elevator. A strange sound followed her, but she was too scared to look. She focused on those silver elevator doors, determined to reach them. The wet sounds behind her continued. Any moment, it would grab her again.

The hallway went on forever, and it felt like she would never make it. There were now pops and cracks joining the wet sounds, and they seemed to be getting closer. Closer.

Darla forced herself to run faster. Only a few more feet.

Something grazed the bottom of her foot as it lifted.

She let out a stifled shriek and kept going.

Just a couple more steps.

It grabbed her foot, but she pulled from its grasp.

The button within reach, she fell forward, slamming her hands against the round surface. She turned, back against the doors, and finally looked at the thing that had been following her.

Rigoberto's body hunched on all fours, its head bent sideways. The fingers looked broken, splayed out across the carpeting. His jaw hung slack, bloodied drool leaking down his chin. The eyes remained unfocused, just as before.

Darla willed the elevator to arrive. Mechanical whirring sounded behind the doors. It was coming, but it would be too late.

"Please, please, please," she begged. Tears ran down her cheeks, splashed onto her chest, leaving pink droplets there.

The Rigoberto thing reached for her, sharp pops sounding as the arm moved forward in jerks. It gurgled and creaked.

Darla slammed her hands back against the elevator and screamed. She kicked forward, striking the outstretched hand. It snapped, the hand hanging from the wrist, but kept coming.

The elevator dinged.

"Oh, thank God."

The doors slid open. She stepped backward, relief filling her.

Her foot touched open space, an abyss. She tumbled backward.

Above her, Rigoberto's bent head poked out, sightless eyes staring downward as she fell. Her last thought was, *What will they tell Stan?*

Your Mother's Eyes

As mother sickened, so did father, though in different ways. Ways that looked more like a haunting than an illness. He hollowed out from the inside, cheeks becoming gaunt, eyes feral. While mother showed a type of strength in her decline, a quiet fortitude, father weakened. It was as if his very essence drained along with her life.

We watched from the sidelines, the six of us. Sally, the youngest at five, didn't fully understand it, but she could sense it all the same. We weren't only mourning for mother.

Father stopped going to work in order to care for her, cashing in long unused vacation time, even though I and my sisters tried to help. He slept in quick snatches—only when she found her deepest slumber—his eyes half open, face slack, lines still burrowed into his brow and around his mouth.

At seventeen, I was the oldest. Unable to do much for mother, I took care of my sisters, making sure they got off to school in the morning, preparing their meals, doing their hair, signing their permission slips, and kissing their wounds after applying the requisite bandages. Father needed caring for, too, but I had to do that more discreetly. So I slipped food onto the side table for him when he wasn't looking, quietly kept his toiletries stocked up, did his laundry, and paid the bills. Things my mother had done, but couldn't any longer.

They touched each other constantly, my parents, holding each other's hands or tracing a finger along the other's exposed skin. The contact soothed them both, as if the only life force that existed for them was shared, charged by touch. They rarely spoke, but when mother was lucid, they looked into each other's eyes, facial expressions changing as if they held a full conversation, one between only the two of them. Smiles and frowns, questioning expressions, mild nods. Sometimes I became entranced by these mute discussions, studying their faces from across the hospital bed she rested upon. They often forgot I was there. I couldn't bring myself to be hurt by that, as their absorption in each other showed me what love must be like, the ethereal connection that reached across space and mortality in a gentle caress.

When mother died on a silent exhale and a drifting of the soul, father slumped, his head upon her shoulder, tears spilling onto the soft white of her nightgown. He caressed her face with one hand, while the other held her hand atop the crisp sheets. His shoulders shook gently, but no sound came from him. We had long been a mute household in deference to the cancer eating away at her.

In the other room, we sisters held each other and cried, afraid to make a sound lest it break the spell around our parents. Even a muffled sob might send her being from the room, shatter our father's last hold on his own soul, which we instinctively knew wanted to go with hers. We dared not breathe or let a single tear drip onto a hard surface, where the tiny plop might echo forth into the next room.

He stayed like that for hours, forcing us to do the same by his very stillness. Dusk had fallen around us, the shadows expanding throughout the house. When I could no longer make out my parents' forms, I silently urged my sisters from the room and got them all into bed. None of us were hungry.

I was the first to wake in the morning, and I found my father in the same spot. Terrified at first, I gasped, covering my mouth with my hand in horror at the sound I'd made, unaccustomed as I was to more than hushed whispers. Was he dead? It took a moment, but finally I made out the slight ebb and flow of his breathing, his ribs expanding in minute increments. Alive, then. Though how much of him remained wasn't clear.

For three days he stayed there. Three days of her body drying out, stiffening then relaxing, blood purpling her arms where they lay against the sheet. Her skin sank, leaving shallow indents around joints, her cheeks hollowed out, collarbone graphically illustrated. Out of her paled face, her eyes stared, empty and soulless. I wanted so desperately to close them, but an irrational fear filled me at the thought of approaching my parents' forms, so still upon that bed. My skin crawled at the image of my father's face if he were to look up from her body. Terror iced its way through my veins at the possibility that mother's death had finally snapped his last tenuous grip on reality, that I would see only madness in his eyes were he to turn my way.

And what if her eyes were to focus again on me?

No, I stayed away, left him to his grief while we shared ours in silence in the living room, huddled together on the sofa. We had slipped into a quiet sort of grief-induced meditation, unwilling to speak after months of non-verbal communication, a linked chain of physical touch and comfort. We moved only for two meals a day and bedtime. I turned off the phones and the doorbell. The sign we'd put out weeks ago warning of an illness in the house remained, a deterrent to those who might knock.

I didn't read to the littles, even in the muffled utterances of the last few months; it felt like blasphemy. Instead, I touched small hands, caressed soft cheeks, brushed golden hair from their faces, and nodded a goodnight before turning out lights and disappearing into my own room. There, I lie awake all night, staring at the ceiling, ears straining for any movement from that room down the hallway. That room of death and grief and suspension in time. My body was as rigid as hers had been in those first twelve hours, my muscles an agony of tension and trepidation. For if I heard movement, what might that mean? Part of me desperately wanted to hear a footfall from that direction, a sigh or moan, a voice perhaps, but the other part of me screamed internally at that very possibility, wondering whose footfall it might be, and what might be approaching down that hallway.

I locked my door each night in an effort to make myself feel safer, knowing full well that it instead left my senses doubly alert lest one of the littles need me for anything. But they slept like the dead, still as mother.

The second night I brought a kitchen knife into my room, sliding it beneath the cool softness of my pillow, within easy reach. I cannot say why I felt such fright, especially why it was my father I feared, not my mother. Perhaps it was the stillness of a still-living body, eerie in its immobility and seeming lack of consciousness. Knowing some spark still existed in there, that it could animate the body at any time for any purpose. Knowing the steel strength of his body from years of manual labor, as evidenced by the ease by which he could pick us up, fly us through the air to elicit giggles and screams. Knowing our comparative vulnerability.

My father had never threatened us. He didn't believe in corporal punishment. He was a quiet, patient man before mother's illness. One who wasn't at home as much as we might have liked, and who, when he *was* home, was often distant, thinking of work. Fearing him was unrealistic, and yet I couldn't help myself. I recognized the irrationality of it, that being the only thing keeping me from dragging all five of my sisters into my room, like a dragon hoarding its gold, protecting it from encroachment. Keeping them separate meant I wasn't going crazy, that I wasn't giving in to my delusions.

On that third day, he lifted his head.

We were in our customary places on the sofa, the youngest two nestled into either side of me. I happened to look up at just the right moment, studying his back as I often did, wondering what more I should do, whether I should call someone. How long it would be before he let go.

It was a slow movement, as of someone waking from a deep slumber. His head moved upward in a motion so minute that at first I thought my eyes deceived me. I blinked, squinting against the blurred light filtering into the room. My sister moved against my side, and I grasped her arm to still her, my hand shaking. A small whimper escaped her, bringing my attention to how tightly I squeezed. I let go, but held my hand up, palm in her direction, hoping she got the message not to move or make a noise. It was like watching a deer, afraid to move or breathe, not wanting to startle it.

Hours may have passed while I watched his gradual progress. He made no sound, his clothes not rustling, so deliberate was the shift in his position. As his head came up, his shoulders turned, back bending, neck twisting, until he faced me fully.

His eyes rose to meet mine, stark and empty, two dark marbles in a gaunt face.

A shudder worked its way up my back, a chill moving outward from my stomach. I saw no recognition in his stare. No soul. It was as if a vacancy remained behind inside his body. My father was not there.

Without a word, I gathered my sisters up, gestured them through the process of putting on shoes and jackets, and urged them toward the front door, my back crawling the entire time. The few times I turned to check on him, he remained in the same position, eyes following my movements, though his head didn't shift. One hand lay clenched in his lap, shaking from the strength of his grip, the quiver working its way up his arm and into his shoulder.

Once outside, the door closed, I felt my shoulders relax, and I straightened my back, which had been bowed with the weight of my tension. It popped several times, and I let out a sigh. "Let's go to the park, girls."

A quiet cheer went up, and the littles darted ahead, the park a straight shot down the sidewalk. The oldest after me at fourteen, Maisy kept pace beside me, waiting for the small ears to be out of hearing distance. Finally, she leaned toward me, hands in her pockets, and asked, "Did you see that? The emptiness?"

I nodded, afraid to speak, torn as to my response to her. As the oldest, it was my job to make them feel safe, to actually keep them safe. Revealing my fears to her would give me someone to talk to, but it would also undermine any comfort I could provide.

"What do you think?" she prompted.

I couldn't look at her, couldn't meet her eyes. "I think it's just grief and exhaustion. Maybe he'll go to bed since we're not there. Maybe he'll eat something. He has to be starving. That's all it is." I could taste the lies as they rolled off my tongue, dark and bitter.

I watched her peripherally as she shook her head, picking up her pace enough to get ahead of me. She recognized my lies. A sick sensation washed over me. Now would be an excellent time for an understanding ally, but fourteen was too young for that sort of alliance. I was the closest thing they had to a mom now, and she'd need that more than she'd need a sister, as would the others. My selfish needs would have to wait.

Even so, I feared I'd broken something between us in that moment. That I'd let her down.

We stayed at the park until after dusk. Everyone but Maisy climbed and ran and shouted, happy to be in the open air, free in the youthful sense of the word. The darker it got, the more they sneaked glances at me, not used to getting to be out as the velvet darkness crept across the sandy lot. No way would they call my attention to the time.

Maisy wandered the edge of the forest surrounding the park. Occasionally, she kicked at items on the ground or bent to examine something she'd seen. She never looked my way, but I could tell she was aware of me, her body a straight wire of tension and resentment, jaw clenched, mouth firm. I wondered if she knew how lovely she'd become, if she was aware of the new curves and shapes of her blossoming body. Of course she was. It hadn't been so long since I'd been in her place, every part of me new, skewed from the normalcy I'd known. I vaguely remembered how even my movements had changed, adjusting to the differences in my body. She seemed so laid back about it all the time, oblivious to the stares and whistles she often received. Was she really, or did she put on a good mask?

When my stomach rumbled for a solid minute, I realized how hungry everyone must be. "All right, guys, time to go home for dinner!"

The groans were half-hearted, telling me that as much they might enjoy this daring time extension, they were definitely hungry. They quickly abandoned their various pursuits and walked sluggishly toward home, nicely tired out, though chattering happily.

The closer we drew to the house, the higher my shoulders climbed, an ache settling into my forehead. Would he still be sitting in that spot, shiny eyes staring from the shadows? Would he say anything?

It wasn't only me showing trepidation. Maisy brought up the rear, falling farther behind as we got closer, the soft telltale scuffs of her shoes on the concrete growing fainter and further between.

As for the littles, their pace slowed and their voices lowered as we approached, tapering off when we reached the path leading to the porch.

The house stood dark against the night, no lights on inside. The friendly warmth of the surrounding houses seemed to disappear into the void that was our home, their bright energy sucked into it like it was a black hole. I flashed on an image of father, sitting in that one spot, eyes fixed on the door. Waiting for us to come home, statue-still in that death-filled room. I desperately wished for somewhere else to go, but we had only this house.

The others fell back, even the littlest, waiting for me to precede them to the front door. I felt myself nearly tip-toeing forward, once again afraid to make a sound. I lifted my right foot with trepidation and placed it upon the lowest step, which creaked with my weight. A gasp sounded from behind me.

Suddenly aware that how I approached the house would set the tone for them, I lifted my head, threw my shoulders back, and threw a smile over my shoulder to reassure them, unsure if they could even see my expression in the twilight. I took the next two steps swiftly and grasped the doorknob, forcing myself to turn it and open the door, which swung inward, revealing the bleak darkness of the living room. Nothing moved. No sounds came to me save the gentle clicking of the refrigerator.

I reached inside for the exterior porch light, but flicking it produced no light at all. The bulb must have burned out.

To get to the light switch for the living room, I'd have to cross the room, something that had been only a minor nuisance in the past, but now bore a heavy weight of threat. Achingly aware of the many small sets of eyes on my back, I stepped into the house, sliding my feet forward so as not to trip on anything. It was a walk I'd taken many times, and I knew instinctively where the switch was at this point, but the walk itself was interminable tonight. At any moment, there might be a movement in that room. Father could be anywhere. He might be crouching in the deeper shadows, knowing full well the need to cross the room to bring light to it.

My eyes swept the darkness, probing the darker recesses, constantly shifting back to that room. Something clicked off to my right, in the direction of the kitchen, and I jumped, freezing in place, staring hard toward that random sound.

The fridge continued its soft tick, my ears almost buzzing from the depth of the silence.

When that click didn't happen again, I proceeded forward, legs shaking. A cold burst of air hit my face, and I jerked my head back, reaching blindly for whatever had stirred it up.

My hand came into contact with something soft and covered in fabric. I pulled it back, stumbling sideways to escape it. Him?

I came to rest against the counter between the living room and the kitchen, gripping the cool surface, willing it to give me strength. I waited for a blow, for hands to grasp me. My nerves registered every change in the air currents, every minute sound. I felt like an amplifier, drawing it all in, tension ratcheting up in preparation for whatever might happen next. The shadows seemed to coalesce, to morph as I stared into them. They took on the shape of father's broad shoulders, his wild curls, an arm splitting the air.

When the attack didn't come, I moved more quickly, throwing caution to the wind. So he would hear my footfalls, be able to track them. What did I really think father was going to do? I felt he must be toying with me now, and anger pushed the fear aside. How dare he force me to walk through this house in the dark. How dare he shut down and leave us to fend for ourselves. How dare he allow us to fear him.

My fingers came into contact with the switch, and I slapped it upward, wincing at the sudden flood of brightness. I looked around, searching for father, expecting to see him looming over me or creeping from a corner, but he was nowhere to be seen. Still filled with my righteous anger, I stormed toward the back room, ready to tell him what I thought of his bizarre and frightening behavior. I started speaking before I could see into the room, shoring up all the bravery I possessed.

"It's time you..."

The room was empty.

Not just of father, but of mother's body. The soiled linens and the pads beneath them were even gone, along with the thin mattress, leaving a bare bed, stripped of everything. The food plates, cups, books, everything had been removed from the room. Had the bed not been there, I might have doubted any of this had ever happened. In fact, even with that small piece of evidence, I began to question what I knew. Had I made up mother's death in my head? Would they arrive home from a date, laughing, cheeks flushed, casting each other those glances that told me more than I ever wanted to know about them?

Unsure what to think, I rushed to their bedroom. The bed was still made from when I'd last changed the sheets, the room exuding the vacancy it had held for so long now, abandoned for the more convenient back room. I turned on the light, just to be sure.

I ran from room to room, turning on every light within reach, bombarding every surface so I could see it, seeking.

No father. No mother.

I glanced at the basement door, pondered checking downstairs, but we weren't allowed in his office, and no light showed beneath the door.

Panting, I leaned against the hallway wall, trying to get myself together. The kids still awaited me outside. What must they be thinking right now?

With one final deep breath, I went to the front door, a smile upon my face. "Come on in, guys. Aren't you hungry?"

Maisy stood on the porch, wary, body tense. She jumped when I spoke, but I pretended not to see it.

"Go get washed up," I told them. "How about chicken fingers tonight?"

Resilient, as kids are, the thought of a favorite meal got them moving. Maisy waited as they traipsed past me. She eyed me warily until I stepped away from the door, her eyes flitting between me and the back room.

"They're not there." I wasn't sure whether I intended this as a comfort or a warning. "I don't know where they are."

Her eyes widened, but she moved past me, making a beeline to the back room. She stilled in the doorway, staring into the room as I had done.

I waited, wondering what she might say, but she only stood there, frozen. It felt like an hour, but must have been only a few minutes, as the sounds of a running faucet and shuffling sneakered feet still trilled down the hall. The moment the water shut off, the spell broke, and I shook my head, moving into the kitchen to get dinner together.

We had to eat.

The normalcy of getting food ready and preparing kids for bed carried me through the rest of the evening. Deep in thought, I at first missed that Bethany had been talking to me for some time. I asked her to repeat something four times before nodding and pretending I'd heard what she'd said. All I could think of was where he might be, and what had happened to mother. He must have called the funeral home, had them pick her up. Mother had placed their number next to the charging base for the phone when she was still able to move about the house. She told me all the arrangements had been made, that it might be me who would have to call if father couldn't. Shame flushed my face when I thought of this, realizing I should have called them when she'd first died. It had been up to me, and I'd left them in that room instead, both of them rotting.

Even so, even if the funeral home had picked her up, where was he? Why no note? Why not leave the lights on for us?

Mother had always been the thoughtful one. That explained it. He simply hadn't thought of us. I'd long noticed that father's biggest concern was mother, even before her illness. It was mother that thought of our needs and welfare. Not that he didn't care. He simply had different priorities. Father loved us in his own way, and he took care of us as a father does, but we had never been his first and last thought, as we probably had been for mother.

Despite these calming thoughts, when it came time to tuck the littles into their beds, I couldn't do it. Instead, I declared a slumber party in my room. They didn't have to know it was so I could lock them in with me, keep a watchful eye. To them, this was something special. We set about building night forts out of pillows, blankets, and stuffies. Books were piled up for reading, and flashlight batteries replaced for reading in the dark.

Maisy refused to sleep with us. "I'd prefer to sleep in my own room," she said as she stormed out of my room.

I followed her, leaving the littles to their eager preparations. As she stepped over her threshold, I grasped her arm, pulling her back. She glared at me, yanking her arm from my grip.

"Lock your door," I whispered.

A variety of emotions crossed her face in the seconds between my request and her nod. Irritation, fear, confusion, disbelief. But I heard the snick of the lock, and felt as much relief as I could that at least she'd taken me seriously.

***

The next morning, I awoke to clattering in the kitchen. The others remained asleep, the door still shut and locked. It wasn't like Maisy to prepare breakfast, or to be up before everyone else, but these were strange circumstances. Perhaps she'd decided to step up and help.

The littles began to stir as I moved around the room to get my clothes for the new day. A shower was in order. Then breakfast. I wondered what she was cooking, and my stomach rumbled in response.

Things felt more normal and hopeful than they had in a while. Perhaps father was home, asleep in his own bed. The thought of him alone in that large bed, mother's side possibly still tucked in, reminded me of our loss, but it was not enough to ruin the thought of a real breakfast for the first time in days. We'd been grieving mother for quite some time, had long said our goodbyes. I didn't think the pain would ever diminish, but it existed now as a dull throbbing in my chest, rather than the sharp agony I'd felt off and on during her decline. The relief of her release made me feel both guilty and lighter. No more pain.

I was passively aware that Maisy's door remained closed when I moved past it to the bathroom. She usually left it open when she was up, unlike me. She was far less possessive of her stuff than me. I always kept my door shut so the littles couldn't go in and ruin anything, a hard learned lesson after losing one too many cherished items to tiny, chubby hands and slobbering mouths.

After my shower, I followed the excitedly babbling voices past Maisy's now open door and into the dining room, but froze at the sight awaiting me. All the kids sat around the table, plates heaped with fluffy eggs and fluffier pancakes drenched in syrup. Father sat at the head of the table, shoveling in his own breakfast. He looked up at my entrance, nodded, and returned to his food.

Maisy looked at me and shrugged, taking a bite of her eggs.

Watching father, I filled my own plate from the abundance of food on the stove and sat down in my customary spot at the table. I continued to watch him from the corner of my eye while I ate, studying him. He seemed pensive, but okay. The fact that he was eating reassured me. He must have needed that time to get himself together.

When he'd finished his food, he pushed his plate back a touch on the table and watched the activity around him. His eyes lingered on Sally, a frown creasing his brow. I studied her, trying to see what had made him frown, figuring she'd have something on her face, but I couldn't tell what he'd reacted to.

Then the frown disappeared, the muscles relaxing. A slight smile graced his mouth, and he seemed truly relaxed for the first time. I felt my own tension ease at this change in him. He looked around at each of us once again and said, "Girls, each of you holds a piece of your mother. I can see it. It's beautiful. *You're* beautiful. And I'm grateful for you."

Father wasn't given to emotional moments, so his reaction took me by surprise. I could see from Maisy's reaction that she felt the same. Still, it felt nice to think I reminded him of mother. That I held some part of her within me. Through the confusion, I felt a warm glow spread from my stomach outward. Father would be okay.

We would be okay.

From then on, father became less remote, warmer. He made it a point to tell wonderful stories about mother, stories we'd never heard before, because mother surely never would have told them.

"One time, your mother saw a duckling straggling along behind the others," he started. "It bobbed a lot in the water and couldn't keep up. She spent the next hour watching it, urging it forward to catch up to its family. We couldn't leave the park, because she needed to know it would be okay. But it fell behind until they'd all disappeared, leaving it behind. She stepped into the pond, mud rising like a murky cloud around her, and lifted her skirt by the hem, so that it floated on the surface. This, she eased under the duckling until she could pick it up and swaddle it in her skirt. It didn't bother her when she stepped out of the water, legs exposed, underwear barely hidden. She walked home that way, dirty water dripping from her fine summer dress.

"We had that duckling for a month while it healed. Fishing wire had gotten wrapped around its legs, cutting into the flesh and separating one of its webbed feet. She fed it, took care of it. She was so kind-hearted..."

His voice drifted away, almost choked. We waited, made of silence, while he thought. Waited to hear more of our mother. But he didn't continue that time, silently getting up and walking from the room, the sound of his bedroom door a sharp rap that startled a jump out of me.

The next morning, Maisy didn't come out of her room. Her door stayed shut. We'd stopped locking our doors once father started acting more normal, the littles sleeping in their own beds, Maisy back to leaving her door open.

"Leave her be," father said, when I mentioned going to check on her after she failed to turn up for breakfast. "She wasn't feeling well this morning."

Great, I thought. *Now we'll all get sick.*

With so many of us, illnesses spread like wildfire. We never had just one person get sick. The others would fall like dominoes.

I took pains to make everyone wash their hands and cover their mouths with their arms when they coughed or sneezed, hoping to stave off the worst of it. It seemed to work at first, but then I awoke to another closed door. It was Sally's and Malin's room. Before I could go in, father stepped out of his room and shook his head. "They've got it now, too. Leave them to rest."

He bustled about, preparing breakfast as he had been each morning. I watched the other two for signs of illness, but saw nothing. It must be a fast acting bug; I hadn't noticed any symptoms in Sally or Malin last night.

Figuring I'd be sick soon, I told father I'd head to the store to stock up on apple juice, chicken noodle soup, and bread for toast.

"Good idea. Can you grab me some more coffee while you're there? And eggs? We've been going through a lot of eggs."

"Definitely. I'll leave after breakfast. If you think of anything else, let me know."

Getting out to the store felt wonderful. Aside from visits to the park with the littles, I hadn't gone anywhere or spoken to anyone who didn't live in the same house with me in far too long. We had no living relatives, and the neighbors had long stopped coming by to check on us. Father had started doing all the shopping and running all the errands when he wasn't working in his basement office. He'd told me I deserved a break.

"Don't think I didn't notice everything you did these last months. It's time you got to be a kid."

"But I'm not a kid anymore. I'll be eighteen in a month."

"Then it's time you got to be a young adult. Enjoy it!"

While it felt nice to get a break from playing mini-mother, I missed it. I'd long become accustomed to running the household. Without that, I felt like I was in limbo, drifting. This, at least, was a taste of normalcy for me. Grocery shopping had provided me with a break from the sick silence of our house while mother lay dying.

As a result, I stayed far longer than necessary, wandering through the aisles, gazing at the shelves without really seeing what sat upon them. I grabbed a few impulse purchases, thinking how nice cookies would be. Chicken fingers and macaroni and cheese for when the girls felt better. Tampons for Maisy and I. Popcorn for a movie night. I even bought a cheap family movie they had near the front.

I got home well after lunch. Silence greeted me when I entered the house. After putting away the groceries, I went to check on Molly and Sam, but found their room empty. All the rooms were empty, even Maisy's and father's. Where could they be? Surely they hadn't all recovered at the same time. I'd had the car, so he couldn't have driven them somewhere.

His office was off-limits, but with the changes he'd made, perhaps he'd lightened up on that, too. He'd gotten so much better about being there for us, taking care of us. Maybe he'd set up a movie so they could relax with him.

Tentatively, I opened the door to the basement. A faint light showed at the bottom of the stairs. All else was dark, the shadows a waiting menace around that one small hint of brightness. The wooden steps to the basement creaked as I made my way down, the musty, metallic smell of concrete walls and metal supports strong in the small space. Air circulated around my ankles, whispering in through the gaps between the stairs.

Gaps that would allow hands through.

A terrible electrical thrill went up my legs, the flesh tightening all the way to my knees. Trepidation filled me, pushed me to turn and flee back up those stairs. Back to the safety of the main floor.

I pressed on.

His office door was closed, light leaking beneath it. Inside, a scuff sounded, followed by a tick as of something being put down on a hard surface.

"Father?" I whispered, knowing full well he couldn't hear me through the door. Not *wanting* him to hear me. My mouth had gone dry, tongue sticking to the roof. My heart pounded frantically in my chest.

I found the cool doorknob with my hand, other hand

pressed to the smooth surface of the door. The knob turned easily, and I pushed the door open.

Father looked up at my entrance. His brows knit together at first, but then he smiled, watching me.

My sisters' tiny bodies lay in a heap on one side of the room, bloodied and broken, discarded like unloved dolls. They were a jumble of limbs and torsos, exposed in their nudity.

Maisy's mouth was a ragged hole. It took me a second to process why. Her lips had been removed.

Where Malin's nose should have been, there was only a cavity and a thin line of cartilage.

Bone showed where Sally's cheeks had been.

Patches of skin were gone from all the bodies, sloppily removed.

Blood painted two of the walls in loops and splatters.

The more I looked, the more damage showed itself. They had been brutalized.

Unwillingly, I allowed my eyes to track to where father stood, dread ballooning up from my stomach. On his desk lay what must once have been mother, her body a patchwork of pieces, stitched together. Where her eyes should have been, there were only black, bloodless holes.

"I'm glad you're home, my darling. You have your mother's eyes."

The Importance of Self-Defense

"**M**en need to know how to defend themselves. While not all women have VV, any woman *can*." The instructor brushed a lock of dark hair back from her angular face. "You must assume you could be in danger in order to stay out of it."

Quinton took in the muscles roping her bronze arms. She was fit and toned, her thighs bigger around than his (and possessing significantly less fat). She wore a fitted tank top and capri workout pants in peach and green. There were nine other men scattered around the blue mats, huddled against their nerves and discomfort. One man repeatedly tapped a hand against his thigh as he listened, sweat glistening on his dark brown forehead.

"The most important aspect of defense is awareness," the instructor continued. "Don't put yourself in dangerous situations. Keep your head up, meet strangers' eyes, especially women's. You want them to know you're paying attention, that you won't be caught unaware." She paced in front of them, meeting each man's eyes as she spoke.

"Women who have contracted VV show no significant outward signs. Yet they are strong, and can easily overpower you. They are also preternaturally fast." She swept her eyes over the men once again. "But if you know how to defend yourself, you stand a better chance at getting away."

She stopped pacing and looked out at them, folding her hands in front of her.

"Before we get into self-defense maneuvers, let's talk sex."

Quinton's mouth went dry. He couldn't look directly at her, instead staring down at his navy blue sweatpants and picking at an imaginary bit of fluff. He heard a man clear his throat off to his left. Another man coughed.

"I know it's not a comfortable topic, which is why I want to get it out of the way." She pulled a chair over and sat in it, crossed her legs, and leaned forward. "Let's look at an example. You meet a woman in the bar. She seems nice, friendly. You talk for hours. By the end of the night, you feel comfortable with her. She couldn't possibly hurt you. She's safe. Surely you would know by now if she intended to harm you. No mental alarms are buzzing."

Quinton felt sick to his stomach. How many times had he done this before the VV outbreak? Always with quiet confidence and no fear. Now he couldn't even meet a woman at the bar without having to worry she'd kill him? Trust was a hard thing to come by five years post outbreak.

"You get back to your place. Everything is going just how you want it to." A pause. "You kiss."

Quinton squirmed. Her eyes were like laser beams. When she looked at him, he felt it burning up his spine.

"The kissing leads to more. Then it's like a switch flips." She snapped her fingers. "You can't get her off you. You say 'no,' but she doesn't listen. You can't fight back in fear that it will cause her to hurt you. After all, she's stronger than you are."

His pulse throbbed in his throat and wrists. In his stomach.

"Forty percent of attacks on men occur in their own homes," she said. "It's important that you take precautions. First of all, don't invite a woman to your apartment until you've been dating awhile. Meet her in public places. Drive yourself. Double date or move in groups when possible."

Quinton thought about Felicia's warm brown eyes. Her full lips and throaty laugh. That image changed to one of her the last time he'd seen her. Those same eyes had been bloodshot, edged with desperation. Her lips chapped, skin ashen. He raised his hand.

The instructor pointed to him. "Yes, Quinton?"

"You said earlier you can't tell someone is infected, but my ex-girlfriend showed signs something was wrong."

She nodded. "There are minor signs, but you have to know the woman well in order to see the difference. And if they've recently fed, those signs disappear."

A light skinned, sandy haired man called out, "What are the signs, just in case?"

"Good question, Tim. Skin and eyes may lighten up the longer she goes without feeding, causing pale skin. If she goes too long without blood, her gums and nail beds may bleed, but this is a rare condition, and typically only seen in women who have been infected a shorter time. During that period, they are most often hiding away, as they become sensitive to light."

A Latino man in the front said, "Is that really all?" Grumbles moved around the room.

"For the most part," she said. "There are little things, like an aversion to garlic, for instance. But it's just an aversion. It can't actually hurt them. Sometimes they exhibit symptoms of iron deficiency, but these are things they feel, not that are necessarily visible to anyone else. Other than, say, the paleness, which I already noted, and cold hands, if you happen to touch them."

A pasty fellow with a buzz cut on Quinton's left laughed. "My mom always had cold hands. So have some of my girlfriends pre-VV. That's not much to go on."

"Which is precisely why you need to learn to defend yourselves," she replied. "There's no way to know if a woman is infected for certain."

"How do we know you're not infected?" asked a man in the back with an oddly high-pitched voice.

"I guess you don't," she said.

***

After the self-defense class, several of the guys decided to go out for a drink. Quinton joined them, ready to blow off some steam after the intense training. Pasty Buzzcut, aka Keith, came, as did the Tapper, who it turned out was named John. Tim came scrabbling up behind them as they walked up the darkened, rain-dampened street toward the bar, his sandy hair sticking up in the back.

They walked slowly at first, but then their footsteps sped up. Quinton looked around, studying the entrances to buildings, alleys. He felt like he might jump out of his skin if a woman approached him right now. An infected woman could be hiding anywhere between here and the bar.

"How far is this place, anyway?" he asked.

John shot him a quick glance. "It's not far. About two blocks up."

Quinton nodded. Two blocks wasn't so bad.

They passed a bank, all red bricks and glass. The lights were out, an ATM blinking inside a set of double glass doors. Something moved within. A shadow flitting across the wall.

He swallowed and picked up his pace, the others automatically adjusting to his speed. They looked around, as well. Wary. Defensive.

A cross street stood between them and the next block. Sounds were drifting down from someplace up the way. Hopefully the bar they were heading to. Laughter, one woman's voice loud and clear above everyone else's, almost a shriek.

The scent of wet asphalt was strong here. They stopped briefly at the crosswalk, but with no cars anywhere in sight, didn't wait for the light to change before rushing across, sneakers slapping through shallow puddles.

Their pace changed as each one hit the sidewalk on the other side. Quinton looked over his shoulder. The only things behind him were brick buildings, street lamps, and traffic lights, casting their vivid reflections in the rain blackened street. Greens and reds played leapfrog in a fight for dominance.

At the very last moment, head turning to face forward, he caught a flicker of something behind him and to his right. He jerked his head back around to look again.

Nothing.

The voices ahead of them were getting louder. Now he could hear a few male voices mixed in, quieter, less sure of themselves. Warm yellow light stretched out from the building, trickling across the wet street. He started to relax, his shoulders easing down away from his neck. They were almost there.

Just ahead of them, a curvy figure with bushy hair stepped out of an alley leading off the sidewalk between two dark buildings. Another figure stepped out of the alleyway to flank the first one. This one was all straight lines and sharp angles in contrast to the first one.

Quinton froze, whispered, "You guys."

John and Tim stopped, but Keith kept walking, head down. Exactly what they'd been taught not to do. He obviously hadn't seen the figures yet.

"Keith," John said, more loudly than Quinton had. "Keith, stop."

Keith slowed, looked up. His steps faltered, and he almost tripped. He came to a full stop about three feet in front of the other men, and what looked to be maybe five from the two figures.

The first person to have stepped out of the alley moved forward until she stood in a pale liquid pool of light from a nearby street lamp. His first impression of bushy hair had been wrong. Rather, her hair was a waterfall of dark, soft curls around her face, where a predatory grin spread slowly.

"Where you going, boys?" she called out.

John cleared his throat, and Quinton's hand twitched, moved forward, as if he could stop him before he spoke. "We're heading up to Top it Off. Are you coming from there? We're hoping to hit while happy hour's still going." His hand began tapping at his thigh.

A sound more a purr than a word exited her throat. "Mmm. You know you have to pay a fine before we can let you go."

"A fine?" John asked. Apparently, he'd been elected their spokesperson now. Quinton certainly had no desire to respond. What he wanted to do was turn and run. The muscles in his legs were twitching, preparing for flight. His pulse pounded, and he placed a cool hand on his throat to quell it. Next to him, Tim's breath chugged out of him, creating quick puffs of fog.

She laughed. "A fine for being fine, Honey. Show us a little something."

The other woman stepped up beside her, curling an arm over her friend's shoulders, fingers twirling a curly lock. She stared at Quinton, licking her full, red lips. She was darker than her friend, olive complected in the street lamp, yet her hair was a light brown, almost blond. Her eyes were dark lakes, no light reflecting from them.

Quinton moved up beside John, and Keith backed up to John's other side. Quinton felt, more than heard, Tim come up behind them.

"They're infected," Tim whispered.

"We don't want any trouble," John said, loudly. "We're just on our way for drinks. You're welcome to join us."

"It's boring in there," the second woman said. "We want to have some fun, don't we, Freesia?"

Freesia nodded, licking her lips.

"Let me guess," Tim said, looking at the second woman. "Your name is Rose? Lily?"

She looked at him oddly, smile replaced by furrowed brows and lips turned down at the corners. "No, it's Benny."

Quinton had to stifle the urge to laugh. Right now, that would make things worse than they already were. He clenched his hands to shore himself up. There were four men, only two women, but if they were VV infected they could overpower the men easily. He couldn't risk turning them pissed instead of playful, so he figured their best bet was to play along.

"What kind of fun were you thinking?" he asked. He shot a timid smile their way, aiming it at Benny, who had once again focused on him.

Benny eased her arm from around the other woman's shoulder and stepped in front of her. She looked Quinton up and down, black eyes leaving a chill everywhere they touched. "I want to play with this one, Freesia." She walked toward him, circling around until she was behind him. "Can I have him?" She pressed herself against his back, breath tickling his ear, drifting down his throat. He could feel her breasts against his back. A shiver ran up his spine. She giggled and ran a sharp fingernail along his throat, pausing over his pulse. His blood pushed back against her finger as it squeezed through the compacted artery.

She brought her other hand along his side to his stomach and up to the open neck of his shirt. Sliding her hand between the fabric and his skin, she rubbed it across his chest, teasing the hair there with a swirling finger. Her skin was soft against his. "I like a man with a hairy chest. It gives me something to hold onto."

Quinton hugged himself and moved forward, away from her. Her hand slid out of his shirt, but she grabbed his arm, tugged him around to face her.

"Where do you think you're going?" she asked.

"I'm not comfortable with this. I just want to go to the bar."

He was now standing between the three women, apart from his friends. This was not at all what he should have allowed to happen. But he couldn't stay back there with her pressed up against him. Her mouth millimeters from his throat. The artery right there.

Quinton shuddered and wrapped his arms tighter around himself. They needed to find a way out of this. The bar was so close he could smell the yeasty scent of beer, but there was music pounding, voices raised. No one would hear if they yelled out here. And if they did, would anyone bother to come check it out? Doubtful.

A whimper sounded behind him, and he turned partway, not wanting to show his back to Benny. Freesia now stood behind Keith. John cast a nervous sideways glance toward them. Tim had backed away, and stood about two feet away from the action.

Freesia licked the length of Keith's neck from shoulder to ear, slow and graceful. Keith screamed. Not a yell, but a full-throated scream. He bolted past Quinton, but Benny grabbed him and pulled him against her. She slid a hand up his shirt. Keith tried to push her away, but she was stronger than he was.

A scuffle broke out behind Quinton, shoes scraping on pavement, but he had to help Keith. Tim and John could take care of Freesia.

Benny worked at Keith's button with one hand, her fingers nimble. "Is this little thing for me, Baby?" she asked. "Don't worry, we can make it bigger. Show me how much you want me." Her other hand was at his neck, the long fingers wrapped around it from behind.

Quinton bolted forward, toward Keith and Benny. He had no idea what he was going to do, but he had point-five seconds to figure it out. He stopped just in front of them. Without thinking, he grabbed her hand away from the other man's pants. She'd gotten the button undone, the zipper partway down. Keith was gripping the hand at his throat with both of his. His struggles didn't budge it.

Benny jerked the arm Quinton held, and he flew sideways, his shoulder hitting the metal street lamp with a clang. He got up, ignoring the throbbing pain in his shoulder blade, and ran at Benny again. This time, he remembered what they'd just learned in the class. He forked his index and middle finger, tucking his thumb against his palm, and shoved the two fingers into her eyes.

She let go of Keith and stumbled backward, grunting in pain, hands going to her eyes. Keith looked at Quinton then ran again, this time straight past the struggling Benny, toward the safety of the bar.

Quinton approached Benny, who stilled. Her hands dropped away from her face, revealing one bloodied eye, the other squinted and tearing. She looked directly at him. When he got close, she was ready. Her foot shot out, and he was knocked to the ground without having a chance to react.

The next thing he knew, she was on top of him, snarling, and grasping his head. Benny slammed his head down on the ground. Tiny, bright white lights exploded in his vision, and his eyes rolled back. It felt like something sharp had been shoved into his brain. Everything was going black, but he couldn't pass out now.

He struggled to focus his eyes. Benny loomed above him, her mouth stretched into a toothy grin. She grabbed the hair on top of his head and pulled his face up to hers, giving him a slow, hard kiss. Her lips ground his against his teeth, but he kept his mouth clamped shut, even once he tasted his own coppery blood. He tried to turn his head, but the pain where his hair pulled was sharp and kept him held fast.

She straddled him, her legs trapping his arms. In fact, she

squeezed so hard he had trouble getting a breath. Conflicting thoughts moved though his head. If he stopped fighting, she might go easier on him. Stop hurting him. But then there was the humiliation of her taking advantage of him in front of the other guys. He felt sick dread at the thought of what she might do to him as he lie there, unable to do anything about it. No, he had to fight if it meant there was a chance to get away from her.

He rolled to his left. When she leaned the other way, her iron leg grip loosened just enough for him to worm his arm up and out. His elbow touching the pavement, he pulled his hand back as far as he could then shot it upward, palm striking her nose. There was an audible crunch, like someone biting into a crisp apple, and blood flooded down over his face and chest in a warm gush. Warm copper invaded his mouth. He sputtered, clamping his lips shut.

Benny was still on top of Quinton, but no longer focused on him. He shoved her off and stood up, turning to see where the other men were. Tim unconscious, lying over Freesia's legs. John, blood dripping from a gash on his head, had pinned Freesia down. She writhed, and it didn't look like she'd stay down for long, even with the weight of two men on her.

Quinton tried to lift Tim, but he was dead weight. He managed to get Tim's arm over his shoulder, but he couldn't quite stand up. Stuck in a hunched position, he could only watch as Freesia threw John off and leaped for him.

There was a loud click, and a small object flew toward her, light glinting off its surface. When it struck her, something sizzled. Her back arched. She stiffened and slammed to the ground, just shy of John, who had his arms crossed over his face.

Freesia twitched on the ground, and now Quinton could hear women's voices. Women in light blue shirts, black pants, and white face masks swarmed them. The police had arrived.

Benny was still on the ground. A female officer cuffed her hands behind her back with silver handcuffs, and dragged her into a reinforced police SUV. Everything Quinton could see looked steel except for the windshield.

Keith came out of the bar, approaching slowly. "I'm the one

who called," he said.

Quinton hadn't had time to wonder what Keith was doing, whether he had deserted them. Relief flooded him, and he began to shake when he realized they were safe now. It was over.

***

An hour later, they'd all been interviewed by the officers. A male victim advocate had brought them blankets, speaking with each in turn to let them know of resources available for assault victims. He spoke in a calm, soothing tone, careful to not step into their space or touch them.

Finally, they were told they could go. Quinton was glad he couldn't see or hear the women in the police SUV. The vehicle shook back and forth, like an animal was throwing itself at the walls, trying to get out.

"You guys still up for a drink?" John asked.

Quinton's first inclination was to turn him down, but then he thought about the two block walk back to his own vehicle. A drink would be good. His nerves needed settling. And then they could all walk back to their cars together.

"Sure," Quinton said. "Just one, though."

"I need a few," Keith said. Tim nodded.

"Alright," Quinton said. A few beers wouldn't go too far, anyway.

People stared at them when they walked into the bar. The music throbbed, though there was a part of Quinton that expected a record to skip, like in the movies. But the sound drove on, pummeling his ears. The scent of beer was stronger in here, and he could smell food. Rich, meaty burgers. Salty, oily fries. That sounded good.

They grabbed a table in the corner, as out of sight as they could find. Most people had looked away when nothing interesting followed them in. Attention spans were short, and while they probably looked hellaciously banged up, there was currently nothing trying to kill them.

This thought made him take stock of everyone. The EMTs had looked them over thoroughly. His head had been poked at, and he'd been told to see his physician tomorrow. He had a mild concussion, but he probably wasn't going to die in his sleep tonight. The EMT had laughed when she told him this, which made him want to curl in on himself and slink away. It humiliated him to be laughed at, for the EMT to not take what had happened to them seriously.

His sweatpants were torn at the knee, and his t-shirt had ripped under the armpit on one side and at his neck. It was crusted with blood, scratchy against his skin. His lips felt swollen, and he imagined they were taking up half his face, a visible sign of what had happened outside.

All but one of the buttons on John's shirt had been ripped off, and he'd buttoned it at his navel. He kept pulling the ends together self-consciously. Tim had one eye swollen shut, his hair sticking up in tufts. His clothes were in disarray, but Quinton couldn't see any real damage to them.

While Keith's clothes were intact, he was the quietest of them all. He couldn't meet anyone's eyes, and kept rubbing at his neck. His hands occasionally strayed to the button of his jeans, as if to make sure it was still fastened.

A waiter came over to get their orders. They ordered a round of beer and shots, and several appetizers. Quinton ordered a burger. He was starving. "Extra fries, please."

The bartender, an attractive woman, looked over at them and winked while she filled their glasses. When the waiter came back over, he said, "This first round of shots is on the house. Mary thought you guys could use it after whatever happened outside."

They raised their glasses to her and took their shots, quickly chased by beer. Quinton reveled in the tang of tequila, followed by the hoppy taste of the beer. When their food arrived, not too much later, it was gone in minutes, the rich taste of beef and salt coating Quinton's tongue. Only Keith didn't eat anything. Instead, he downed his second shot and beer.

"You sure you don't want anything to eat, Keith?" John asked.

"I'm not hungry." His voice was subdued.

"Okay, man. No problem."

A woman in a flannel shirt and jeans sauntered over. Her stiff hair was moussed to oblivion. "Careful, boys. You don't want anyone taking advantage of you because you're drunk."

"Thanks for your concern, but there's no chance of that," Tim said.

"There's no reason to be rude. If you're going to come out in public, you have to expect some attention." She turned and stalked away, calling back over her shoulder, "You're a bunch of fatasses, anyway."

"What is it with women?" Quinton asked. "Can't they just leave us alone and let us drink in peace?" He took another big slug of his beer. It was getting warm, and near the bottom. He didn't especially think he needed another, but he wanted one, so he caught the waiter's eye and raised his glass. The waiter nodded, went to the bar, and quickly arrived at the table with a fresh beer, just the right amount of foam on top.

Quinton felt relaxed, languid even. He looked around the room. A woman sitting at the bar smiled and nodded. Then she turned away. She was dark skinned, her hair short, cropped close to her head. Her eyes were large, deep brown, with thick lashes. She looked familiar for some reason. He looked away when she glanced back at him.

When he turned back, she happened to look at the same time. She held her glass up in a toast. He lifted his fresh beer to her and took a drink, ducking his head to hide the shy smile that had crept onto his face.

"How can you look at a woman after tonight?" Tim asked.

Quinton hadn't realized they'd stopped talking and were looking at him.

"I'm not."

"You are," John said, then shrugged. "She's cute."

"What if she has VV?" asked Tim.

"I'm not sleeping with her," Quinton said, in exasperation. "I just raised my glass."

Tim threw his hands up. "Yeah, that's how it starts."

Quinton sighed. "Back off, okay?"

"Alright, but don't say I didn't warn you."

"I won't," Quinton said. "Besides, I think I might know her."

Conversation started again, mostly about the defense training, sports, anything but the attack. He was sure he'd want to talk about what had happened later, probably with his brother, but not right now.

Keith's speech was slurred, and his head kept dipping.

John cast a worried look his way, face scrunched. "We should probably leave soon."

"Agreed," Tim said. "Let's get the bill."

Quinton was ready to go, too.

Except.

Except she was looking at him again. Those gorgeous eyes meeting his. Everything about her looked soft, sweet.

She wasn't pale. Her eyes weren't bloodshot. She sure didn't look cold. He'd seen her eat the garlic parmesan fries. And she was sitting right at the bar, where the lights were brightest, a change they'd made after VV broke out.

No way she was infected.

And right now he felt the need for intimacy. Something to wash away what had happened. To drive it out like a demon before a priest.

What he needed was an emotional exorcism.

"Excuse me," he said to the guys. He stood up, fresh beer in hand, and approached her. She sucked in her lower lip, pressing her front teeth to it in a gentle smile.

"Hi," she said.

"Hi," he replied. "Have we met?"

There was a moment of silence, and then she stuck her hand out. "I'm Candy."

"Candy? I'm Quinton."

"I think we belong to the same gym. Lucky's?"

He snapped his fingers. "That's it! I couldn't figure out where I knew you from."

"Why don't you take a seat?" She gestured to the stool beside her.

"Thanks." He slid into the chair. A gentle scent of lavender surrounded her like an aura.

Risking a glance at the guys, he saw Tim shake his head, a frown on his face, lips pursed. Keith lay back, head resting on the back of the booth, mouth wide open. He appeared to be asleep. John was looking down at his beer, but Quinton could see his hand tapping his thigh under the table.

"So...what do you do?" she asked him.

"I'm a teacher," he said. "Middle school."

"Oh! What subject do you teach?"

"Language Arts."

"Do you like to write, or do you just like grammar?" She laughed, eyes sparkling in the bright lights of the bar.

He laughed, too. It felt good. "I like to write a bit, but I'm not published or anything." He ran a thumb over the condensation on the outside of his glass. "What do you do?"

"Oh, it's boring really. I've got a corporate job. Briefcase, power suit, the whole shebang."

"Yeah? Where do you work?"

"VenCon," she said. "It's a pharmaceutical company. Need any good drugs?"

He laughed again. "No, I'm good."

"Good, because if you'd said yes, I would have had to end this right here."

VenCon was the company in the media all the time for the research they were doing on VV. There was no way they'd be employing infected women, not when they were working to eradicate the virus. This realization helped him relax further.

***

They'd been talking for about fifteen minutes when John approached. "Hey, we're heading out." He looked at Candy then back to Quinton. "You ready to go?"

"I'm going to stay, thanks." He gestured toward the table. "You guys should go, though. I'm okay."

John lowered his voice. "You sure?"

Quinton nodded. "I'm sure."

"Okay. I'll see you at class next week?"

"Yep. See you then."

John went back to the table and helped rouse Keith. He and Tim got Keith up between them, and half carried him out the door. Tim never looked at Quinton, but John glanced back one more time, a question on his face. Quinton smiled what he hoped was a reassuring smile. He waved, and turned back to Candy.

"Thanks for trusting me," she said. "It's hard to get to know anyone these days. VV changed everything, huh?"

"Definitely." He put a hand over hers on the bar. It was smooth, but cold. "But sometimes you have to go with your gut."

She smiled, the corners of her eyes crinkling. Then she leaned forward. He met her halfway, and they kissed. Her lips were soft on his bruised mouth, the kiss tender and sweet. She tasted of mint.

***

Quinton yawned, mouth stretching wide. He brought a hand up to cover his mouth.

"Tired?" she asked.

"Yeah, and I have to get up early for work. I should probably go."

"How far away are you parked?"

"It was a couple blocks away," he said. "Back by the community center."

"Why don't I walk you to your car? It's a bad idea for you to walk alone."

He had to admit, the thought of walking alone to his car terrified him. It was after one in the morning. The bar crowd had thinned significantly. He nodded. "Thanks. That would be great."

It didn't take too long to get to his car. Shadows puddled around it. He'd parked away from the lights, his blue sedan tucked away in a corner of the empty lot. When he'd first parked there, it had been nearly full, lots of foot traffic moving through.

"This is me," he said. "Thanks for walking me."

"No problem." She reached up, wrapping her arms around his neck. He leaned into her, his hands coming up to her hips. She ran a hand through the hair at the nape of his neck, sending tingles down his spine, and back up.

She pressed him backward into the cold, damp side of the

car. Her mouth found his in a quick kiss, and then she moved back, running a hand down his chest. She let her coat slide down her arms to puddle on the ground, and nudged a knee between his legs. Bringing her head down, she pressed her lips to his again. This time, the kiss was harder, but the blood pumping through his body gave the pain a pleasant, dull edge.

He moved his hands up her thighs, the ample mound of her ass, to the small of her back. She pulled back and eased his shirt off over his head, throwing it behind her.

"You won't be needing that anymore," she said.

Part of him registered the insanity of doing this in public, but he didn't care.

She grasped his hands, still at her back, and brought them around in front of her. Using his arms and her knee, she maneuvered him sideways until they were at the hood of the car, where she pushed him back onto it. He eased backward, ignoring the creak of the shocks as the front end dipped under his weight. She climbed up, straddling him. Then she put his hands over his head and leaned on them, trapping him there.

"Kinky," he said. He tried to move his arms, but she was strong. He was pinned. Anxiety began to well up within his chest. He worked harder at moving, but couldn't budge her.

"You don't know the half of it." She brought her face down to nuzzle at his neck, the pulse beating against her tongue and the teeth she had pressed to his skin. When she spoke, her voice vibrated against his throat. "Didn't anyone tell you not to be alone with a woman you've just met?"

He struggled harder, thrashing his entire body in hopes of shucking her off him. "Please."

Her face was still buried against his throat. "I can smell your blood through the skin. Did you know that's how it works?"

He shook his head, swallowed deeply.

"It's so hard to resist. Impossible, really. I keep trying, but the virus wins every time. I can't control it."

"All you have to do is let me get in my car and drive away," he said. "I'll be gone, and the temptation will be gone with me."

"It doesn't work that way." She pulled back, looked at him,

her eyes filling with bloody tears. "I'm sick. There's nothing I can do."

"Please, just let me go. I haven't done anything to deserve this."

"I'm sorry." She plunged her face back into his throat, gnawing at the skin over his pulse.

He fought, screamed, thrashed, kicked, but nothing stopped her. The pain was sharp. The moment she broke through the artery's surface, he felt a release of pressure, the blood pumping out of his throat. Cold and weak, he looked at her, his struggles ceasing.

She'd been so nice. Normal looking. No warning sings.

The last thing he felt was shame.

Message of the Night-Gaunts

Out of what crypt they crawl, I cannot tell,
But every night I see the rubbery things,
Black, horned, and slender, with membranous wings,
They come in legions on the north wind's swell
With obscene clutch that titillates and stings,
Snatching me off on monstrous voyagings
To grey worlds hidden deep in nightmare's well.

Over the jagged peaks of Thok they sweep,
Heedless of all the cries I try to make,
And down the nether pits to that foul lake
Where the puffed shoggoths splash in doubtful sleep.
But ho! If only they would make some sound,
Or wear a face where faces should be found!

-HP Lovecraft, Night-Gaunts, Fungi From Yuggoth

Man has long pondered dreams and their meanings. Discussing them among friends, journaling them to seek some hidden deeper understanding, drawing the images represented within. But what of the dreams that come during waking or in the in-between? These faceless monstrosities that haunt the tranquil hours when one is supposed to be deeply sleeping, that appear when least expected...and least wanted.

They've been coming to me for months now, in those

formerly restful hours during which I toss and turn and reach for pleasant, healing dreams or, even better, the dreamless sleep of the pure and content. It began with a shadow along the far wall. A draped figure that didn't move, merely stared back at me as I sat up in bed, jerked from the dullness of near sleep by a feeling as of being watched. Born of shadows, still there was a sense of being, of solidity and substance.

On that particular night, it did nothing more. I made no sound, merely waiting for it to fade into obscurity. Once it had dissolved, I again slipped beneath the covers in repose and closed my eyes, now firmly shut lest I reopen them and see something more. The pounding of my heart faded after a time, and I once again drifted to the in-between, floating there until blissful slumber took me under.

Would that this had been the last I saw of it.

It did not come each night, but when it did, there were minute changes as if to prove that it was not a mere shade. Upon its third appearance, I was awakened from that murky in-between by that sensation again, only to find it at the foot of my bed. There, it lurked, the velvet blackness of night's dark shadow moving about it in forms I could not contemplate, taking one shape and then another, the being unwavering in the center. Ever still. Ever faceless.

My breathing quickened, and I fought against a sudden paralysis. No matter my effort, I could not move, nor could I make a sound beyond the chug of my own breaths. This time, it did not fade so much as splinter, fragmenting into deeper shadow.

Sleep was long in coming that night.

Doubting my own sanity, I embarked upon a journey of exploration into this phantasm. My research led me through hauntings, possessions, schizophrenia, and more—all disturbing possibilities. I sweated, anxiety filling me. The preferable diagnosis was unknown to me, for none seemed reasonable. Mouth dry, I could not even wet a fingertip with my sandpaper tongue to aid in the turning of a page. I moved through my daily life with darting glances, full of guilt and fear. In desperation, I searched all sources I could locate, afraid to speak with other people lest they see the burgeoning insanity within me.

Finally, my heart in my throat, I discovered something called parasomnia, in which a person who is deprived of sleep may see strange things between waking and dreaming, ofttimes accompanied by a paralysis of the body. Being a sufferer of insomnia, I frequently reached a point of utter exhaustion, and had recently had more trouble than usual, causing constant fatigue.

Hope swelled in my breast. Not crazy, nor haunted. Just overtired. I returned home, determined to get some real sleep. I could face anything if there was a solution awaiting me beyond it. To ensure sleep, I used an elixir, doubling the dosage. If anything tried to wake me that night, it failed, for I tumbled into the deepest of slumbers within moments of my head hitting the pillow. A dreamless sleep, or at least one I departed with no memory of dreams.

Infused with a new energy from that favorable night, I went about my day confident of another restful night to come, sure that these haunts of mine would be long gone. I ate well, smiled at everyone I met, and marched to bed as one approaching a wondrous event. Pajamas on, I slipped my feet under the covers. A silken glide of fabric against fabric saw me prone in bed, head embraced by my soft pillow. I reached over, turned the light off, and closed my eyes, a contented smile curling my lips.

Then I felt it. That sensation again. Something was in my room, somewhere in the depths of darkness surrounding me. Instead of looking, I kept my eyes clamped tightly shut; there was no reason to look. A tingle of awareness spread up my spine, my neck, and my scalp prickled. The longer I tried to ignore it, the more the sensations increased, my entire body a current of tension and fright. My flesh buzzed with the feel of something getting closer. Closer.

When I could stand it no longer, I opened my eyes, straining against the night. The end of my bed revealed nothing; it was not there. A sense of relief flooded me, causing first a sensation of pins and needles, followed by a wash of warmth. I stretched out an arm, eyes closed, and curled up onto my side. Blinking my eyes, I stared straight ahead.

There it was. Rather than at the foot of my bed, it stood against the wall beside me. Once again, the shadows swirled about it, as of floating fabrics, but this form was masculine, whereas the last had felt decidedly feminine to me, at least in retrospect. There was no face, only deeper shadow, yet I felt watched by eyes that did not appear to exist. The hairs on my arms stood to attention, a sickness filling my stomach. My blood, gone ice cold, forced its way through my veins at an accelerated rate.

No sound came from it, but still my ears reacted as if there were sound, straining and vibrating against a pressure that was not there. As I watched the figure, it moved forward, holding a shadowy appendage out toward me. I yelped and slid backward across the bed, eyes shutting for but a single second, aware that at any moment it might grab hold of me, take me up in those dark, shifting arms.

I opened my eyes, knowing it would be there before me, waiting.

The figure was gone. I was alone again within my bedchamber. All negative sensation had departed with it, and I felt emptied. Exhaustion overtook me, and I slept.

Upon waking, I had forgotten the worst of it, shaking my head at this silly nightmare. It wasn't even so frightening upon reflection. A shadow in a room was nothing to fear. I went through my day embracing the sunshine. A bright world surrounded me, and everything was as it should be. But as night fell, my skin began to crawl. I found every excuse possible to stay up, approaching the wee hours with no need for rest. Until, that is, my eyes began to droop, my head to nod. Now, rather than cough syrup to aid in slumber, I undertook a determination to avoid sleep at all costs. Truly, it was the time just before sleep that was the problem, but with no knowledge of how to skip this phase, I had no recourse save not to sleep. I caffeinated myself until my eyes swam with the liquids within me, yet sleep crept up on me anyway, drawing me down onto the sofa, where it ensnared me in dreams of forms about a flame.

These forms at first appeared to be human, arms waving about in a slow, fluid dance. I watched the beauty of their movements, a part of me registering the wrong, the other, about them, but hiding it from my conscious mind. The forms appeared to be both male and female, clad in flowing garments. Aside from this, they were mere shadows against the fire's light. Their movements overlapped, a blur of limbs and fabric, until I realized with a start that there were extra limbs within the circle that my mind could not account for.

I feared both movement and stillness, for at any moment they might discover my presence. What would occur then was unknown to me; these were neither friend nor foe as far as I was concerned. Until I could learn more of them, I had no desire to approach them. Wait, this is untrue. My mind still wishes to cover the base truth, but I must be honest in this accounting. I did want to approach them, even to join them. There was a pull within me as that of the endless ocean tides upon the beach. A desire that swelled against my own wishes, urging me toward the flames although my conscious mind did protest. It took on a physical sensation of cramping at my center, and my flesh was energized with forces that drifted from the thralls before me.

I resisted these urges, but still I was undecided as to whether to move away from them or stay where I was, for how had I arrived here? Last I'd known I was safe within my abode. With no clear answer, I squatted down into dry grasses that tickled my legs beneath loose breeches. Squinting, I examined the beings about the fire, but still could not ascertain who or what they might be. Scents of smoke and grass invaded my nose, and a cool breeze shifted the hair on my forehead.

It was some moments before I thought to look at the flames, whereupon I saw something moving within them. This was no image born of the fire, but an entity standing in its midst, wide of shoulder and long of arm, if my eyes did not deceive. No face was visible from this great distance, merely form, much as with the dancers. Whatever this creature was, it was at least twice the size of those around the fire, perchance thrice.

Next I was aware, I was coming to in my living quarters. I sat up with a gasp, looking about, but there were no figures, no fiery fiend. My heart pounded, and an odor of smoke flitted through my sinuses, tickling and enticing with the mystery of a scent brought forth from a dream. My flesh tingled with the sensation of static electricity, a dance across my skin. When I stood to head to my bedchamber, a brown blade of grass fell from my cuffed pant leg. I left it there, having no desire to test out the validity of what I had seen and felt.

My slumber the rest of that night was uninterrupted.

Once more enshrouded in the light of day, I pondered what I had dreamt, for that's surely all it had been. Exterior sensations are often enveloped within dreams, and I convinced myself this was all that had occurred. My dream was a product of these items, not the other way around. Over the days that followed, I considered the souls viewed around the fire. In retrospect, one might think they had been worshipping that entity within the flames, but there remained the question of what this creature had been. As well, I wondered who the figures were or, if my sight had been accurate, what they were, for something had been wrong with them, something I still could not put a finger on.

It was perhaps a week hence before I was once again visited during the in-between. I had decided that if it came back, I would seek to learn what it was trying to tell me. Whether my unconscious mind or a real entity, a message was obviously being put forth. I had only to interpret it, and perhaps all of this would cease. Anything that would halt these night visitations was worth an attempt.

This night, I drifted in the murk of near sleep for quite some time, the ticks and creaks of my room playing a night symphony of distraction. These were familiar sounds, so I held no fear of them, though they did keep me awake with the randomness of their play. Warm and cozy, I was content enough to enjoy the sensation of my body sunken into the mattress, fluffy covers atop me.

Then came the moment when the feel of the room changed. The buzz and tingle began, pressure filling my ears. The sensation of something right in front of me was a physical electricity upon my skin. A puff of smoke-scented air caressed my face. The small hairs covering my body stood on end simultaneously, and I swallowed deeply before opening my eyes.

For the first time, a scream was forced from my throat. There was a black swirl directly before me in the shape of a face, but with no clear demarcations that indicated any sort of humanity. A void of sensation emitted from it.

I shot backward across the bed, tumbling off it onto the hardwood floor with an impact I would likely feel for days. Pain shot along my hip and elbow, and I rolled off them, pushing myself up to sitting. In this position, my head came just above the level of the bed, and I could see the form was still there; it had not disappeared this time.

Long hair drifted about the dark oval that was its face, and the fabric of its gown did the same, defying gravity in a way that seemed most natural. It did not move except to cock its head to the side in an implied query as to my new location upon the floor. I gripped the edge of the bed and peered over at the figure, unsure how to proceed. Finally, I asked, "What is it you want of me?"

It was as if my voice had broken whatever calm filled the room. The figure shook its head, appearing to grow even as it hunched there on the bed's edge. Soon, it had filled the shadows, a seamless meeting of the two, black against black. And then it was gone, an implosion that happened in mere seconds.

How could I find answers if I could not speak with the entities? This was the answer I endeavored to find, and it was not until the next full dream of fire-enthralled capering that I found a clue that might lead me to the location of the fire. It may sound odd, but this clue was a lightning struck tree of a distinctive shape, with which I was familiar. It stroked a dim memory of my childhood, hidden deep within myself, a remembrance of a strange experience near my birthplace.

I mentally worried at this thread until the details became clearer. It was around the age of six or seven that I happened across a burnt clearing within a short distance of my home. This clearing was accessible by wandering through a copse of trees atop a hill, a journey I often took in those days, desperate to find my independence in any way possible. Its location meant it was invisible from our home despite its proximity.

The burn was new, a thick smell of ash hanging about the area like a fog, clinging to the ground. I scuffed at the blackened grasses with the toe of my shoe, upsetting ash that rested there, and sending it a short distance into the air, where it clung to my breeches. Something sparkled near the center of this large circle, and I undertook a slog through the dense, burned grasses. I recall the ashes moving higher, beginning to swirl as a breeze picked them up. It coated my mouth and tongue, burned my eyes, yet still I persisted, the curiosity of childhood too strong to resist.

There may have been more to it than curiosity, as well. Within my reminiscence, there came that same urge I'd felt when watching the figures about the flame. It was a sensation that touched just above my navel and beckoned me forward, as a puppet on a string, while at the same time making my guts clench in a mild cramp. Even when I began coughing against the ghastly tickle in my throat, I moved ever forward, eyes only for that vague sparkle in the midst of the circle. Then the cramping spread, reaching outward from my navel, filling me within. My progression slowed, legs becoming weighted, and it felt like I was moving through water.

This was where my memory ended. Whether I had ultimately grasped that sparkling item in the circle's center was unknown. But thinking of it, I discovered my hand was pressed into my stomach, an echo of that cramping stirring within me. Nausea filled me, and I retched onto the floor.

But the tree. I was trying to remember the tree.

It had stood there, apart from the others, forsaken. Blackened by lightning, it had always struck me as looking like a gnarled hand, five thick branches thrusting from the twisted stump. In my memory, it rose above the ashen circle, standing guard at the edge, a looming monument against the sky. The burned grasses were indistinguishable from the black base of the tree. When I had waded into the circle, gaze upon that sparkling item, the tree had been a presence at the edge of my awareness, taking on an aspect of life. I'd felt it there, a tingling sensation across my skin, just as with the haunts beside my bed.

In the visions—for now I knew them for what they were—

the tree stood near the fire, the flames lighting its cracked exterior, a hand reaching up into the night sky, beseeching.

A compulsion overtook me, and I knew I must return to the place of my birth. There was only one option open to me, and it was to end the presence of these night-gaunts that tormented my slumber. If I was ever to sleep again without fear, I would have to discover what these beings were trying to show me, and that tree was the key.

Home.

Sadly, it was no longer a home to me, but the property was unoccupied. This had always struck me as strange, seeing as how the rest of the surrounding land had long been built upon. The dip below the treed hill had remained open and untouched, that circle of ash having healed over. I wondered now if that tree would still be standing, or if it had long fallen over, consumed again into the earth it had grown from.

I drove for two days straight, stopping for nourishment and relief solely once per day. On the second day of my drive, my eyes gritty from exhaustion, a flicker caught my attention, and I turned toward the passenger seat wherein one of the forms drifted. The tendrils I had glimpsed around the fire were clearer to me than they had been at any time previous, and it was made clear to me that it was not, in fact, clothing, but appendages of some manner that moved on their own, freely waving away from the main body of the form. Even in the dim light of evening, there existed no face, merely that dark oval of absence.

"I'm coming," I said.

It sunk into the seat, disappearing from my vision just as my tires on that side left the road, a pole looming up outside the window. I jerked the wheel to right myself back upon the road, shaking my head to remove the vestiges of sleep creeping up on me. I had nearly succumbed to slumber, which surely would have meant my death. A prickle of energy flowed through me, flushed into my veins by the panic now driving me forward, eyes wide and on the road.

My arrival fell shortly after nightfall, a large, waxing moon hovering at the horizon's edge. Everything around me was in shades of gray, and no insect or animal call sounded. It felt unnaturally still, no lights shining from the surrounding abodes. Within my limited vision, the buildings appeared rundown, crooked. Wrong. Where had all the people gone? And what of the animals?

The now familiar energy crawled across my exposed flesh, and I rubbed my arms, failing to tame the sensations there. I stepped into the grass, eliciting a crisp crunch and the feel of brittle fragility beneath my shoe. Even the scents of the night were stale, musty, smoke drifting beneath it all. A glow showed to the west, and I pointed myself in that direction. I registered the cool of the night air, yet was not bothered by the cold.

I should have been afraid. Instead, I buzzed with a sick energy, a faint thrill of excitement as of something familiar and favorable coming my way. The glow increased, framing the hill that now grew before me, furred at the top by skeletal trees that groped skyward. It was bright and orange, indicative of a flame of great size. Upon reaching the crest of the hill, I peered down through the trees, hopeful that their craggy trunks would keep me hidden away from what lay below. For there were the dancers, bodies undulating against the yellow-orange of the flames. And within those flames stood that giant entity. Once more I was pulled toward it, cramping deep within.

This time I hearkened to its call.

I bore no recollection of the trip down the hill, or of my approach to the fire. Instead, I found myself there as if in an instant, surrounded by the forms, who I now found to be larger than myself. Unlike the creatures who had haunted me, these forms had faces, but they were off. Rather than the linear aptitude of the human face, these appeared melted, features running in irregular lines. No two faces were the same. One might have an eyeball near the top, and another at the chin. Another might have only a single eye, or perhaps three. There were no noses, just slits somewhere in the mass that made up the face. And their mouths were lipless, jagged teeth located in seemingly random patterns. I could now see the appendages I'd noticed previously, their tips razor sharp and scaled.

Though they should have been frightening, their energy was directed toward the central figure writhing within the flames. It was to this entity that I directed my own attentions, intent upon discovering what it was and what it wanted with me. Goose pimples crept across my flesh as I studied it. While the thralls looked somewhat humanoid, there was nothing human in the creature they worshipped. It was, in fact, entirely alien, a mass of tentacles, scales, and tumors that appeared to breathe on their own, growing and shrinking at different rates. One tentacle reached through the wall of fire, moving in a serpentine fashion toward me. At its tip was a single bright orb that sparkled in the light of the flames. A dark, swirling maelstrom was at the center of this orb, and as I looked into it, I saw everything.

Within the maelstrom was the beginning and the end of all things. In mere seconds, I saw infinite universes built then destroyed, cataclysmic events, birth and death, rebirth. I saw the end of civilization as I knew it, the destruction of Earth. There was more than I could possibly have imagined, and my blood ran cold at the sheer immensity of what I was being shown. At the center of all this was the creature, feeding off the horrors perpetuated in an endless loop of carnage. The extinction of the human race was but one small element of the annihilation of All.

Whether this anathema was the creator of all I saw, or merely a parasite feeding off the aftermath I could not discern. What became clear was that I played some part in all of this, though I could not see in what way that might come to pass. I was filled with utter loathing and dismay, with no notion of whether it was aimed at myself or the being before me.

With a suddenness that was shocking, everything was gone. The creature, the fire, the worshippers. Dawn peeked above the hill in shades of pink and orange, and there I lay, swathed in black ash that smeared across my skin and clothing. I climbed to my feet, shaken, and ventured toward a home that no longer held any meaning, for I had seen the terminus of all I knew, and all I had never known.

My goal had been to save my dreams and sanity, but now I realized my slumber would always be haunted by these night-gaunts, for I was one of them, a bearer of destruction and plague. I was the creature within the flames, the end of mankind. And it was all of us.

- 190 -

Treading Water

Voices rang out from all directions, bouncing between the lake's mild waves, making it hard to track what sound came from which person. Young kids stuck close to shore, tired helicopter parents dressed in stretched out bathing suits and saggy shorts hovering at the edges. Older kids ventured farther, eager to prove their maturity, but afraid to stray too far from the relative safety of the shore.

Alice reclined on the large, wooden float tethered in the middle of the lake, soaking in the warmth of the sun. She tugged at the waistband of her navy blue bikini, pulling it up to a more comfortable spot. Around her, teen boys jostled, shoving each other into the water with raucous cries and playful taunts from deep voices that sometimes still broke. Other girls lounged beside her, toasting lithe, still developing bodies. The collective energy of fifteen youths shifted the float about in a constant sway.

Alice had just rolled over onto her stomach to warm her back when a crack sounded, deep and throaty. She sat up, wrenching her sunglasses off to look in the direction from which the sound had come.

The teens around her froze, as did everyone around the lake except those too young to care.

The water shook as if contained in a bowl set down too hard, sloshing onto the beach and the float. Cold water slapped onto Alice's feet and legs, a shock against the sun-kissed heat of her skin, and she gasped. The air felt thinner, like everyone had sucked the oxygen up into their lungs when the crack sounded, and had yet to release it.

For a moment, all was calm. The water stilled.

It took just long enough for everyone to exhale, for their bodies to relax by a single degree. For children to splash one more time.

There was another loud crack, a sound as of boulders splitting. This time, the water leapt and splashed, knocking teens off the float and children from their feet. It covered their heads, attempted to pull them down. Alice managed to hang on to the wood, a splinter sliding painfully into the pad of her middle finger.

At first, the whirlpool was small, a tiny funnel, inconsequential. She squinted at it, thinking there was no way she actually saw what she thought she saw. It had to be a trick of the light.

A redheaded girl next to Alice pointed, ponytail swinging with the motion of her arm. "Look! What's that?"

One of the boys, a jovial brunette with pink cheeks and a body newly converted from chub to muscle, swam toward it. The other boys and a few of the girls cheered him on.

Alice called out, "Sam, don't!" Worry filled her.

Then it grew, doubling in size in a matter of seconds, sucking hungrily at the water around it, guzzling and slurping. Sam stopped in mid-stroke, forcing his chest backward before turning and trying to swim away. Though his arms and legs pumped, he made no forward progress, frozen in place by the force of the suction. One of his friends swam for him, calling out, "Swim harder, Sam!"

Sam was the first to disappear down the whirlpool.

Bedlam broke out. Panicked, the cold sensation of fear sliding up her spine and enwrapping her gut, Alice looked to the shore for help, but what she saw was parents running for their children, calling for the older ones too far to reach. One man chucked his toddler onto the shore and dove into the water before the diapered body hit the sand, swimming for a boy around ten now flailing in the choppy waves, pizza-shaped floaty forgotten behind him.

Teens clamored for the float, calling to each other, playful taunts from earlier long forgotten. They worked to help each other onto the float, those still on it pulling them up, ignoring the splinters now edging into knees, feet, and hands. Alice and the redhead helped a girl who'd lost her bikini top back onto the float. It took only moments to get everyone back up, and they panted, heaped together in the center, unsure of what to do next.

The proximity of the float to the whirlpool kept them in the path of danger, and it pulled at its moorings, the weight of so many teenagers too great when it already fought a mighty battle against the strains of the water swirling around.

With a jolt, one of the cables snapped, spinning the float around, jerking when it caught at the other cable. The teens screamed, falling over each other. Alice got out one shriek as a boy slammed into her, sending her off the side and into the water, which quickly closed over her head.

Instantly, her ears filled with water, muffling the voices of those above her. She saw one boy lean out and fall in, but the others pulled him back onto the float right away. She reached for him, anyway, kicking her legs, fighting the pull of the whirlpool, but unable to reach the surface. Rays of sun fell around her, tinted green by the water.

It sounded like a bathtub draining, a sucking roar that grew louder as she was pulled downward and sideways. She strained against the pull. Alice was a strong swimmer, a member of the school's swim team and lifeguard at the local pool during the summer season, but she was no match for the power of draining water.

Pieces of wood and other detritus slashed at her body, lacerating the skin. Dirty water scoured her eyes. The water down here was dark and murky, the swirling debris making it all the harder to make out anything. Fish flashed past her in a silvery panic, making more headway than she could, but still pulled backward.

Above her, the float crouched, a dark, unreachable mass, furred with algae resembling reaching tentacles. Light faded, and she lost sight of it, eyes burning from the dirt.

A large chunk of wood struck Alice on the side of the head. Her vision went black momentarily, but she fought against it, forcing her eyes to clear. Her lungs burned and strained, panic fluttering at the edges of every thought like a poisonous butterfly.

The wood had knocked her deeper into the whirlpool, and she now began to spin in place, no longer on a protracted course around the outside of it. She couldn't make out anything except the dark shapes swirling around her, looming near then pulling away. Some hit her, but none with the force of the wood that had put her here.

She closed her eyes, focusing on keeping her mouth closed, her lungs full, but her body deceived her, and she sucked in a breath against her will. Water filled her lungs, ice cold against the fire of her chest. She tried to expel it, her diaphragm desperate to do its job.

Then it consumed her, filled her. It felt as if the water would burst from her, tear her apart.

I will not pass out, she thought. She hated movies where the women fainted. Where they screamed and flailed and did nothing to save themselves. Alice wasn't one of those idiots. Only she could save herself. Still, it was impossible to claw her way out of the water. Nor could she will the fluid out of her lungs.

Alice was going to drown, whether she fainted or screamed or flailed. All she could think about now was how badly she needed oxygen.

There was a moment where the touch of water disappeared from her face, warm air caressing her cheek. She opened her eyes. Around her raged a swirling cone of dark green water leading down to a black hole surrounded by rocks. Objects danced beneath the rippled, foamy surface of the water all the way down.

She coughed, expelling some of the water, though it did little to ease the burn and strain of her lungs. She dragged greedily at the air before it was ripped away again, water closing over her face. It hadn't been long enough to get all the water clear of her lungs, but it had gained her precious seconds.

Awash with the fresh influx of oxygen into her veins, energized by the adrenaline coursing through her body, Alice tried once more to swim. She switched to a version of the breast stroke, using both hands and legs in a uniform maneuver meant to thrust her out of the greatest pull of the whirlpool. For a moment she thought it had worked, the pull on her weakening limbs lessening.

In the next moment her head slammed into the ground, rock hard against her skull. Pain burst through her left temple, expanding across every inch of her skull and beyond. Her neck throbbed from the blow. She drifted, stunned into stillness.

Now the sound of rushing water took over the sucking noise, and her legs fell, surrounded by a waterfall. She clawed at the ground, tried to find purchase, but anything big enough to grab had already gone down the hole. She felt the earth slide away under her, first up to her waist, legs dangling, then to her chest, her armpits.

Alice slipped the rest of the way, hanging in midair for what felt like a full minute before crashing down onto hard water below in a graceless, painful belly flop. The force of it knocked both air and water from her lungs, but paralyzed them so she couldn't draw in another breath. Her head went under, she twisted, body flung in every direction at once, limbs twirling out of her control.

She slammed into a hard surface and finally did as all those girls she hated in the movies, and passed out.

***

When Alice came to, she heard the distant rush of falling water and the lap of waves against stone. Her head pounded. Every part of her hurt, even her lungs, which ached. She floated face up, feet lower than her chest. All was darkness.

Panic gripped her at the loss of sight, and her already ravaged lungs pumped oxygen in and out.

Something wet and scratchy rested on her face, and she batted at it. The thin substance grabbed her fingers, twining through them, tight against her skin.

She yanked at it, pulling it away from her face. A garbled shriek escaped her throat.

Pain shot through her scalp, and she realized it was her hair, messed up from her time under the water. She pulled it away from her face, tucking as much as possible around her ears. When that didn't work, she ducked her head backwards into the water just enough to get the hair wet, then smoothed it back as well as she could.

These actions calmed her some, and she straightened, trying to touch the ground. All she felt was a void. The lapping sounds told her there were surfaces somewhere around her.

Something splashed off to her right, and she jerked her head toward it, even though she couldn't see. Pain lashed through her head and neck. Without her sight, her other senses felt more alert. Everything seemed loud, and she felt the miniscule ripples formed by whatever had broken the surface.

One of the tests she'd had to pass to become a lifeguard was to tread water for five minutes. Luckily, it had been easy for her, and she was certain she could tread water for quite a bit longer. She did so now, straining her ears to follow the closest sound of water against rock. Somehow it felt safer this way, less vulnerable than floating with her back exposed to whatever lurked below her. It felt like she was doing something instead of just lying there. Corpses floated; she wasn't dead yet. People would be looking for her. The lake had been full of people, many of whom she knew. They'd know she was missing.

Her thoughts drifted to Sam, who had disappeared before her. Had he survived? "Sam? Are you in here?" Her voice sounded loud and stark in the space. No answer came. "Sam, are you there?"

What if he was in here, but unconscious? Or dead?

Was his body floating feet away from her, swollen and soft, ready to bump into her? Would he be cold and clammy, or would his body still be warm to the touch?

Her skin crawled at the thought, fear making her voice come out quieter than she'd intended. "Is anyone in here?" Someone could have been sucked under after her. Surely, they would have said something by now, though.

The scent of rot, fish, and algae rode the currents, but stale air subdued it, as if the outside world hadn't touched this space in a long time. Her tongue felt dry, despite being surrounded by water, and tasted stale like the air. Cold penetrated her skin to the bones, and she shivered against it, muscle rubbing muscle in an attempt to warm her. She felt deeply exposed without a wall to put her back to, and no idea where the ground was.

Something rough brushed against her calf, a quick dart of movement that did not linger.

She whipped around in the water, reaching out with a shaking hand to make sure nothing hovered nearby.

She touched only water and grit. It occurred to her that whatever it was might be able to see in this darkness in a way she couldn't, that it might be floating just out of her reach.

She jerked her hand back.

"It's just a fish." Her voice echoed back at her, not at all convincing. She figured the quick echo meant it was a smaller space, like an underground cavern perhaps. The water was mostly still, but had a slight current to it, a consistent soft streaming, indicating it might move outside of this cavern. That meant she could, too.

If someone was lost in the wilderness, they were supposed to stay in place so they could be rescued, but what was someone supposed to do when trapped in water in an underground cavern beneath a draining lake? She couldn't tread water forever. She couldn't float forever, either, especially with the cold temperature. No, she would have to take matters into her own hands and at least try to find a way out of here or to a surface she could rest upon. Would trying to find where she had entered the cavern be a good idea? It was hard to decide, wrapped in the darkness, unsure if she was alone.

Desperate, she called out again. "Is anyone there? Can you hear me?" She strained for the slightest moan or shift in the water, but nothing came. Another person would mean they could hover together for warmth or work together to find a way out.

Another person would mean she wasn't alone in the dark.

This time she screamed as loudly as she could. "Help me! I'm in here!"

No one called back.

Her skin, despite or because of the cold, was a painful

receiving board for sensation. Something touched her again, this time a slow drag past her thigh. It stung. She didn't fish, and wasn't certain how rough scales were, but surely that was the explanation for the stinging. Rough scales against cold, sensitive skin.

Now something tapped her toe.

She jerked her foot away before kicking out. There was no impact, and panic overtook her, causing her to flail, to kick, to hit out with her hands.

Water splashed onto her face, the thick flavor of minerals and dead plants filling her mouth.

Her head went below the surface, and she came back up with a gasp, the cold shock bringing the panic down a notch.

"The fish are getting restless." Yes, the fish. Fish, fish, fish. That would be the only thing down here. Right?

But what about water snakes? Water moccasins? Her skin crawled once again at this thought. She hated snakes way down deep where she couldn't rationalize away the fear. If there were poisonous ones down here, it wouldn't be an irrational fear at all.

But it hadn't felt like a snake. Snakes were long. There'd be more contact, and it would feel different, smooth. Even though she was scared of snakes, she had touched one at the zoo, its scales velvety soft against her fingers. "There are no snakes down here. It's too cold."

Saying that word out loud actually made it worse.

Snakes.

Water snakes couldn't need the same kind of warmth as regular snakes, or they wouldn't be able to swim around in cold water. Then again, the water they inhabited might not be that cold. The ponds she usually saw them in were murky and shallow, and probably tepid. Whether they could exist in water this temperature or not was one more thing she didn't know, and wished she hadn't thought about in the first place.

Her mind seized on this phobia, amplifying her fear and compounding the fright she already felt at being stuck underground and surrounded by water. There could be snakes moving all around her, sizing her up. With their sinuous movements, they could be touching her now, matching the temperature of the water, wrapping around her, seeking her vulnerabilities. She'd never know until they bit or reared up out of the water.

The ever-present panic crawled up her spine, curled up in her stomach. She started to swim, fast, heedless of what she might run into. Every tiny object that brushed her skin was a snake's tail, a fang, a tongue.

She inhaled water, spluttered, kept swimming. Something big bumped into her, and she pictured Sam, his face black and bloated, a hand straining toward her, eyes eaten by fish or snakes, his skin loose and wrinkled as hers must be.

Some instinct must have kicked in, because she felt something before her and pulled back abruptly. She stayed perfectly still, only moving her feet the minimum required to keep her head above water.

With trepidation, she reached out, forcing her hand forward despite her desire to roll up into a ball, to avoid whatever it might be.

It felt like hours passed as her arm stretched out, fingers spread. She could feel something in front of her. Something large.

Her hand came to rest on slick, cold rock. She ran her hand up and down the surface. Her fingers came away slimy. She allowed a small amount of hope to trickle through the fear. A wall. She'd found a wall. Now to see if there was a ledge on which to rest and possibly bring her body temperature up.

She splayed her fingers out and began to move along the wall to her left, following the mild current she'd felt earlier. She proceeded slowly, running her hands over every reachable surface. The areas above the water were covered in a thin film of slickness, but those under the water boasted a fringe of plant material that tickled her legs like tiny fingers as she slid along the surface. She moved her body farther from the wall, attempting to keep away from the wet fuzz reaching for her beneath the water.

It struck her that plants couldn't form somewhere with no light. Could they? Did that mean light penetrated this area somewhere? If so, was it night? She would have had to be unconscious for hours if that was so. It had been late afternoon when the sinkhole had opened up and pulled her down. Almost time to go home for dinner, yet still bright out.

A sinkhole, yes. That's what it must have been. They'd learned a little about sinkholes in geology last year. This area was rife with pockets formed by water moving through the stone, a perfect place for sinkholes to appear. That didn't explain how light might get down here, but perhaps she'd been moving the whole time she'd been out, shifting through various caverns and pockets. In that case, Sam could be anywhere. The same went for anyone else who had been sucked down after her.

Solid objects bumped into her as she moved. The first time, she threw an arm out to send the object away, terrified of what it might be. When it happened again, she put her hand out slowly, the skin on her hand and arm crawling in the opposite direction, her entire being urging her to pull it back. She tapped it with her outstretched index finger and jerked back.

Nothing attacked her, and she touched it harder, pressing against it. It sunk below the surface and bobbed back up with a mild splash. Now she reached out again and wrapped a hand around it, wary that at any moment it would shift, that it would move against her, attack her, touch her.

It didn't.

It was light in her hand when she lifted it from the water, and pliable. Oblong and a little slick, it had give to it. A firm, rigid flap rested under her thumb. Her pinkie touched something round and smooth. An eye?

A dead fish. Had it died on the way down with her, or were they dying off around her?

Time was questionable down here. She had no idea how long she'd been passed out or how long had passed since waking. It could have been hours or minutes, but the algae told her it had been longer than mere minutes since there was no light. It felt like it took forever to circle the cavern and all its alcoves, and she had no idea if she'd made it all the way around or if she'd made a circuit multiple times. Her senses were so screwed up that she would have figured she'd passed into an entirely new space, what with the inconsistent feel of the walls, if not for the fact that a familiarity had formed as she'd moved. A bit of rock jutted out that felt like it had cat ears on the top, two sharp, triangular pieces that had cut her the second time across them. Either there were two such rocks, or she'd gone around at least three times, because here they were a third time. She couldn't be sure if she'd passed it more than three times, but had her hands in a different position the other times.

At no point did she find a ledge or surface she could pull herself up on. There was no hole allowing an underground stream in or out, despite the sensation of movement in one direction. Water dripped somewhere, and as she'd first noticed upon coming to, there was a louder rush somewhere in the distance, but she couldn't figure out how to get to it. The rushing came from high above her, as if there was a hole up there, allowing her to hear that piece of freedom far away, but not giving her physical access to it. It was possible she'd come in from above on a rush of water. Or that she was in the same place she'd initially fallen, but it had somehow sealed up.

"Why hasn't anyone found me?" Were her parents looking for her? The authorities? Her friends? Would they be able to find her? She thought about home, a warm shower, a fire, hot chocolate. She thought about her little brother, who had been so sad to not be able to come to the lake today. But he'd had a runny nose and a nasty cough, and mom had insisted he stay home, even though Alice had been willing to bring him out to the lake to hang out with her. At twelve years old, he loved the lake, loved to feel like one of the big kids when Alice's friends helped him out to the float.

She decided to make another circuit from the cat-eared rock, full circle, and this time she would pay closer attention to the current than to the rock surface climbing above her head. She'd become numb to the cold, the shivering long gone. Sluggishness overtook her. Something told her this wasn't a good thing, her body no longer fighting to keep her warm. Confusion settled over her like a net, dragging her down. She hadn't paid much attention to hypothermia training since she worked at a heated pool, but it felt like this was a sign of progression. She tried to remember more details about hypothermia, but they evaded her.

With her limited sensation, she wanted to try this current tracking now, while she still had any way to feel.

Alice drifted parallel to the wall with one hand dragging over the surface. The other hand floated in the water so she could sense the current. Eventually she felt it going the same direction she was, and she followed this until the direction changed a little. Going back to where it had been aligned with her, she took a deep breath, hard with her breaths coming in short pants due to her cooling body and the exhaustion setting in. The cold was a shock when her head went under, despite her thoroughly chilled body temperature, and she almost gulped water, but managed to stop it from happening. She kept her hands on the rock and dove, trying to find whatever hole the water moved through.

She didn't have to go too deep to find it. The hole was small, not much bigger around than her thigh. She shoved an arm through it, battering her shoulder against the rock, not caring about scrapes or bruises. No matter which way she twisted her body, she couldn't maneuver her shoulders through the hole. Short on breath, she surfaced, breathing raggedly. The shivers had not returned. Her skin felt like marble, like a foreign object draped over her bones. She was almost entirely numb to outside sensations.

The small hole explained the lack of major current. Maybe the entry hole was bigger. Though if it was, wouldn't the cave be filling up instead of staying level? The cat-eared rock hadn't appeared to be any higher or lower the second time she'd found it.

She tried twice more. Each plunge under the water made her that much colder, yet she couldn't shiver even when she tried. It was like her body had given up before her mind wanted it to. It felt like she was floating outside herself, an awareness outside the physical entity.

It disturbed her that she could no longer feel if anything touched her. Something could take a massive chunk out of her and she wouldn't know it. Snakes could wrap around her body, twine in her hair, and she'd have no idea unless they hissed in her ear. It felt like her eyes had doubled in size from widening in an attempt to find light by which to see. Her ears felt like satellite dishes. She knew this must be her imagination, that the numbness must extend to those parts of her body, that it would take far longer to evolve in a new environment, that it probably couldn't happen at all, but she couldn't remember or reconcile what her brain told her was happening. Her body no longer felt like her own.

Why was she here? How had she arrived? Where was here? Her thoughts were fuzzy, memories floating just out of reach. Her arms and legs were chunks of wood, knocking about her body. She lay on her back, allowing the water to move her as it willed. Floating felt peaceful. Water muffled her hearing, lapped at her eardrums. She thought about swimming in the pool, surrounded by friends and familiar faces. Warm sun beating down on her face, her body. It felt right. She was floating, and when she opened her eyes she'd see the sun, the edges of the pool, the lifeguard's chair.

Wasn't she supposed to be in that chair, high above the people splashing in the water below? Watching them, protecting them. Working on her tan. Watching the boys check her out while she discreetly looked back from behind her mirrored lenses. Waiting until close of day so she could frolic in the darkened pool with her fellow lifeguards and pool staff, and whatever friends the manager let them sneak in.

Yes, night had fallen. That's why it was so dark. She floated in the pool. All she had to do was hold her breath and let herself sink. Then she'd feel the bottom, be able to push off it back into the moonlight.

Back into the light.

The water closed over her head and she drifted down, down, down, felt the comforting heat.

But she never touched the bottom.

Alice drifted.

Good Girls Don't Swallow

Keri tripped, causing her gum to shoot into the back of her throat like a chewable missile. She gasped past the sticky obstruction, choking until it shifted and popped back into her mouth. A blush warmed her cheeks, and she looked around to see if anyone had seen her klutz ballet. To her relief, no one looked her way. Hundreds of people on this concrete-filled city block, and they were all so engrossed in their own goings on that they probably had no idea she existed in their space. Even with the flirty summer dress she'd worn to combat the heat, and the cute haircut she'd just gotten, which had her hair gliding silkily over her shoulders.

She huffed out a breathy laugh, looked around one more time, and returned to chewing the large wad of tasteless bubble gum. The mock mystery fruit flavor had long worn off. *Guess I really can't walk and chew gum at the same time.* Keri looked around for a garbage can, but didn't see any. Shrugging, she swallowed the gum. It slipped down her throat at a snail's pace, briefly lodging against her voice box before struggling into her stomach by way of her esophagus.

Maybe I shouldn't have swallowed such a big piece of gum. Mama always said not to swallow gum at all or it would remain in my stomach forever. Too late now.

Of course, she'd swallowed tons of gum over the years. Better than leaving it on the ground to ruin someone's shoes or choke a bird. Besides, in this concrete jungle the only place she had to spit it was pavement. Urban legends aside, there couldn't be any harm in swallowing a piece of gum. Everything exits eventually.

Keri passed a shop front with a dark blue canopy over the entrance. The large window exhibited a variety of fresh fruits in vivid yellows, oranges, reds, purples, and greens. Her mouth watered, and she went through the slim glass door to look around. It was a small shop containing fresh produce and a few grocery staples. A short refrigerated cabinet stood by the front desk, full of energy drinks. It struck her how run down she felt, with a long day still ahead of her. Missing the beginning of the work day for her hair appointment meant she'd be working late tonight to make up the hours.

She grabbed a red apple and another pack of bubble gum, looking around for a drink to give her an energy boost. There weren't any coffee drinks, but an obnoxiously neon sign looked promising: "All new Oxi-Blast! Unleash the antioxidant power of acai and goji berry to battle free radicals and energize you like no other!" Antioxidant properties—as if that were a legitimate health boon. The magic of antioxidants fixing all ills was about as likely as swallowed gum solidifying in your guts and stopping up your stomach, she figured. And what were free radicals, anyway? All she cared about was the burst of energy the drink would give her to hopefully get through the next hour until lunch. She grabbed an orange bottle with "MANGO" written across the label.

The apple tasted perfectly sweet until she took a swig of the energy drink. The fake sugars in it made the apple taste bland, with a bitter edge. She put the lid back on the drink, face scrunched in disgust at the awful taste, and powered her way through the apple as she continued her walk to work. The apple's juices ran down her palm to her wrist, drying into a stickywet patch. When she got it down to the core, she once again looked around for a garbage can without luck. A patch of grass stood off to the side, and she lightly tossed the apple core onto it, figuring animals would eat it. No harm, no foul.

The heat of the day beat down on her, and she gulped the Oxi-Blast. The building housing her office dominated the skyline before her, its shadow falling over the sidewalk and chilling the temperature a good ten degrees. It was even colder inside when she moved through the revolving door. Pushing with one hand, she tilted her head back to finish the drink from the wide-mouthed bottle. She barely registered when her hand lost contact with the door. It moved away from her a split second before the door coming up behind her slammed into her back, knocking the drink from her hand. The bottle flipped end-over-end onto the tiled floor of the lobby. The last dregs of the container formed a pale orange puddle that engulfed a flattened piece of mint-green gum that looked like it had been left there off the bottom of someone's shoe. It even had tread marks. As she watched, it began to swell, as if it were absorbing the liquid of the Oxi-Blast.

Irritated, Keri turned to confront the asshole that had pushed the revolving door into her. He stepped out, calm as can be, and said, "You should really pay attention when you're in one of these." With a smug curl of his lip, he stalked off toward the bank of elevators, not turning to look back at her.

She spluttered, but failed to find anything hurtful to hurl at his back. Instead, she muttered, "Asshole" before bending down to pick up the bottle and throw it away. After a quick stop at the front desk to let them know about the spill, she climbed the stairs to the third floor, embraced by the familiar scents of paper, ink, and misery that signified she'd reached her office.

Doris, the two-hundred year old receptionist who always managed to remind Keri of a sloth-owl hybrid, looked over at her in slow motion. She blinked her massive round eyes twice in her wizened face before greeting Keri. "Good afternoon, Ms. Hubil."

"Hi, Doris. Is Mandy in yet?" This elicited exactly five thought-blinks. Keri counted. "Yes, she's in your office."

"Great, thanks!"

While Doris was still thought-blinking her way through a response, Keri booked it for her and Mandy's office. The back of Mandy's shaved head greeted her, a spiral carved about her perfectly rounded dome. Her bare shoulders peeked above the back of the chair.

"So you've completely given up on wearing clothes to work?" Keri asked.

Mandy swiveled to face Keri, fully clothed in a strapless romper. "Not quite yet. If this heat keeps up, I may get there."

A smile curved over her face. "How was ol' Doris?"

"As witty as ever."

With a snort, Mandy turned back to her computer, grabbed her mouse, and got back to work.

Keri put her things down on the desk across the way from Mandy's, then hit the power button on her own machine. "You working on the Severson ad?"

"Yep. It's due tomorrow. You got the deodorant one?"

"On that now." Keri grabbed her notes from the last marketing meeting and slid them under her keyboard. She popped a fresh piece of gum into her mouth to help with focus. The sweet taste hit her tongue, the soft texture exactly what she needed to sink her teeth into.

Her stomach rumbled then gurgled.

"Was that you?" Mandy asked.

"You heard that? Jeez, my stomach's grumbling."

"I've got a granola bar in my bag if you need it."

"Thanks, but I'm good. It's not that long until lunch." An ache started just above her belly button. "I may need Tums or something."

"Got that, too." Mandy's chair squeaked as she shifted in her seat then ruffled through her bag. "Here you go."

Keri turned and reached for the bottle of Tums. "Thanks. Not sure what would have upset my stomach. I just had an apple and a fruit drink."

Keri tried to focus on the happy, smiling idiots on her computer screen. The models were all highly attractive and wearing dark colored clothing. The better to show that the deodorant wouldn't leave marks. She'd gotten a free sample, and that was a blatant lie. It had flaked all over the black dress she'd worn to test it out, leaving a white smear across the dark material. It had also clumped up in scales on her underarms, a decidedly unflattering look. She'd felt like a leper.

Her stomach gurgled again, louder this time. Discomfort churned in her gut. Red faced, she started some music to cover up any further sounds. No need for the two of them to have to listen to the stomach acid choir.

It continued to gurgle and growl for the next hour. Instead of hunger, she began to feel full, the sensation growing as more time passed. When she put a hand to her stomach, she touched a small lump. The screen blurred before her eyes, and nausea overtook her. She spit her gum into a tissue and threw it away.

"I'm going to hit the bathroom, Mandy. You need anything when I come back?"

"Nah. It's almost lunch time. You up for tacos?"

The thought of food made Keri want to throw up. "I'm not hungry. Can you get food poisoning from an apple?"

"I don't think so. Maybe if you don't wash it?" Mandy grabbed her purse and headed out the door. "Text me if you change your mind about tacos. I can bring some back."

Too distracted by her probable apple-related food poisoning Keri just grunted in response. Great. She hadn't washed the apple. Maybe there'd been some sort of bacteria on the skin. *See what good eating healthy does for a person? So much for Mama's advice that an apple a day keeps the doctor away.*

In the bathroom, Keri peed then waited to see if anything would develop. The gurgling inside her sounded wet and violent.

When nothing happened, she hiked up her panties, flushed, and squatted in front of the toilet. Maybe the porcelain god required some prayers. The full sensation had crept up into her chest, the pain moving with it. Stomach acid leached into her mouth, but nothing more.

It seemed like an hour had passed, though it couldn't have been more than twenty or so minutes. If she wasn't going to be sick, she might as well get back to work. The ad wouldn't create itself. If she'd worn the sample deodorant today, it would be getting quite a test. Sweat rolled off her forehead, between her breasts, down the center of her back, and from under her arms. Her flowery dress dampened in crescents.

The queasiness increased, drawing a moan from her. Flushing the toilet, she went to one of the sinks to wash her hands and splash some water on her face. Her eyes stared back at her, bloodshot and droopy. Could she have a fever? She placed her hand to her forehead, but couldn't tell.

If she hadn't walked to work, she'd go home, but the idea of walking while this miserable had zero appeal. Better to sit at her desk and get something done. Plus, she was a bit short of breath. Surely this would pass if she gave it some time.

Back at her desk, Keri looked through possible backgrounds. The client had wanted at least one ad showing users were sophisticated. Should they be at an upscale restaurant? A garden party? A business meeting?

How the hell was she supposed to care about a stupid ad for a crappy product when her stomach was about to digest her throat? She touched her belly, unable to resist the urge, as if it would quell the pain by magical touch. The lump had grown bigger, now the size of a grapefruit.

Keri picked up the phone and dialed her doctor's office.

"Centurion Health, how may I help you?" came the voice on the other end. The chipper sound irritated her.

"I think I need an emergency appointment. Something's wrong with my stomach."

"The doctor has a full schedule today. If you're concerned, head into the urgent care on State Street."

"Okay." She hung up. "Thanks for nothing." What was the point of having a doctor if she couldn't help in an emergency?

A quick search on the computer revealed the phone number for urgent care. They had an opening in an hour. She'd have to arrange for a ride.

Sharp pains spread through her stomach and up her chest. Something tickled at the back of her throat, and she gagged. Her breaths wheezed in and out. The lump had swelled to the size of a cantaloupe. She could see the bulge. It grew as she watched, stretching her dress out. Her skin tightened.

Stomach discomfort was the worst. Helplessness engulfed her. Tears leaked from her eyes. She blinked to get rid of them with little success. The screen of her phone blurred.

Angrily, she dashed the tears away and pulled up the app that would net her a ride to urgent care. If Mandy were here, she'd do it, but she'd gone to lunch.

The tickle returned to the back of her throat and Keri attempted to clear it, which only made it worse. Something swelled into the back of her mouth, shoving more acid in front of it. Keri grabbed her trashcan and heaved over it, but nothing came out other than a bitter trickle of bile.

Goosebumps rose on her arms and an icy chill ran up her back. Her heart pounded like an off-balance tap dancer in her chest, the rhythm stilted. She gagged and heaved again, the item swelling further into her mouth. It lay heavy on her tongue, pressing it down, choking her.

Keri reached a shaking finger to her mouth and explored inside. There was something in her mouth! Something soft and sticky. She jerked her finger back and looked at it, not sure what she expected to see. Saliva glistened on her fingertip, but nothing else.

This time when she gagged, the substance pushed out through her lips, sticking to the dry, flaky skin. She put her fingertip to it again, this time pressing. It gave, enveloping her finger.

It felt like gum.

She pinched a small amount and pulled, eyes widening at the pink string stretching away from her mouth. She gripped more, pulling as fast as she could, but it kept thinning into strings that drooped and broke. Her thighs were covered with broken threads of gum. It looked like someone had sprayed her with silly string.

Still she pulled, and still it swelled. Her stomach stuck out like a beach ball, her ribs straining and aching above the bulge. Breathing became harder. Panic fluttered along with the irregular beat of her heart. This couldn't be happening.

Desperate, she ran from the office, both hands wrapped in gum. She stumbled then tripped, sprawling across the floor, hands raised to shield her face. The smell of stomach acid and fruit hit as she face planted into the gum. It stuck to her cheek when she raised her head, more pushing out of her mouth.

Doris turned her way, mouth opening in slow motion, eyes blinking. Her eyes widened even more than usual, mouth gaping open several seconds before the scream emitted from her throat.

Keri tried to ask for help, but only managed to produce a bubble. Her eyes crossed, watching the bubble grow. Her nose tickled, and two more bubbles expanded from her nostrils, blocking her airway.

She reached up and popped the bubbles, dragging in a miniscule breath that whistled over the gum. Her lungs burned, desperate for more air, but she couldn't get any. Her organs were being crushed, like something large sat on her chest and stomach.

Doris still screamed. She hadn't moved. Her mouth stretched, tongue flapping with the ululations of her voice. Her eyes still blinked slowly like the most idiotic Morse code ever.

It struck Keri with some minor, hysterical hilarity that she was going to die watching Doris blink stupidly at her, gawping like a freaked out turtle. She would have laughed if she weren't so busy suffocating to death on the rapidly expanding gum. Of all the people to have near her in an emergency, Doris was the last person on Earth who could be of help.

Keri held her hand up to her ear and attempted to make the universal phone sign, but the gum made it impossible. She was rapidly becoming a formless pink blob, gum on every surface. Her belly distended so much that she now balanced on it, wobbling.

It took her a moment to get on her feet. She stumbled the few steps to Doris's desk and batted the phone at the stupid woman, whose eyes just now moved to where she stood. It felt like Keri weighed one hundred extra pounds, the gum pulling her down toward the ground, dragging at her every movement. It stuck to the floor, acting like an anchor.

Breathing became impossible. The gum filled her lungs, her stomach, her mouth, her nose, everything. She couldn't pull it out fast enough.

She sunk to the floor, the only sounds Doris's high-pitched scream and her own heartbeat.

Then there were footsteps. Several pairs. Responding to the scream, no doubt.

Hands touched her body, turned her over.

Her boss, Arnold, hovered over her, concern and disgust on his face.

"What is this?" he asked.

She couldn't answer. He spoke to someone she couldn't see. "This looks like the stuff blocking the revolving door downstairs."

What stuff blocking the door? She tore at her throat, her chest. Sharp pain traced the line of each scratch from her nails, a fiery grid of misery. Her lungs burned, panic her only emotion now.

"Call 911!" Arnold called to Doris, but the scream didn't end.

Everything started to go black, a tunnel closing in on Keri's vision. She fought to stay conscious.

I should have listened to Mama.

The Dating Game

Scharl climbed the stool, sitting down with a *squelch*. A tall, tan-skinned man with kohl around his eyes sat down to his right, close to a white panel that blocked the other side of the stage from view. The man smelled of mushrooms.

A wet slopping noise drew Scharl's attention to his left, where a gelatinous black blob oozed its way up the metal leg of the stool before circling the padded seat and sucking the rest of its form up into a single mass. A set of eyes bobbed to the top of the blob and stared at Scharl, a second set popping out of the side and floating around in a circle to check out the surroundings.

An overly cheerful voice sounded from the other side of a large red curtain in front of them. "Welcome to Take Out, a new dating game for those hip to our dark overseers. I'm Bill Eldritch, your host. Tonight, a human female will ask our eligible, yet questionable, bachelors three questions before making her choice. The winner joins our bachelorette for dinner. Are we ready?"

The audience cheered.

Bright lights flooded the stage where the three males sat. The tan man stared straight ahead, while the blob undulated, constantly shifting its body to keep it on the stool. One set of eyes glided around in frantic motions, sinking then popping back up again.

Scharl looked down at his tail, a dry white scale catching his attention. He scratched at it with a side fin, trying to extricate the scale, but making it more obvious instead. The curtain started to rise, and Scharl slapped his fin over the loose scale, locking his body into an uncomfortable position.

The lights blazed enough that he couldn't make out individual faces in the audience, but he could see their dark shapes through the white-hot glare. Instantly, Scharl felt the moisture evaporating from his body. He tried to shift on the stool without moving his fin from the dry scale, almost toppling over backwards, but he stilled when the voice came again, this time from a closer shadow that paced in front of the light.

"Before we bring out our bachelorette, let's meet the three bachelors. Bachelor Number One hails from Egypt and fancies himself a pharaoh, though he admits to reinventing himself often. Welcome Nyarlathotep."

The audience applauded politely.

"Bachelor Number Two comes to us from the depths of the ocean. His people call themselves The Deep Ones, but he says he can be pretty shallow. Please welcome Scharl."

More applause.

"Bachelor Number Three has been to both Egypt and the ocean, but he's sometimes described as spineless. Welcome Shoggoth."

A final smattering of applause.

"Now let's bring out our bachelorette. Layla, a shark lobotomist, loves to dance a jig and eat stinky cheese."

"The stinkier the better, Bill," a high female voice called from the other side of the panel.

Bill laughed. "That's what I thought, Layla."

The audience laughed with them.

Bill spoke again. "I'm sure you're hungry. Go ahead with your first question, my dear."

Microphones rose from the stage floor, tall and skinny. Nyarlathotep's was at just the right height, but the other two mics loomed above Scharl and Shoggoth. Shoggoth shot out an oozing tentacle and pulled his microphone down to just below one set of eyeballs. Scharl couldn't reach his at all.

"Let's start with Bachelor Number Three," Layla said. "If I were a vegetable, how would you peel me?"

One set of Shoggoth's eyes moved toward the partition,

while another stared out at the audience. A raspberry noise emitted from somewhere inside him, causing bubbles to rise to the surface of the ooze, followed by a gurgle that made the entire creature vibrate.

Layla said, "Bachelor Number Two?"

Scharl ripped the offending scale off and held it up, tired of the crick trying to form in his back. He strained toward the microphone. "I'd surround you with my fins and rub my scales over you to loosen your skin as gently as possible."

"Bachelor Number One?"

Nyarlathotep leaned forward, full lips almost touching the black sponge of the mic head. "In ancient times, we had a crescent blade called a khopesh. I would use this to peel your skin from you in one long, sensual piece."

The audience gasped in harmony with Layla.

"Bachelor Number One, if I were a stew what seasoning would you use on me?"

"I'd roast you up in a mix of coriander and cumin. Not only would you be delectable, but the aphrodisiac powers of coriander would make for a spicy night."

The audience "Oooooooohed" then applauded.

"That sounds amazing. Bachelor Number Two?"

Scharl gulped. How could he beat that answer? He searched his mind for something sexy to say about spices. "I, uh, would cover you in olive oil so I could massage some pepper into the, uh, you. Into you. And some salt, so you'd taste like the ocean and call me home."

Almost total silence greeted this, but one man yelled out, "What?"

A pause, then, "Bachelor Number Three?"

"Phbbbbbbbbbbbbbbbbbblt. Fut. Lllllllbbbb."

The audience applauded.

Scharl rolled his eyes.

"Bachelor Number Two, describe your perfect date?"

Scharl had this one. "The perfect date would be a picnic at the beach and a lovely swim in the sun and brine."

"Number Three?"

"Pbbbbbbbbbbb."

"Number One."

"A delectable meal by a raging and powerful river, followed by antics not proper for television."

A buzzer sounded, and Bill spoke. "That's time. Layla, which bachelor would you like to have dinner with?"

"Bill, that's a hard one, but I love the ocean, so I think I'm going to go with Bachelor Number Two."

Scharl gasped. He'd fully expected Nyarlathotep to win. His answers had been so good. Exhilaration filled him at this wondrous surprise. He'd won!

Speaking of Bachelor Number One, his human form rippled then changed, leaving behind a towering, dark body with wings and talons. The creature flung out its wings and flapped them over Scharl's head, lifting off the stool and flying away, screeching as he crossed the partition. He didn't sound happy.

Something wet hit Scharl's foot, drawing his attention downward. A piece of Bachelor Number Three had landed on his tail fin. Scharl grimaced, jerking his fin back and shaking it. The ooze ran off, but didn't touch the floor before Shoggoth sucked it back into his body on his way down the stool. The oozing mass hit the ground with a *sploosh*, pausing in front of Scharl's stool. This time, the raspberry noise sounded personal. One set of eyes moved around the blob to keep Scharl in view as Shoggoth moved around the partition.

A startled, feminine "Oh!" sounded.

Bill said, "Come on out and meet your date, Bachelor Number Two!"

Scharl carefully climbed down from the stool, his tail fins flattening against the cold hardwood. He teetered his way around the partition to find a beautiful rubicund woman with golden curls and kewpie doll lips standing before him. Oddly, she wore a bib with the basic image of a fish on it, and sat at a table decorated with a red tablecloth, plastic utensils, and a Styrofoam container. He hadn't realized dinner would be served right there on stage. Perhaps he should have watched the show before volunteering to go on it, but a free meal was a free meal, and he had a thing for human women.

Oddly, there was only one chair.

"Layla, meet Scharl, your Take Out for tonight."

He held out a fin to Layla, who took it firmly in her soft hands and said, "I'm delighted to meet you. You know every part of you is a delicacy, from fins to eyeballs?"

This struck Scharl as an odd come on, yet his dorsal fin rose when a purr rumbled from her throat.

"Ah, we've got to clean you up first," Bill, no longer just a shadow, said. He held a long, thin microphone, his pinky sticking out. His suit was gray, his form hirsute, and his grin predatory. He gestured backstage. "This way."

Scharl pulled his fin from Layla's grasp. He followed a slight man with giant headphones toward the curtain, struggling to keep up. A rich, spicy scent reached his gills, causing his stomachs to rumble in unison. Dinner smelled delectable.

Giant Headphones stopped at a large round container. From inside, Scharl heard an urgent bubbling, as of boiling water. A large woman with the face of a porcelain doll and a stench of wild yam stepped forward and picked Scharl up without warning. The skin of her hands felt rough and calloused.

"Hey!" Scharl yelped.

The heady scent was stronger here, but even more so when his body impacted the surface of a brown liquid full of thick cut carrots, potatoes, and celery. The spicy, meaty taste of broth filled his mouth. Burning pain seared through his body, and he had a moment to think, *Oh, Take Out*, before merciful darkness overtook him.

Story Notes

Stuck With Me – While reading about the famous conjoined twins, Chang and Eng Bunker (of Chinese heritage, they were born in Thailand, inspiring the term "Siamese twins") I discovered that they died hours apart. Horrified at what it would be like for the longer living twin, I decided to explore it with this story. I originally submitted this for a magazine, but the editor contacted me back and asked me to re-submit it to an anthology he would soon be opening. I did, and he accepted it! The theme of that anthology was "doubles." How timely was that initial submission?

Miss Etta's B&B – I actually wrote this one to a specific anthology call, which required it to heavily involve food. I'm sure they got a billion stories dealing with cannibalism. I got a very nice personal rejection on the call. It was inspired by a woman who really had a handyman (or so she called him), who buried the bodies of her pensioner tenants. Her motive was collecting the pension checks. As far as we know, the real woman didn't eat any of them... (Look up Dorothea Puente, if you're curious.) My critique group was split half and half on how many got the whole tongue thing at the end. Did you?

Unwelcome Guests – This came from a late night jaunt across the internet. I happened across a story about Black Eyed Kids (BEKs). Upon further research, I found all kinds of claims by people that they had experienced real-life interactions with BEKs. Usually, it was simple sightings, but sometimes it went further. But what would happen if they were able to get into your house?

Tent City Horror – After Hurricane Katrina, the city of Colorado Springs became overrun with people fleeing the storm-ravaged areas in the south. Tent cities popped up, and the newspapers were constantly trying to find ways to deal with the vagrancy issues. One particular park was heavily populated by the homeless, with tents and other makeshift shelters along Fountain Creek visible from the Interstate. I wanted to look at how far a city government might go to rid themselves of what they considered an eyesore and embarrassment. The migraines suffered by the main character were inspired by a migraine condition I have, and the research I did in the first couple years of the problem, where I discovered how many people with chronic migraines lose their jobs, marriages, homes, and lives due to their constant suffering and the associated depression.

Let's Play a Game – This was inspired by the very real practice during the London bombings of parents who couldn't afford to leave their jobs in the city sending their children off to live with people out in the country who were willing to take those children in. Knowing full well how situations like this can go, with there always being adults wanting to take advantage where children are concerned, I wondered what would happen if one of those children was pure evil. The caretaker in this story was inspired by the foster parent of one of my employees, when I managed a theater back in my 20s. I repeatedly tried to report the abuses this foster teen dealt with, but nothing was ever done. All I could do was be as kind as possible, and do what I could for her when she was at work. I hope she's doing well now.

Dearest – This one doesn't have any major inspiration. I just thought it would be fun to write a love letter from a stalker, but bury that particular lead. The rest developed as I wrote.

Beneath – I have a thing about murky water. If something can swim up on me and not be seen, I want no part of it. I was fascinated as a child to learn that a town my grandpa lived in during his youth had been flooded, buildings intact, to create a reservoir. The thought of swimming in a lake, unaware of a ghost town below your feet stuck in my head. This was another one where the editor I submitted it to for one thing (an anthology with a specific theme) rejected it with a note to resubmit when another anthology opened up. The anthology it ended up getting accepted into had a water theme. Again, lucky timing. The best kind of rejection is the one that comes with a request to submit to something else by the same editor.

Night Shift – It's been pointed out to me that my stories tend to be circular. This one is more obvious than others, in that it starts and ends with some of the same sentences, which I believe Shirley Jackson did in *The Haunting of Hill House*. I enjoyed the matter-of-factness of the repeated statements. Something about the coldness of it makes what has occurred, sandwiched between those lines, all the more horrifying. This was actually born of an anthology call for horror in an asylum I didn't have time to write to, but upon seeing the call, I got the idea. Revisiting it later, I wrote the story, even though the call no longer existed.

Where I Woke Up – I have a long-term, mental love affair with the book *The Girl in the Box*, by Ouida Sebestyen. I even got to exchange letters with Sebestyen while putting together an author day for my middle school (I had the coolest English teacher ever!). Sadly, she couldn't make it to the event, but she was so sweet and supportive. The story involved a girl, plucked up by a stranger while walking angrily from her friend's house, typewriter in hand. He stuck her in some sort of cellar, with some water and bread, and never came back. In the darkness, she types journals on her typewriter as she runs out of food and water. Given, I haven't read it since middle school, so I may be remembering it wrong, but I found the situation and lack of a real ending or motive completely unsettling, especially as I had multiple times escaped kidnapping attempts in real life. I thought it would be unsettling in a different way to wake up in a strange, unescapable house, with no idea who you were, no memory of the "normal" world you must have come from.

A Doomed Affair – This story was written for an anthology call dealing with hotel horror. It was accepted, but never saw publication. The editors of the publication, frustrated with the publisher's inaction, withdrew the stories for the authors, returning the rights to us. I was excited to be in the anthology, because I'd met the publisher before, and because a friend was also in the book, but publishers have real-life issues, too. One of the things that will instantly turn me against a character is adultery. I wanted to see if I could write a sympathetic character, despite her intention to commit adultery.

Your Mother's Eyes – I wanted to try my hand at a quieter type of horror. I was also doing a bit of a role reversal concerning an ill parent, with the other parent acting as a caretaker, as my mom was caring for my dad, who had ALS, full time. My parents were soul mates. So are the parents in this story. The thing is, the person who's dying often comes to terms with it before the rest of their family. But even of the family, caretakers have it the hardest. Their lives revolve around the care of their loved one. When that is taken away, they've not only lost a loved one, they've lost their purpose, the thing their entire life has revolved around for however long the illness lasted.

The Importance of Self-Defense – I imagine this one is pretty obvious. I wrote it during the beginning of the #METOO movement, while watching women try to explain to men what it's like to be female in the world at large. The things we have to check for when going out in public that men probably don't give a second thought to. The fact that were taught how to use our keys to defend ourselves, as if that's all it would take. What would happen if a virus flipped it all? This is also the closest I've come to writing a vampire story.

Message of the Night-Gaunts – I was invited to contribute to an anthology of Colorado authors, many of whom were friends and acquaintances. It had to be Lovecraft themed. The only problem? I'd never read Lovecraft. When I researched him, I discovered he had the same sort of night terrors I do, where a figure would stand over his bed. He called these Night-Gaunts. How could I resist? I've since found that many people have this very same night terror, often accompanied by sleep paralysis (like me!). I read a couple of his short stories to try to get a feel for his writing, then wrote this story.

Treading Water – Oh, hey, look, another water one! What if it wasn't that the water was murky, but that the victim was somewhere without light, unable to see what else might be in the water with her? I should mention that sinkholes freak me out. They can open anywhere, at any time. How are you supposed to prepare for that? They're especially common in Colorado, for several reasons. Because we have an underground spring that meanders along beside our house, I used to have nightmares of it eating away the porous rock beneath us, causing a sinkhole to swallow us up in the middle of the night. While that particular story may happen at some point in the future, I wanted this one to involve water. I also wanted it to be a quieter type of horror. Sad instead of terrifying.

Good Girls Don't Swallow – I was invited to submit for a horror comedy anthology. The plot had to revolve around something your mama might have told you not to do, a wives tale. There were so many good ones, but they weren't funny to me. Then I thought about the threat of swallowing your bubble gum (don't swallow your gum, or it will stick in your intestines!). What if it didn't stick in your intestines? What if, instead, a chemical reaction occurred that caused it to grow and grow and grow inside you?

The Dating Game – This one was also written for the Lovecraft anthology. I'd already done serious, but there were so many interesting characters Lovecraft had created. Dating games aren't a stranger to horror; a famous serial killer was once selected on the real Dating Game (Rodney Alcala). The woman who'd chosen him from behind the partition was so freaked out, she refused to go out with him. Lucky for her. But I wanted this to be funny, to be a bit of fun while I explored the weird creatures, and I wanted the anonymous "man" behind the partition to be the one putting himself at risk. I put this and *Good Girls Don't Swallow* at the end of the collection to hopefully let readers ultimately leave on a higher note. Just this once.

Acknowledgments

"Stuck With Me" © 2019 Shannon Lawrence (*Twice-Told: A Collection of Doubles*, ed. C.M. Muller, Chthonic Matter)

"Miss Etta's B&B" © 2020 Shannon Lawrence

"Unwelcome Guests" © 2017 Shannon Lawrence (*Bards and Sages Pubishing*)

"Tent City Horror" © 2019 Shannon Lawrence (*Sanitarium: Issue No. 02*)

"Let's Play a Game" © 2017 Shannon Lawrence (*Space and Time Magazine, Issue #128*)

"Dearest" © 2019 Shannon Lawrence (*Tales From the Moonlit Path*)

"Beneath" © 2018 Shannon Lawrence (*Beneath the Waves: Tales From the Deep*, ed. Steve Dillon, Things in the Well Publishing)

"Night Shift" © 2020 Shannon Lawrence

"Where I Woke Up" © 2019 Shannon Lawrence (*The Desperate and the Damned*, ed. Sandra Ruttan, Toe Six Press)

"A Doomed Affair" © 2020 Shannon Lawrence

"Your Mother's Eyes" © 2020 Shannon Lawrence

"The Importance of Self-Defense" © 2019 Shannon Lawrence (*Bloodbond, January 2019*)

"Message of the Night-Gaunts" © 2018 Shannon Lawrence (*The Necro-Om-Nom-Nom-Icon*, ed. Jason Dias, Sol Nigris Press)

"Treading Water" © 2020 Shannon Lawrence

"Good Girls Don't Swallow" © 2019 Shannon Lawrence (*Don't Cry to Mama*, ed. Jonathan Lambert and Lori Titus, Jolly Horror Press)

"The Dating Game" © 2018 Shannon Lawrence (*The Necro-Om-Nom-Nom-Icon*, ed. Jason Dias, Sol Nigris Press)

In Memory

Instead of thanks this time around, I would like to dedicate this book to two family members I lost in the last year.

My dad (Greg Kenoyer) died in May 2019 after battling ALS for six-and-a-half years. I've been told by well-meaning people that it was a blessing he passed, but here's the thing: it wasn't. He wasn't done. Yes, his body had failed him, but his mind was still sharp, and we still had a husband, a dad, a grandfather, and a friend.

We knew that he had been reaching out to others with ALS via online forums, and I had done some light editing for him on a guide for those newly diagnosed, but we didn't know the scope of what he'd been doing. Using his eye-gaze computer, he not only wrote a thorough guide for those needing more information on ALS, but he led a weekly online group, helped people in forums, ran an informational Facebook page, and helped create a protocol for emergency responders dealing with ALS patients (they need different care, and some things an emergency responder might do for a patient without ALS could kill someone who has it.)

I AM ALS (iamals.org) will be launching the protocol my dad and Juan Reyes created, and they asked me for permission to name it after him. The Kenoyer Protocol will hopefully help save many lives, and my dad will not only live on through us, but through his actions in his final years. Instead of feeling sorry for himself, he did constant research in order to better fight this disease, and he found ways to help and educate others.

I'm grateful to all the wonderful people who reached out to our family to let us know what my dad had done for them and how much he had impacted their lives.

Of course, before he had ALS my dad was still an amazing man. He was always there for me, always pushing me to be better, to achieve more. He taught me how to fight for myself, how to be responsible for my own actions, and all the little things, like how to ride a bike or how to change the oil and a tire in a car. He mowed the lawn every week when I was pregnant and my husband was out of town. He introduced me to sci-fi horror. We used to watch V, The X-Files, Dr. Who, and Twin Peaks together. Because of him, I'm a smartass and have a twisted sense of humor.

I miss you, dad, and I will always love you. I will never forget everything you did for me.

***

My grandma died February 2019 of cancer. She was my mom's step-mom, but she was there for her just as a mom should be. She had three children of her own and three step-children. She was a western farm-girl, who married young, as was so often the case in those days. Her husband was abusive, but when he developed cancer, she nursed him until the end.

She married my grandpa, and they led a simple life together. Her sons both ended up with the same form of cancer that had killed her first husband. She survived the loss of her sons, my uncles, and continued taking care of everyone else. Of the three grandmothers I had, she was the one who acted most like what I imagined a grandma should. She was there for her grandchildren, kept our pictures on her walls and furniture, sent us birthday cards without fail, wrote us letters. She was tough when she needed to be, and soft when she needed to be. While I'm glad her pain is gone now, I'll miss her.

About the Author

A fan of all things fantastical and frightening, Shannon Lawrence writes in her dungeon when her minions allow, often accompanied by her familiars. She writes primarily horror and fantasy. Her stories can be found in over forty anthologies and magazines, and her first collection, Blue Sludge Blues & Other Abominations, is available in stores. When she's not writing, she's hiking through the wilds of Colorado and photographing her magnificent surroundings. Though she often misses the Oregon coast, the majestic and rugged Rockies are a sight she could never part with. Besides, in Colorado there's always a place to hide a body or birth a monster. What more could she ask for?

Website: thewarriormuse.com

Facebook: www.facebook.com/thewarriormuse/

Twitter: @thewarriormuse

Pinterest: www.pinterest.com/thewarriormuse/

Instagram: https://www.instagram.com/thewarriormuse/

Amazon Author Page: https://www.amazon.com/Shannon-Lawrence

Goodreads: https://www.goodreads.com/shannondkl

For past and upcoming publications:
thewarriormuse.blogspot.com/p/publications.html

www.ingramcontent.com/pod-product-compliance
Lightning Source LLC
Chambersburg PA
CBHW021134190726
48288CB00008B/2656